DAMAGED GOODS

A JACK McMORROW MYSTERY

Other books by Gerry Boyle

Jack McMorrow Mystery Series

Deadline

Bloodline

Lifeline

Potshot

Borderline

Cover Story

Home Body

Pretty Dead

Once Burned

Straw Man

Brandon Blake Mysteries

Port City Black and White

Port City Shakedown

DAMAGED GOODS

A JACK McMORROW MYSTERY

GERRY BOYLE

ISLANDPORT PRESS

Damaged Goods
A Jack McMorrow Mystery

First Islandport Edition / September 2018

All Rights Reserved.

Copyright © 2010, 2018 by Gerry Boyle

ISBN: 978-1-944762-66-7
ISBN: 978-1-944762-67-4 (ebook)
Library of Congress Control Number: 2018952715

Islandport Press
P.O. Box 10
Yarmouth, Maine 04096
www.islandportpress.com
books@islandportpress.com

Publisher: Dean Lunt
Book Design: Teresa Lagrange, Islandport Press
Cover image courtesy of iStock.com/sarayut

Printed in the USA

For my growing family. Life is good.

INTRODUCTION

This is a story I carried in my head for a long, long time. When it was time, I put it on paper in one take. No mulling the plot. No need to ponder to get to know the characters. No alternate beginnings or endings. Even the title. It was *Damaged Goods* right from conception.

Background: The seed was planted at a time when people didn't turn to the internet to find "companionship." Sometimes they went to the newspaper, the one printed on paper. The notices appeared in the "personals" section, alongside items stating stuff had been lost or found, somebody was no longer responsible for their ex's debts, and an AA meeting was scheduled at the local church.

"Companionship" was an actual sub-section, and the purveyors of this service hawked their wares like growers at a farmer's market. The names were likely pseudonyms: Tawny, Ginger, and Destinee described their respective styles: patient and loving, ferocious wildcat, classy and elegant. They did in-calls or out-calls or both. Rates were by the hour.

I was fascinated by these items, not in a prurient sense, but because the items were in small newspapers that served small communities. Did Tawny's 2 o'clock turn out to be Raymond from ninth-grade science class? What did they say when they met? "Oh, hey, Sandra. I didn't know it was you. Wow. Small world. . . . Hi, Ray. I heard you got married. . . . So what else you been up to? . . . Oh, a little of this, a little of that."

How could these businesses survive in communities where most people knew each other? How did they keep their secret just that? Were they worried about blackmail? Wasn't it just awkward all around?

I was a newspaper columnist this whole time but I didn't write about this more exotic section of the personals. I don't think I knew it at the time, not consciously, but I think I was saving it for a novel. That novel, *Damaged Goods*, emerged when I covered a real-life murder that propelled me—and the community and region—into horror of another magnitude. The two subjects melded in a seamless way and the story that was created seemed so natural it could have been torn from the headlines, as they say.

I can't say more about that aspect of the genesis of the book without spoiling it for readers, so I won't. I will say that Mandi is a character I still think about often. As does McMorrow, I find her mysterious, sympathetic, and an intriguing blend of vulnerable and independent. Unfortunately for McMorrow, his wife Roxanne meets Mandi and concludes the young woman is nothing but trouble. Does Roxanne know best? Read on.

I'll let you decide which camp to choose. But I hope that Mandi and the characters who cross her path in Galway, Maine—some good, some bad—will engage you as well. Remember, it's only a story but they are out there now, in real life. In a way, Mandi is, too.

—Gerry Boyle, September 2018

1

I made my way down the trail through the pinewoods toward the house. Sophie was on my shoulders, her legs tucked under my arms, her arms around my neck, one small hand clutching a droopy bouquet, strangled in her sweaty grip.

"So it was a good day," I said. "We picked flowers."

"For Mommy."

"Yes. And we found arrowheads—"

"—the Indian kids lost them," Sophie said, whispering into my ear.

"Right. The Indian kids lost them. And we had a picnic at the swimming spot and you went swimming—"

"And we had a nap," she said.

"Right. We went to sleep in the mossy spot."

"A bug, he crawled on me."

"But he didn't hurt you," I said.

"No, Daddy," Sophie said. "He was a nice bug."

Down the path we went, Sophie's face brushing against mine as she leaned forward while we passed under low-hanging branches. I could smell her fresh Sophie smell, feel her soft-smooth skin. I bent under the branch of an old maple, craggy and dying, dating to when Prosperity, Maine was all farms, these woods were pasture, and this maple was spared the axe. Its roots had come to the surface, as if the old tree was trying to get up and move, sick of the same old place after a hundred years.

I stumbled, Sophie hung on, and after a few more lurching steps, we emerged from the shadows of the woods into tall grass, then onto a broad swath of lawn. Beyond the lawn was the Varneys' big, shingled barn. A door swung open.

"Hey, Pumpkin."

Sophie slipped her leg over my shoulder, her legs pumping as I lowered her to the ground.

"Clair," she said, running on her little sandaled feet. "We were in the forest."

Clair held his arms out and she hit them at full stride. He swung her up and around and she was chattering now, about the Indians and the bug, then she was down again, racing back to me as I crossed the lawn, saying, "I need the arrows. Clair needs to see."

I took three stones from my shorts pocket. Sophie took them and ran back, held them out. Clair bent down, his head of white hair close to her dark curls, his big, tanned hand picked up one stone and turned it.

"Whoa, Pumpkin," he said. "Where were the Indians?"

"They left," Sophie said, jumping up and down on one foot, then the other. "They left a long time ago."

Clair looked up at me and smiled.

"I know where there's some dinosaur bones out there," he said, picking her up and holding her so she sat on his bicep, just above his Semper Fi tattoo.

"Wow," Sophie said. "Can we go get them?"

Then two chickens came around the corner of the barn and she squirmed to the ground, following them and clucking as they fled back toward the coop.

"A lesser paleontologist might mistake them for moose bones," Clair said.

"Or pointed rocks," I said.

"Good thing we know what we're doing."

"A very good thing."

"She's gonna be in trouble if she ever needs to know about video games," Clair said.

The chickens came back around the end of the barn, heads bobbing. Sophie was behind them, saying, "Peckety peck," bobbing her head, too.

"You want to come in? Mary'll make us some lemonade," Clair said.

"Sure," I said. "We worked up a thirst, didn't we, Soph?"

Walking along the gravel path that led from the barn, we started for the house. We were by the back door, closer to the road, when we heard a familiar sound: Roxanne's Subaru approaching. The car flashed past, headed for home, leaving a billow of dust in its wake.

"Mommy's home," Sophie said.

"Yeah," I said. "And she's early."

Clair and I exchanged glances. I said we'd take a raincheck on the lemonade, go see Roxanne. Sophie was already trotting down the drive, and I followed, caught up with her, swung her into my arms and hurried out to the dirt road.

It was five hundred yards to the house, and when we walked up the drive, Roxanne's Subaru was parked by my truck. We went inside and as soon as I put Sophie down she dashed for the kitchen, and I heard Roxanne say, "Sweetie." When I came into the room she was holding Sophie in her arms and the wilted bouquet as Sophie briefed her on our day.

"Indians," Roxanne said. "Really. Did you see them?"

Sophie said no, slipped down, and said she had to put her arrowheads in a secret spot. She ran out of the kitchen and we heard her shoes slap on the stairs. I walked over to Roxanne, gave her a squeeze and a kiss. Behind her on the counter, there was a bottle of white wine already out of the refrigerator.

"Three o'clock," I said. "They let you start the weekend early?"

"I'd had enough."

"Everything okay?"

"Oh, yeah, it's just—"

Roxanne closed her eyes. Swallowed hard. A tear showed at the corner of her eye like a tiny pearl.

"A crummy day," she said.

"Why?" I said.

"Oh—"

She paused. Sighed.

"We pulled these two little kids down in Appleton. People down the road found them rummaging for food in their trash cans. Thought it was raccoons."

"So why—"

"Why is that so crappy?" Roxanne said, turning and uncorking the wine, pouring a glass. She took a quick sip. Swallowed.

"Kids didn't want to come with us, of course. Skinny little things, dirty. Their teeth, oh my god."

"And?"

"Welts all over them. They said it was from 'the belt.' Parents live in this compound sort of place way out in the boonies. Filthy house.

Dogs on chains you had to get by. Deputy had to Mace one of them. Inside there's dishes covered with mold. Blankets over the windows, dark and stuffy and smelly. Mother was clearly an abuse victim, scared to death of the dad."

"Was he screaming at you?"

"No, the deputies held him back, and then——"

Roxanne drank again. Her face was drained and gray, dark shadows under her eyes. She swallowed.

"And then what?"

"He's going on, saying he'll see us in court. Usual stuff. State won't get away with this."

Roxanne looked at me.

"And then he gets really quiet, he's this tall skinny guy, going bald, really creepy pale blue eyes."

She shuddered.

"Marilyn, she takes the younger one, a little boy, five-year-old. They go outside. I'm inside with the older one, he's seven or eight."

"Where are the cops?" I said.

"They're right there but then the dogs—one of the chains pulled out or something and the dog attacks Marilyn in the yard and the deputies take off, their guns out and everything and Marilyn is screaming and the younger boy is yelling. Oh, God."

Another sip. A quick breath. I'd rarely seen her this upset.

"So you're alone with the boy."

"And the parents. They clearly hate my guts, I mean really hate me."

"Who are these people?"

"Harland and Cheree Wilton. With two E's. But you don't know that."

"These things don't usually bother you like this."

"I know. I mean, they shouldn't. But this wasn't just normal angry. The guy especially, just staring so hard, and then out of nowhere he calls me a Jew bitch."

"Huh."

"And then I'm headed for the door, I've got the boy by the shoulder and he isn't saying a word. But the father gets close to me, he's right behind me and the door won't open, it's this heavy wooden thing, and I was about to yell for help."

"You should have."

"And he's right next to me, Jack. I can smell him. And he says, in this awful low voice, calm and slow. He says, 'You're dead. The power of Satan will destroy your body and soul.' Those exact words. And then he lets out this awful bellow and raises his arms up, like he's going to make lightning strike and he says, 'Satan. I will do your bidding,' or something, and then he's ranting about filthy Christians and Jews, and oh, my God."

I put my arm around her shoulders.

"It's okay, honey," I said. "He's just some nut. You've seen hundreds of them."

Roxanne closed her eyes.

"This one just shook me."

"Sure, but it's okay now."

"Jack," Roxanne said.

"Yeah?"

She looked at me, eyes wide open, tears welling in her lashes.

"I don't want to do this anymore."

"Alright," I said.

"Baby, I just want to stay home."

"Fine. Then you'll stay home. I'll pick up the pace on the freelancing, cut wood with Clair. We'll be okay."

I held her close, felt her sigh again and shudder. Then we heard Sophie come back down the stairs, one step at a time. We broke our embrace and Sophie ran into the kitchen, launched herself at Roxanne, who caught her, lifted her up and held her tightly. Sophie pushed herself back and looked at her mother.

"No being sad allowed, Mommy," Sophie said.

"I'm not, honey," Roxanne said.

"Where did you go today?"

"A place called Appleton."

"Is the apple place far, far away?"

"No," Roxanne said.

About ten miles from Prosperity, I thought, if you took the back ridge roads. Just the other side of Searsmont.

"Do you have to go there tomorrow?" Sophie said.

"No, honey," Roxanne said. "I don't."

Twenty minutes, I thought. Shorter if they were in North Appleton.

"Why did the apple place make you sad?" Sophie asked.

Because some psycho devil worshipper scared the crap out of her, I thought.

I patted Sophie's shoulder.

"Mommy just missed us," I said.

2

The rain began sometime after midnight and when I got up at five, it was falling steadily, a storm with staying power, the kind that goes on for days. I grabbed jeans and a T-shirt and slipped out of the room, leaving Roxanne—dark hair spread on the pillow, beautiful in her stillness— to her Saturday sleep-in. When I passed Sophie's room, I went in and checked on her. She was on her stomach, stuffed animals sprawled around her like they were sleeping off a wild party. Her breaths came quickly, each one a miracle. The "arrowheads" were on her bedside table.

I leaned over her, watched and listened. Then I went downstairs, dressed in the kitchen as the water heated in the kettle. When it had boiled, I made a cup of Irish breakfast tea, went to the study end of the big room. Chickadees were already at the feeder, flitting in and out of the rain. I watched them through the sliding glass door, then turned to my desk.

I sat. Opened the right-hand top drawer and took out a leather-bound notebook. I flipped it open and scanned the list, flipped through the clippings and notes scrawled on sticky-notes about stories I wanted to do someday.

Someday was here.

There was an old news clipping about a schooner that had sunk off Deer Isle in the 1950s. That one I'd pitched to *Down East*. A note about a mother who had reportedly visited her son, a murderer doing life at the Maine State Prison, every Friday for twenty-three years.

A letter (addressed to "Jack McMorrow, the reporter, Prosperity, Maine") somebody wrote me about a state trooper who delivered twins in the back seat of his cruiser in a snowstorm. They were twelve and he had cancer and they mowed his lawn. A note about a guy alleged to be the biggest outlaw woodcutter in Maine, cutting trees on out-of-staters' land. A clipping about a guy who claimed to have seen a mountain lion in his backyard in the little town of Swanville, how everybody thought he was nuts.

And a torn piece of classified ad from the *Waldo County News* a few weeks back. Personals offering recreational massage and erotic entertainment. Who were these people? What financial pressures drove them to this? How did they remain anonymous in this small-town place? Did they know their clients from junior high? The ads were circled. One was underlined, "Mandi. Companionship. 298-9630."

I looked at it. Remembered why that had caught my eye, that word. What was the going rate for being a companion? By the hour or the day? What did that mean?

I spread the stuff out, considered it. If Roxanne was going to stay home, I needed to start cranking out the stories. If I made a couple of grand for a magazine feature, eight-hundred for a section-front news story for the *Times*, started pitching stuff to the *Globe*, even the travel section—maybe we could do this.

That and cutting wood.

Turning from the desk, I looked back outside. The rain was heavier, the chickadees at the feeder had turned to soggy feathered balls. Clair and I, thinning a woodlot in West Montville, wouldn't be working today. I turned back. I'd missed the mother at the prison. I could try the guy with the mountain lion.

I picked up the classified ads. Looked at my watch. I wondered what time Mandi opened for business.

Sophie woke up at seven and made a beeline for our room, climbed in bed with Roxanne. They slept for an hour and then Sophie was up, chattering away. I listened from the kitchen as I made scrambled eggs, home fries and English muffins—our Saturday morning ritual. They came downstairs, Sophie skipping ahead in her pajamas, Roxanne behind her in one of my T-shirts, a big one that said Red Sox, 2007 World Champions.

"Daddy, you made special eggs," Sophie said, running to her chair at the table. Roxanne went to the counter and poured herself coffee. She held the cup in her hands, turned to me.

"Hey," she said.

"Hay is for horses," I said, and Sophie repeated it, kicking her legs in the air and whinnying. I got her plate, scooped eggs and potatoes, and put them in front of her. Added apple juice, a fork, a half of muffin with jam. She drank the juice. Bit into the muffin. Drank some more and started on her eggs.

"You ready?" I said to Roxanne.

"Just give me a minute," she said.

"You okay? You look tired."

"I didn't sleep well."

"Why? Because you were—"

"I don't know. Thinking."

"Don't," I said.

"I'm sorry I was so whiny. I'll be okay."

"You'll be okay when you can take a break," I said. "Eight years of looking out for everybody else, including me. Time to take care of yourself."

"I'll take care of you, Momma," Sophie said.

"I know you will," Roxanne said. "And I'll take care of Daddy, too."

We smiled, and Sophie took another bite of eggs, then a drink, holding the glass with two hands.

"I'm going to work some today," I said.

"You're leaving?" Roxanne said, looking into her coffee mug.

"Just for a while. You okay?"

"Sure."

"Those people?"

"What people?" Sophie said.

"It's work, honey," Roxanne said. "No, Jack. I'm just fine."

"I'll talk to Clair," I said.

"No, don't be silly," Roxanne said.

"I like being silly," Sophie said. "Daddy's silly a lot."

"And he's being silly again," Roxanne said.

But she didn't object any more, and an hour later, when I left, I drove down the road and pulled the truck into Clair's drive, parked by the big barn, where lights glowed in the rain.

I went in the side door, across the garage and into the workshop. There was music playing, Gershwin, *American Spring*. Clair was bent over a chainsaw on the bench vise, running a file over the teeth of the chain.

"Morning," I said.

"Morning? It's afternoon, isn't it? Some of us are ready to knock off, day's work done."

I smiled.

"If you call tinkering and puttering work," I said.

"Got to have my saws tip-top. I slow down out there, that'll make two of us."

"My section, the trees were all tangled up."

"Always an excuse," Clair said. "You sure you were never in the Army?"

"For tough guys, you Marines are awfully petty."

"Comes from having to carry everybody else."

I grinned, walked over.

"I'm going to Belfast for a few hours for work," I said.

"If you can call it that, scribbling in a little notebook," Clair said, filing the chain. "What a racket."

"Roxanne and Sophie will be home, just hanging out. Can you keep an eye on the road?"

"Sure. What is it?"

I told him about the devil people, the kids in the trash cans. The guy in Roxanne's face.

"She doesn't scare easy," I said, "but these people shook her up."

"I'll keep an eye on her. I'll tell Mary, she'll have them come for lunch."

"No big deal," I said, as the music stopped. Clair reached for the CD player and clarinet notes floated through the shop.

"If Roxanne's worried, it's big enough," he said.

"She's better today."

"Where in Appleton?"

"She didn't say. And it's probably nothing. They're probably back down in the cellar in their Halloween costumes."

"Take somebody's kids, they don't tend to forget it."

He loosened the jaws of the vise and lifted the saw out.

"I could let these dirtbags know, they come over here, they're playing with fire," Clair said, his voice low and flat, the way it got when he was slipping into combat mode. Forty years after Vietnam, a switch flipped in his head and he was again the emotionless Force Recon Marine.

"I know you could."

"Just say the word," Clair said.

"We'll see," I said.

3

Good stories didn't usually walk up to your desk. It didn't happen at the *Times*, in the thick of Manhattan, and it sure as hell didn't happen here, reporting from the Maine woods. You had to always be moving, eyes and ears open. Ready to stop at the whiff of a story.

Like a predator.

Of course, there were real predators in the woods in Waldo County: coyotes, some big enough to be called wolves; bobcats working the ridges and alder thickets; mountain lions, at least according to a few trappers and loggers who claimed to have seen the big cats bounding across a road at dawn.

From the truck, I called the mountain lion guy, left a message on a machine at his house in Swanville, north of Belfast. The trick would be convincing him to tell a few hundred thousand people that his neighbors thought he was crazy.

My job was one-third writing, two-thirds sales. As I drove, I was gearing up.

The route to Belfast wound over wooded hills, past small ponds, through intersections named for farmers who were dead and gone, their pastures mostly grown up, their barns sagging to the ground.

As you closed in on the coast, the signs of money began to appear. New houses, shingles unweathered like untanned skin, with new cars and trucks parked in front of big garages. Closer to the bay, the boats began to appear. Big sailboats on spindly metal stands, lobster boats parked by stacks of traps.

I pulled over in front of one of the lobsterman's houses, shut off the motor, and opened my folder. I took out the page from the *Waldo County News*. Started at the top.

I called Amber, who offered "playtime." Left a message with a robotic voice on a cell phone. I called Mercedes, who offered "two-girl specials." A guy answered, interrupted when I started to talk, said to call another number, which he recited, then hung up. I called that number, and a woman answered.

"Mercedes?" I said.

"Who's this?" she said, her voice raspy, a smoker.

"My name is Jack McMorrow. I'm a writer for newspapers. I saw your ad in the *Waldo County News* and I'm hoping to—"

Mercedes hung up, too.

After Mercedes was Katrina, then Destinee. Katrina had a real answering machine, with a sultry voice promising she'd call back. Destinee's voice mailbox was full. Finally, it was on to Mandi, the one who offered "companionship."

"Yes," a young woman said.

"Is this Mandi?" I said.

"Who is this?"

She sounded youngish, twenties. I could hear music in the background. Acoustic guitar, a woman singing.

"This is Jack McMorrow," I said. "I'm a reporter. I live in Maine and I write sometimes for the *New York Times*."

For a long moment she didn't answer, and then she said, "What do you want?" She sounded frightened but stayed on the line.

"I'm hoping to talk to Mandi."

"Why?"

"It's nothing to worry about," I said. "I'm just interested in what she's been doing."

"Since what?" It was an odd response.

"Not since anything. Is this Mandi?"

A long pause, and then she said, "Yes."

"I don't mean to bother you. I just was curious about the companionship thing. I wondered about how it works, who takes you up on it."

"Why me?"

"I saw your ad in the paper."

"There are lots of ads in the paper," she said.

"I know. I called all of them."

"What did they say?"

"I left messages. One of them hung up on me."

"I think I better hang up," Mandi said.

"Wait," I said. "Let me buy you lunch. We can just talk about talking."

I heard her exhale, a long deep breath.

"Well," she said. "Maybe. But it's only eleven o'clock. Where are you?" "Outside of Belfast. Where are you?"

"It doesn't matter," Mandi said.

Another pause. The woman had stopped singing in the background and an announcer had come on. Public Radio. Then there was traffic sound. A truck, beeping as it backed up.

"You there?" I said.

"Yes. But I don't know about this."

"No commitment. Just a preliminary chat. I promise."

"You don't have a camera, do you?"

"No. I just write the stories."

"And you don't take pictures?"

"No. I just have a notebook. But I won't even write anything down. Not unless you say it's okay."

"What was your name again?"

"Jack. Jack McMorrow."

Another pause, the woman singing again in the background.

"It's usually fifty dollars for an hour," Mandi said. "For this, it's a hundred."

"It's more to talk?"

"Talking's harder," she said.

I hesitated, reached for my wallet and flipped through the bills. A hundred and eight dollars, some change in the ashtray. I considered it. I wondered if I could get a receipt and expense it.

"Okay," I said.

"There's a pizza place in Belfast, right downtown. As you come into town, it's on the left on the corner. It's called Big Mamma's."

"I'll meet you there," I said. "When?"

"It'll take me a while to drive there," Mandi said. "Say twelve."

"Okay."

"What do you look like?" she said.

"Forty. Dark hair. No beard, no glasses. Not big, not small."

"So now I know what you don't look like."

"Jeans and tan Topsiders and a dark blue polo shirt. I'll put my reporter's notebook on the table. The page will say, 'Jack.'"

"Okay."

How will I know you?" I said.

"You won't," Mandi said, "unless I want you to."

Big Mamma's was as Mandi described, on the left on the main street headed down hill to the harbor. I parked across the street, adjusted the mirror to watch the restaurant. It was early, and I was, too, and the shop was just opening, no big mamma, though. Just a skinny guy in shorts and a black T-shirt unlocking the doors.

I looked down the block toward the water. The shops had awnings. There were two new pubs, a couple of cafes. Facing me was a gallery that sold paintings of the harbor, the real thing just down the street. I wondered if they'd done paintings of the harbor when it had a smelly fish-processing plant, with its cloud of hovering gulls. That was a painting I might buy.

The fish plant was gone, closed then razed, antique shops built in its place. The idea was to change the town into what summer people thought Maine should be, so now there were restaurants with chefs who had worked in New York, and only one of the old bars left, a place for the locals to drink and commiserate.

Big Mamma's was a holdout, still the kind of place real locals would go. I watched them in the car mirror: shopworkers, high school kids, an older man and woman in shorts and sneakers, the guy toting a camera. Rare tourists on a budget.

I waited until noon, then got out of the truck and crossed the street. The pizza shop was half full and I went in and took a seat at the back, away from the window. I sat facing the door and the skinny kid brought me a glass of water and a menu. I took my notebook from my back pocket. I scrawled my name on a blank page and left it out, like a chauffeur's sign at an airport.

And then I waited. Waited some more.

At 12:15, a woman came in alone, but she was in her thirties, ordered takeout and left. At 12:25, a young woman came in with a guy—Mandi and her bodyguard? They sat two booths away, the woman's tank-topped back to me, a butterfly tattoo on her shoulder blade.

Or maybe it was a moth. They talked; she never turned around. And then, at 12:35, another woman came in. Alone.

She was in her mid-20s. Tall with dark hair pulled back, wearing a denim skirt and leather sandals, a long-sleeved knit pullover, cream with thin blue horizontal stripes. Her straw bag was slung over her shoulder. Stopping in front of the counter, she glanced up at the menu on the wall.

Then she turned and looked across the restaurant. Our eyes met. She smiled and headed over. I slipped the money—four twenties and two tens—inside the notebook, then stood. She approached and quickly sat. I sat, too, and she said, loud enough for the next table to hear, "It's so nice to see you, Jack. It's been a long time."

"Yes, it has," I said. "Too long."

"I'm glad you called. It was such a fun surprise."

I looked at her. Pretty face in an old-fashioned sort of way, like a movie star from the forties. Big, dark brown eyes, a broad nose, and a wide mouth with full lips. She was big, not heavy but solidly built, like she'd played high school basketball. Her makeup was a bit obvious— dark eyeliner, up and down, bluish eye shadow—like a young teenage girl would wear. There was a tiny gold stud in her nose.

"I've been meaning to call," I said. "Just never got around to it."

"Oh, I know. We're all so busy," Mandi said. "How's Lucy?"

"She's good. She's going to have a baby."

"Oh, my God. Tell her I'm so happy for her."

She smiled. I did, too, feeling like I was in a play. The kid came with another menu and a glass of water and put them in front of her. She didn't acknowledge him and when she looked up at me, the curtain had just fallen.

"I Googled you," Mandi said softly, picking up the menu.

"So you know about Jack McMorrow, the Scottish physicist."

"You really are a reporter."

"Yes. I've been doing this for a long time."

"Why would the *New York Times* care about me?"

"It's an interesting story," I said.

She raised an eyebrow. I tried again.

"It's an aspect of small-town life you don't think about much."

"It may not be what you think," she said, still staring at the menu.

"Most stories aren't. That's what I like about doing this."

"People are complicated, you know what I'm saying?" she said. "They aren't what they seem."

"I know that," I said. "It's the one thing you can count on."

She looked up at me.

"The clock's ticking," Mandi said.

I slid the notebook over, the bills sticking out. She lifted the page and slipped the money out, tucked the bills in her bag. She slid the notebook back.

"I'm not hungry," she said. "Let's go for a walk."

We left the pizza shop and started down the street toward the water. The sidewalk was busy on a summer Saturday, and we stepped around people as they paused to look into shop windows. A couple of guys outside a pub turned to glance at Mandi. She ignored them and didn't talk to me, either.

We walked to the end of the street, past a big seafood restaurant that overlooked the harbor, lobsters traps screwed to the restaurant roof like they'd been blown up there in a tornado. There was a boardwalk, ramps leading down to the floats. A couple leaned against the railing as their young kids tossed chips to squawking, squabbling gulls. We detoured around them and I was beginning to wonder what I was going to get for my hundred dollars. I could see a receipt was not in the cards.

Mandi crossed to a bench on a patch of lawn across from the boat launch. She sat down and crossed her legs, pretty legs, with toenails painted red. I sat beside her, but not close. Pulled a small digital recorder, slightly bigger than a cigarette lighter, from my front pocket.

"No," she said. "You can write, but no recording. No voice."

I put the recorder away, took out the notebook and pen. I smiled, I hoped disarmingly. I was about to ask her a question when she beat me to it.

"Why aren't you a reporter for the *New York Times* in New York?"

"I was. I left."

"Why?"

"Something happened."

"They fired you?"

"Something like that," I said.

"So you ran away to the boonies of Maine?"

"Maybe at first. Now I like it here."

"What do you like about it?"

"Who's the reporter?"

She smiled, looked out at the water.

"You answer my questions, maybe I'll answer yours," Mandi said.

She was right. People were not what they seemed.

"I like the woods. I like the people. There's something true about this place."

"I think truth is way overrated," she said.

I wrote in my notebook, kept one eye on her. She didn't react.

"Why?"

"I think people spend most of their time trying to get away from the truth. Watching movies. Those reality shows on TV. You know they're made up? Not true at all. That's why I watch them. They're acting."

"Are you acting?" I said.

"Now?" she said.

"When you do what you do."

She didn't answer. I could see her biting the inside of her lip, the first hint of some sort of agitation.

"We're all acting, more or less," Mandi said. "Life is just an act anyway, don't you think? We pick out a part, who we're gonna play, and then we try to be that person. If we get tired of that one, we try another one. You used to be the big-city reporter. Now you're playing the country reporter. You just learn new lines."

She looked at the couple with the kids feeding the gulls.

"They're playing the parents."

"What part are you playing?" I said.

She shrugged.

"I'm playing the companion," she said. "My character is a girl. Men pay her for my time."

"For sex?"

Mandi glanced sideways at me.

"Sorry, but I have to ask."

"That's what it's supposed to be," she said. "But you know what?"

"What?"

"Mostly they pay me so they can tell me their troubles, have me laugh at their jokes."

She held my gaze for a three count, looked away.

"I'm a good listener. I bet if we sit here long enough you'll tell me why you really left New York."

"Maybe," I said. "But let me ask you another question. Why do you do this at all?"

"Do what, Jack? Sit on benches talking to strange men?"

"And everything else."

She stared out at the harbor, the boats, the gulls, the kids with the chips. I waited, let the silence linger

"You don't waste any time, do you?"

"You want me to beat around the bush?"

Mandi shrugged. "It's your nickel."

"That's an old-fashioned expression," I said.

"I guess I'm old-fashioned, too," she said.

"So why?"

"Why what?"

"Why do this?"

She looked out at the boats.

"You'd be surprised," she said.

Scribbling quickly, I said, "What about it would surprise me?"

"How lonely people are."

"The men who call you?"

"Yeah. If I had to describe them—I mean, if you asked me what they have in common, it's that they're all lonely."

"But aren't they married, some of them?"

"Sure. But they're still alone."

"So your ad isn't really a euphemism? A nice way of—"

"I know what a euphemism is, Jack. I read books. For a hundred bucks, you can ask me questions but you don't get to patronize me."

"Sorry."

We sat. For a while, we didn't talk. She ran her hands over her hair, slipped it out of the scrunchy and tightened it back up. Suddenly she started up again.

"Sure, it's partly that, euphemistic I mean. But not totally. You know what it does, my ad?"

"No."

"It says this is more than an afternoon quickie, some guy can't wait for his wife. This is temporary but it's still a relationship."

"Interesting way to put it."

"You know what the ad should say?"

"No, what?" I said.

"It should say, 'I'll pretend to like you.'"

"People would respond to that?"

"No, but it's true. It's what most guys want. Some women, too. Everybody just wants somebody to care about them, not to have sex with them, necessarily. But somebody to find them interesting."

"And do you?"

"What? Find them interesting?"

"Yeah."

"Sometimes. For an hour or two. Or a day. A couple of weeks ago a guy took me to Fun Town. It's this amusement park, down past Portland. You been there?"

I shook my head.

"We had a date. We went on rides and ate popcorn and pizza. He had a great time, ate this gross sausage sandwich. Guys like the most disgusting food, I've noticed. Anyway, the end of the day, he kissed me goodbye on the cheek, asked if he could call me again."

"That's it?"

"That's it," Mandi said. "Cost him three-hundred bucks. Plus the rides and popcorn."

"What did you say?"

"I said no," Mandi said.

"Why? You didn't like him?"

"He was fine. Kind of boring but nice enough."

"But what?"

"It's still business, Jack."

"Why?"

"Why is it business? Because they pay me money, I provide a service."

"Why is it a business? This may be too personal, but why aren't you going to places with guys you really care about. Or do you?"

Mandi stood up, pulled her sleeves down and crossed her arms.

"You're right," she said. "It's personal."

She crossed to the boardwalk, started back toward the restaurant. I walked beside her as gulls swooped over us, hoping for chips. At the end of the walkway, she stopped, leaned over the railing and looked out at the boats. I leaned next to her and we stood for a while and didn't talk. Gulls circled. Boats chugged into the harbor and out. Two people pushed off from one of the biggest sailboats, two masts, dark green hull and matching green and white canvas over the stern, and motored over in an inflatable dinghy. We looked down as they eased up to the dock. The guy held the boat still while the woman stepped up on to the dock.

She was tanned and lithe. He was handsome as a catalog model.

"Money," Mandi said.

"Serious money," I said.

"You ever wonder," she said, "what it would be like to have everything go your way?"

"Don't think they don't have problems."

"I know," she said. "I have a client like that. Rich as hell. Never even had a job. But he knows."

"Knows what?"

"What it's like. To be really down and out. His family's all screwed up. Parents never wanted him around, shipped him off to some fancy school when he was eight. His father's been married, like, five times. Mother's a cokehead, tried to commit suicide."

"Is that what you have in common?" I said.

She smiled. "Screwed up families?"

"Yeah."

No reply. I waited. She looked out on the harbor, lost in thought.

"Did I offend you?" I said.

She laughed. "Offend me? Hard to do."

"If I did, I apologize. I didn't mean to."

"No prob, Jack." She turned and looked at me and I felt her eyes, her smile drawing me in.

"I don't even know you, Jack," Mandi said. "When did we meet, twenty minutes ago? But you're like me. Easy to talk to. "

"Goes with the territory, I guess," I said, more business-like, stepping back. "Let me ask you a couple more questions, before my time runs out."

"Go ahead."

"How old are you?"

"Twenty-four, give or take a year."

"Do you live alone?"

"No, I have a cat."

"What's the cat's name?"

"If I tell you, how will you know it's true?" She grinned.

"Trust," I said.

"She's black and long-haired. You can brush her like a doll."

"Indoor cat?"

"Oh, yeah. She wouldn't know what to do on the outside."

I wrote that down. "Where'd you grow up?"

"A bunch of places, none of them worth ever going back to."

I scribbled more.

"Have you had other jobs?"

"Sure. Worked full-time and I was on food stamps."

"Go to college?"

"No."

"Finish high school?"

"Yes."

"Where?"

"It doesn't matter."

She suddenly looked weary, discouraged, like some sort of medication was wearing off. And then her mind was someplace else, not on Belfast, Maine or Jack McMorrow or the gulls trailing the lobster boats into the harbor. She twisted her hands like she was cold.

And I saw them.

Both wrists. Scars that made pale pink hash marks, like she had been keeping score in some sad and horrible game.

"I should go," Mandi said, turning away, starting up the walk.

"I didn't get my full hour."

"Call me again."

"I will. Because I have more questions."

"So do I," she said. "Are you married?"

"Yes."

"Kids?"

"One. She's almost four."

"You love her?"

"More than life itself."

"How 'bout your wife?"

"Her, too."

She smiled, wistfully, I thought.

"That's sweet," Mandi said. She quickened her pace and I did the same. Side by side, we walked past the lobster restaurant, back up the street.

"Where are you parked?" I said.

"Around the corner. Up a ways. But I gotta go to the store, as long as I'm in town."

"Okay."

We were halfway up the block. There was a hardware store ahead on the right, rubber rain boots and flowerpots set out on the sidewalk.

Mandi stopped at the door. Held out her hand. I clasped it, gave it a shake. It was soft but her grip was firm. She looked me in the eye, then turned away, walked past the flower pots and into the store. I hesitated, then continued up the block. Crossing at the corner, I walked out of sight, then stopped and walked back.

Leaning against the brick wall of an old hotel, I watched and waited. After a couple of minutes, Mandi came out of the store, empty handed. She looked both ways, then crossed the street. Halfway down the block, back toward the water, she stepped into a doorway and out of sight.

I waited another minute, then walked down the brick sidewalk. The doorway was next to a pottery shop. The door was painted pale green, a lace curtain covering the window from the inside. I turned the ornate iron knob.

The door was locked. I pressed my face to the glass and peered in. Stairs.

I stepped out onto the sidewalk to the curb. Glanced up.

There were three windows on the second floor with the same lace curtains. I walked down the block, crossed again, then went to the adjacent corner, next to the pizza shop. I went in and the same kid gave me a look. I took a bottle of water from a rack, flipped a couple of dollars onto the counter. And then I went to one of the window booths and sat.

And watched.

After five minutes, one of the curtains moved. Ten minutes later, a black cat jumped up and sat on the sill. Five minutes after that, the curtain brushed aside. Arms encircled the cat and picked it up. A face flashed in the window, just for a moment.

Mandi was home.

4

They weren't devil worshippers, Roxanne said. She'd been on the phone to the deputy. The deputy said the couple were into some religion that had them worshipping Satan, except he wasn't the devil. Christianity invented the devil we knew, the one with the pitchfork and horns.

"Then what is he?" I said.

I was holding a can of Ballantine Ale. I opened it. Sophie looked up from the floor of the porch, then reached for another crayon.

"He's something that came before Judaism and Islam and Christianity," Roxanne said.

"Ra, the Sun God?"

"No, he's Satan, except it was these other religions that turned him into something evil and crowded him out."

I took a swallow of ale. Roxanne was drinking iced tea. We were sitting in Adirondack chairs, overlooking the lawn, the apple trees. A blue bird flew to the roof of one of the bird boxes at the far edge of the lawn, flipped down and stuffed its babies with bugs.

"And that's why they didn't feed their kids?" I said.

"They don't believe in buying food that will make a profit for Jewish and Christian companies. That's what the dad told the deputies. He said they raise their own pure food."

"Harder than it looks."

"Deer ate the lettuce. Woodchucks got most of their broccoli. Potatoes weren't ready 'cause they planted too late. Kids were living on green tomatoes and wormy spinach."

"Can't Satan just whip up some barbecue?" I said. "Must make a mean hot sauce."

We both sipped. Sophie was stretched out on her belly, coloring something brown.

"What is it, Soph?" I said.

"It's deers," she said. "It was bears but I changed it. I gave them horns."

"Very nice, honey," Roxanne said.

"You're a good artist," I said.

"I need to show Brownie," Sophie said, and she got up, took off on sandaled feet, paper flapping in her hand.

Brownie was a toy stuffed bear, all the fur loved off it. A gift from Clair and Mary.

"Where are they now?" I said, asking the question that had been hovering.

"Parents went home," Roxanne said. "Kids have been placed, but they'll be moved after they're assessed. Hearing is Monday."

"Did they calm down? The parents, I mean?"

"The deputy said the mom's okay, the dad's on another planet. Went into a rant about how they don't recognize the authority of our Christian government. He won't even begin talking about a safety plan. Won't listen to anything we try to say. He said he'll 'await spiritual guidance.'"

"From Lucifer?"

"I guess," Roxanne said.

"They know your name?" I said.

"Yes. It's on all the documents. I'll have to testify at the hearing next week."

"Will they show up?"

Roxanne shrugged.

If they don't, I thought, where will they be?

I took a swallow of ale. Thought of my conversation with Clair. I wondered if I should load the rifle before I turned in.

Sophie went up at 7:30 for books and then bed. She propped Brownie on one side of her and a big blonde doll named Twinnie, so called because she was the size of a two-year-old and Sophie had decided then that they were twins. I read them a story about mice that lived in a treehouse. A weasel tried to get into the house and the mouse manned (moused?) the barricades. . . .

We had at least one weasel, maybe more.

Sophie asked me to read the story again because Brownie hadn't been paying attention. Halfway through the encore she was asleep. I took Twinnie down and propped her up in the corner by the bookshelf. Brownie stayed put. I kissed Sophie's silken cheek, stared at her for a minute, and then I walked downstairs, silently in bare feet. Roxanne had gotten a blanket and a glass of wine and had gone back out to the porch. She was sitting with her feet tucked underneath her.

I kissed her cheek, too.

"So tell me," she said.

"The girl?"

"Yes. Start at the beginning."

I did, from the pizza shop to the talk on the water, and back to the pizza shop, watching the apartment.

"That's so sad," Roxanne said.

"It is. You wonder what brought her to this place. She seemed smart. Quite nice. Very likeable. I mean, if you didn't know her, what she did, maybe you'd like her, too."

"Most women in any sort of sex trade were sexually abused when they were young. They go on to repeat it. Maybe out of some sort of self-abasement. Maybe because they think that's all they're good for."

"Or they're drug addicts."

"Or both."

"The scars tell you something was seriously wrong with her at some point," I said.

"Yes," Roxanne said. "Very."

"It's a good story though."

"I guess, but why are your stories never simple?"

"Life isn't simple," I said.

Roxanne sipped her wine, looked out on the lawn, the apple trees, the woods beyond. From the edge of the woods, a red-eyed vireo sang, the last bird to call it quits.

"We're okay, you know," I said.

"I know. But it's a big mess. Everything, except for us."

"There's Clair and Mary."

"I know. But sometimes I feel like we're the only thing staying in place, our little part of the world. Everything else is just swirling around, all this chaos. I just want to stop the merry go round and get off."

"Can I help you?" I said.

Roxanne turned to me, smiled. Stretched her legs in front of her. Her lips opened. Her eyes softened. "Yes."

"Right now?"

"I think I need you. I need to be that close to you."

"We're pretty close anyway," I said, and we stood and kissed, then walked upstairs, my arm around her waist. We looked in on Sophie, sleeping on her back with Brownie beside her. We closed her door and went to bed. Dusk deepened as we made love, and when it grew dark, Roxanne got up and lit a candle. For a moment, she stood in its light, and I smiled as she came back to bed and melted into my arms.

Ten o'clock. Roxanne was asleep, her back to me, her bare shoulders showing above the sheet. I eased off of the bed, found my boxers on the floor and put them on. I blew out the candle and went downstairs. I walked to the kitchen, turned on a light, and opened the closet door. My deer rifle, a Remington 30-06, was leaning in the back.

I took it out, went to the counter and, standing on a chair, reached a box of shells from the top shelf of the cupboard. From a jar on the shelf above the slate sink, I took out a key, unlocked the trigger lock.

I loaded the gun, four rounds clicking into the magazine, the metallic clack loud in the silent house. I put the lock back on, kept the key out. Walking to the study, I looked out the window at the darkness. I could hear the rustle of the night woods, the distant yelp of a fox.

I walked to the dining room, looked out the front window to the road. It was empty and all was still.

The rifle cradled in my arms, I walked up the stairs, opened Sophie's door and listened to her breathing—soft and regular as a clock tick. I left the door open and went to our room. Roxanne was still asleep and I opened the closet door, leaned the rifle against the wall inside. I closed the door and hooked it shut at the top.

I went to the side of the bed, put the key on the top of the earthenware base of the lamp on the bedside table.

Making a mental note to show Roxanne the key in the morning, I lay back on the pillows. Eyes wide open in the darkness, I stared. Listened. Heard a car approaching, coming down the road from the east. Loud exhaust. A manual transmission. Probably a pickup. American.

It slowed slightly as it passed the house but continued on until the night was quiet again.

I listened, waiting.

And then the truck returned, slowed, continued on.

5

The hearing was Monday morning at eleven in Belfast District Court. Roxanne left early for a prepping meeting at her office in Rockland, kissing me on the fly as she went out the door.

"You can do this," I said.

"Thanks," she said, looking back. "For everything."

I made oatmeal and Sophie and I chatted as we ate. She said she wanted to go back into the deep woods to see if we could find more arrows, maybe even some Indian kids. I said I had to do some work and asked if she would like to visit Clair and Mary.

She was out of the chair and on her way to the door when I reminded her she was still in her pajamas. She changed direction, little feet sliding on the pine floor, and ran for her room.

I went to the phone and called. Mary answered and I asked if I could leave Sophie with her for three hours or so.

"You could leave her for three weeks," Mary said.

She was at the kitchen door when we arrived, Sophie carrying Brownie, me handing off her backpack filled with toys and books and crayons. Mary said she was making cookies and needed a helper.

Sophie ran in, saw her "cooking chair" pulled up at the counter, and started to climb up.

"Is Clair here today?" I said.

Mary, her salt-and-pepper hair pulled back, her face tanned from the garden, gave me one of her gentle and reassuring smiles.

"He's here. He told me what was going on. She'll be fine, Jack. Hard part for you will be getting her back."

"Between one and two," I said.

"Take your time. Do what you have to do."

I hoped it wouldn't come to that.

It was a little after 10:30 when I drove down the hill into Belfast. I drove down Main Street toward the salt-smelling bay, looked up and down the sidewalks for Mandi, but didn't see her. When I passed her building, I slowed and looked up. The black cat was in the window.

I circled back, took a left at the light and drove a block and parked the truck on a side street diagonally across from the courthouse. There were cars parked up and down the block in front of the building, and three women smoking on the sidewalk out front. I settled into my seat and watched.

The women—middle-aged, young and younger—resembled each other. Three generations, I decided. The family that goes to court together . . . After a couple of minutes, they flicked their cigarette butts into the gutter and walked into the courthouse. A jail van pulled away from the back of the building and turned the corner. Orange-suited inmates looked out of the windows sullenly, their field trip soon coming to an end.

A couple arrived with a teen-aged boy, the father rigid, the mother patting the kid on the back. Belfast cops came and went, then two Waldo County deputies pulled in, followed by a state trooper, a young woman. She adjusted her round-brimmed hat and went into the courthouse just as Roxanne's Subaru pulled up.

She was with a guy in khakis and a blazer. They got out, retrieved their briefcases from the back seat, and started up the walk. As they neared the door, an old Chevy pickup came down the block from downtown. It was dark green, patched on the doors. The exhaust was loud and the motor throbbed as the truck rolled up to the curb.

It was the truck I'd heard on our road.

A woman got out of the passenger side, took a canvas tote off of the seat and slammed the door shut. She was wearing glasses, baggy jeans and sneakers, a shapeless print shirt. Her hair was long and straight, nondescript brown, and tied back in a ponytail.

She crossed in front of the truck and walked toward the entrance. The truck pulled away, started down the block. I eased down in the seat as it passed, got a good look at Mr. Satan himself.

He was forty, maybe younger, but thin and hawk-nosed, a face out of the Depression-era Dust Bowl. At a glance, I saw a green work shirt, a tattoo on his left arm. He was wearing sunglasses. He was smiling, a self-satisfied grin, as if everything was going according to plan.

The truck rumbled away, and a minute later it rumbled back. He parked across and up the street from me, in front of a turreted old Victorian house, now apartments. He shut off the truck's motor and sat.

He didn't appear to notice me, didn't look in my direction. His gaze was fixed on the courthouse doors. I watched him—and the courthouse. The radio played Beethoven, a violin concerto; the three smoking women came out, lit up in unison, raised their heads and blew out a big puff. It hovered over them as they walked down the block, got in an old Ford Taurus and left. Then it was Vivaldi and the couple with the kid. The mother was crying, wiping her eyes, and the kid was hanging his head. The father walked ten feet ahead like they were suddenly not related.

Mister Satan watched the door.

For a while nobody came or went. Gulls flew over, headed for the bay. Vivaldi gave way to Strauss, a sappy waltz. I shut off the radio. Then the courthouse doors swung open. Roxanne came out, followed by her colleague in the blazer, two deputies and the woman trooper, another older guy who looked like a lawyer. They all walked to the street, paused and talked.

Where was Mrs. Satan? Still inside?

The lawyer was talking to Roxanne; she was shaking her head, disagreeing. Her face was hard, a look I'd seen before. No deal, no way.

The cops said something, then started for their cruisers. The lawyer started walking up the street toward downtown. Roxanne and the blazer guy got in her Subaru as the cruisers pulled away.

Mister Satan started his truck. I started mine.

Roxanne pulled out, started north, headed for the road that would lead to Route 1 and south to Rockland. The Chevy approached the courthouse as Mrs. Satan came out of the front door, but her husband didn't slow, didn't even seem to look at her. He passed the courthouse, following Roxanne. As I fell in behind them, Mrs. Satan started walking up the block.

Roxanne turned, headed up the hill and out of town. She was driving fast, as she did when she was upset, agitated. The old truck accelerated, puffing blue smoke. I cruised along a hundred yards behind the Chevy, saw Roxanne signal to make the left onto Route 1.

The truck's blinker went on. We all turned, merging into the summer traffic, moving slowly southward in a tourist procession.

A mile from town, Roxanne swung out and passed. The truck pulled up close behind a slow-moving Mercedes with New Jersey plates. I closed in as he pulled alongside the Mercedes, smoke trailing behind the pickup as he passed and pulled back in. We crossed a bridge and the Mercedes braked, turned off to the left. Cars pulled into the procession from side roads, restaurants, and I was five cars back now, watching Roxanne and Mr. Satan pull away from me.

A tractor trailer with a yacht on a flatbed pulled out ahead of my group of cars, followed by a wide-load warning car with flashing yellow lights.

I grabbed my phone from the seat, dialed Roxanne. I got her voice mail.

"Your Satan guy. He's following you in a green Chevy pickup," I said. "I'm a few cars back. If he gets close, call the police."

I put the phone down. Slapped the wheel. The boat hauler slowed on an upgrade, then pulled to the side. I pulled out, punched the accelerator, and passed.

One car. Two. Three and four, and then the truck began to edge back into the travel lane. There was a car coming in the other direction and I floored the truck, hit the horn. The wide-load car swerved right and the driver flipped me off as I passed. The truck and boat kept moving to the left, and I hit the lights as the car sped toward me.

It swerved right. I passed it in a blare of horns from all sides, kept the gas down, hit eighty just past Northport. Slowing for ferry traffic in Lincolnville, I called Roxanne again, got voice mail. Probably reporting back to Rockland about the hearing. I passed an old couple in a Volvo wagon, saw the man shake his fist as I pulled back in.

I picked up the phone again, started to punch in 911.

And I saw the Chevy, a glimpse, a mile ahead.

We were north of Camden, traffic slowing for hikers turning into Mount Battie. I was two cars back as we eased down the hill into Camden. Mr. Satan was separated from Roxanne by a box truck hauling lobsters. We rolled past the big captains' houses, into the downtown traffic, cars slowing for shoppers on Main Street, braking at the sight of gift shops.

The Chevy swung around a BMW, pressed up close behind Roxanne. A gaggle of shoppers crossed in front of me, taking their time. I eased through them like they were sheep in a road in Ireland, a woman saying, "What is your problem?" and then the BMW turned right.

I sped up, closed on the Chevy, now just six feet from Roxanne's bumper. I could see Mr. Satan reaching for something on the truck seat, turning away from the road, then back. A big knot of shoppers, all khaki shorts and polo shirts, stepped into the crosswalk in front of the truck and he slammed on the brakes. As he waited, I pulled over, parked in front of a hydrant. Got out and trotted up to the Chevy.

I yanked the passenger door open. He looked up wide-eyed as I grabbed the sawed-off baseball bat from the seat, slid in and sat.

I slammed the door shut. Held the club across my lap.

"Okay, Beelzebub," I said. "We're gonna have a talk."

6

"Take the next right and pull in someplace," I said.

He looked at me and smiled, that same smug grin. His eyes were a pale gray that looked almost white against his dark, weathered skin. The crosswalk cleared and he eased up to the intersection, took a right on the red light, pulled in behind the shops in a space that said "Employees only." He put the truck in park and reached up and shut off the engine.

"You're following the people from the state," I said.

"I'm looking for my children," he said.

"What's this for?" I said, waving the club at him.

"We have a dog. He's turned mean. Sometimes he won't let us get to the truck. I need to hold him off."

"Bullshit," I said.

He smiled again. Shrugged. His hands were still on the wheel and I could see his arm muscles flexing. Long, sinewy arms. Hands tanned with pale scars. On the left wrist was a tattoo of a snake. There was something on the right hand but I couldn't make it out.

"Back off," I said.

"I have a right to my own children," he said.

"Tell it to the judge."

"The judge is a Judeo-Christian puppet. He's a pawn of the Christian dictators."

"Should have thought of that sooner."

"I also have a right to practice my religion. And there's only one road south from Belfast. I have a right to drive down the road."

"Tell that to the judge, too."

Another slow shake of his head.

"It's all so predictable," he said. "The Jews invented Christianity to keep the masses in check, keep them down. Now they're all threatened when the true religion surfaces. It scares all of you to the bone. You Jews. Papists. Perpetrators of the Nazarean hoax."

"Your religion is your business," I said. "Show up in court, have your say. Just stay away from her."

"You work for the Jewess," he said.

I didn't answer.

"She must be afraid," he said. "That's what happens when you build your life on lies. Nothing frightens a liar more than the truth. And Father Satan is the whole truth. The only truth. In ancient Egypt, he was an ancient religion. But he's been slandered by the Jews and the Christians for centuries. Muslims, too. Nothing but lies. But his true nature has been revealed to some of us."

"Goody for you."

"You're one of her minions."

"Doesn't matter what I am, just so you get the message. Stay the hell away."

"Hell. Ha," he grinned. "Hell is a Jew/Christian invention. There's no such thing. No fire. No devils with horns and pitchforks. All a fabrication. Bullshit. Invented to keep the people ignorant and afraid. It's true. I've done research."

"A little Internet is a dangerous thing," I said.

"Did you know Father Satan has minions, too? They're called demons, but true believers can communicate with Satan directly. There is no Christian hierarchy for Satanists. No kissing the Pope's filthy feet. Sending money to some whoremonger television minister. Praise the lord and screw the harlots."

He smiled, pleased with that line.

"Whatever. But if you come near Ms. Masterson, if I think you're going to try to hurt her, I'll stop you."

He turned toward me for the first time since the moment I'd climbed into the truck.

"I won't let my kids be turned into Christian slaves," he said.

"So feed them," I said.

"First thing a Judeo-Christian ruler does when confronted by a society that won't buckle under. Steal their children and enslave them. The French and English did it to the native peoples here. Spanish in Mexico. European conquerers did it to most of Africa. It continues today. Aboriginal children in Australia. Stolen away, brainwashed with the whole preposterous Christian hoax." His eyes were shining.

"Do what you want," I said. "Run around the woods in a goddamn robe. Sacrifice a goat, pal, I don't care. But don't ever come near my house again."

His smile melted away. His eyes still shone.

"Terrible things befall those who mock Satan," he said. "It's true. I've seen it happen. Diseases. Accidents."

"Terrible things happen to anybody who threatens my family," I said. "I've seen that happen, too."

His smile reappeared, like I was amusing. His eyes narrowed as though he were examining me. A woman walked by and frowned at us, parked in somebody's space.

"What's your name, anyway?" he said.

"Jack," I said. "What's yours?"

"Harland," he said.

"Okay, Harland. Last warning.

You come near her, you'd better hope you're right about Hell."

I reached for the door handle, pulled it and the door creaked open. I got out of the truck, still holding the club. He reached for the key in the ignition.

I looked back at him and the motor started.

"I'm not alone, Jack," he said, over the rumbling. "You'd be surprised to find out how many of us have come to know Satan. You don't hear about us because we don't proselytize, sell a package of lies to the ignorant masses."

"Good for you."

He looked at me as I swung the truck door shut. No smile, just a hard, unblinking stare like a mask had fallen away. "But we're right here, all around," he said. "Right in your own backyard."

7

I was back in my truck, still parked on Main Street. While I was talking to Harland, Roxanne had called back. Six times.

I rang her number, waited with the billy club on the seat, the tourists tromping by, boat shoes and whale belts.

"Jack," Roxanne said. "What happened? I was on the phone but I didn't see any truck."

"He stopped in Camden."

"Harland Wilton?"

"Yeah. We talked."

"You talked to him? Jack, you can't—"

"He was stuck in traffic. It seemed like a good opportunity. Where are you?"

"The office. Jack, what did you say to him? Oh, God, I could get—"

"I don't think he'll complain. I took his billy club away."

"Jack—"

"He says you kidnapped his kids to make them Christian slaves."

"Right, but what were you doing in Belfast? How do you even know who he—"

"I went over to see if I could find Mandi."

Silence, the first of the conversation.

"Just to follow up. Then I swung by the court, see if I could get a look at them. He dropped his wife off, then parked and waited outside for you. When you left, he trailed you out of town, all the way to Camden."

There was a long pause. "You there?" I said.

"Yeah."

"So how was court?"

"She read this thing in court that said we were persecuting her because she's a Satanist. Said the judge was a puppet of the Jews and the Pope."

"Interesting legal strategy. Bit of a gamble."

"Worship however you want," Roxanne said. "Just don't have your kids rooting for food in garbage cans. Don't whip them with belts."

"Guy have a job?"

"Flag person for a construction company."

"Huh. What's he do? Get Satan on his walkie-talkie? He says he can talk directly to him, you know."

"They're totally whacko," Roxanne said. "Both of them."

"Yeah, but I have to admit parts of it are kind of interesting, in a paranoid sort of way. Egyptians, Satan getting slandered by Christians."

"How long did you talk to him for, Jack?"

"A few minutes."

"Did you—"

"Threaten him? I said if he came near you, I'd stop him."

A voice in the background, somebody in the office in Rockland.

"This puts me in a very difficult position, Jack," Roxanne said, her voice hushed. "I mean you can't just—"

"I did," I said. "And I will. This guy isn't just your average angry parent."

"I know."

Another pause.

"Where's Sophie?" Roxanne said.

"With Clair and Mary."

"Did you—"

"Tell them? Yes."

Roxanne let out a long, audible breath.

"I'm stopping in Belfast on the way home," I said. "A few more questions for Mandi and then I can write that story, move on to the next one. You can think about staying home."

There were more voices in the background, a man and a woman.

"Not today, Jack," Roxanne said.

"Then soon," I said.

"I gotta go," she said, and I started to tell her I loved her but she'd hung up. I put the phone down on the seat by the club and started the truck, turning at the light. Harland was gone.

I'd danced around the question with Mandi—or maybe she had danced around it with me—but Myra at the *Times* would zero in on it in a minute: "What does she actually do with these men? Yeah, I get all this companionship stuff, but are they paying her for sex or what?"

I assumed, but as newspaper editors said, when you assume you make an ass out of you and me.

A half-hour back to Belfast, traffic slow and steady, cars pulling in and out as tourists stopped to spend money. I drove, one hand on the wheel, my mind jumping from Mandi to Harland and back. Escorts and Satanists. They'd love me at the Maine Chamber of Commerce.

I turned off of Route 1 and drove into town, calling Mandi as I sat at the light on Route 3. The phone went right to voice mail—no message, just a beep. I told Mandi I had a couple of more questions, and I was in Belfast. Did she want to have coffee?

She didn't call right back, and I drove down the hill into downtown, quieter now late on a Monday morning. A few people were coming and going and I drove slowly all the way down to the harbor, where the boats were riding on their moorings, bows pointing south. I stopped and looked out, watched a lobster boat coming in from the bay, a cloud of gulls hovering over the stern like bugs. I started back up the street and parked in front of the pizza shop.

I called. Got voice mail again.

 Got out of the truck and looked over at Mandi's apartment.

It was nearly noon and her shades were drawn. A late night? An early start to the day? I turned and walked up the block, crossed at the corner and started back. As I approached Mandi's door, I slowed.

The door was open, more than just a crack. I paused at the doorway and peered into the gloom of the hallway. There was a beer can on the floor, Bud Lite.

I looked more closely.

At the bottom of the stairs there was a wine bottle, empty, lying on its side.

A big party the night before? The door left open by departing guests?

I couldn't picture it, but then I'd only seen the Mandi she'd wanted to show me.

I hesitated, looked up and down the block. I pushed the door open and it creaked. As I stepped in, something brushed past my feet.

The black cat, skipping up the dark stairwell like a ghost.

I waited. Listened. Nothing.

Why was the cat out? Should I let it back in?

I stepped into the hallway, left the door open behind me. Listened again and started up the stairs. At the landing, I paused. Listened again. I heard the cat crying, but the meow was faint. From inside the apartment? The door still open?

I started up the stairs, slowed as I approached the landing. There was a woman's shoe on the floor, a black stilleto. I stepped onto the landing. The inside of the shoe was flesh-colored.

With a brown stain.

Blood.

I turned. The door to the apartment was open six inches. I put my hand into my pocket and slipped out a pocketknife, pried out the main blade. Holding the knife close to my leg I eased inside the door.

It was a living room. Couch. End table stacked with books. Plants on a set of shelves by the window, where the shades were drawn. The cat dashed out of a cracked door to my left—the bedroom? It saw me and ran back in, its tail a black plume.

I listened. Took five steps across the room to the door. Held the knife firmly and pushed the door open. My eyes adjusted.

A bureau to the left. To the right, by the windows, a double bed, sheets disheveled. A bare foot poking out from beyond the bed.

8

Mandi was on the floor, on her stomach. She was wearing black underwear and the other black shoe. I turned away, scanned the room. Moved quickly across and yanked the door back, knife ready.

There was no one. I did the same with the closet. Empty. I went back to Mandi, crouched over her.

"Hey," I said. "It's Jack. It's okay."

There were drops of blood on the floor by her head. Her wrist was purple and twisted. Her ankle, the one with the foot in the shoe, was a black-blue bruise and swollen twice its size.

As I took out my phone, she moaned and turned her head.

Her eyes were blackened and there were scrapes on her cheeks and temples. Crusted blood flecked her nose and chin.

"Hey," I said. "It's okay."

She looked at me, squinting as she tried to focus.

"He hit me, Jack," she said.

"I know," I said. "It's okay now."

I closed my knife and dropped it in my pocket. Took my phone from the other pocket and called 911.

"My ankle," Mandi said.

"I know. Just stay still."

"And my wrist. I think it's broken."

"When was this?" I said.

"When is it now?"

"It's about noon. Monday."

"It was last night."

The cat rubbed against me, slipped past, and flopped on the floor by Mandi's side. It purred.

"Hey, Lu," Mandi said weakly.

"Who was he?" I said.

"I don't know. He seemed nice. He said he came off a boat. But then he . . . he changed. All of a sudden he got all angry. He started hitting me. He hit me with my shoe. Where is it? Did you see it?"

"It's in the hallway," I said. "What's his name?"

"His name? Roger. That's what he said. They're really nice shoes. Prada pumps. Originally three-hundred and fifty dollars. I got them for twenty-two at TJ Maxx."

"You can get some new ones."

"Maybe I can wash them off."

"I think the police will want to look at that shoe," I said.

A flicker of fright passed over her, and she started to lift herself up, cried out in pain and fell back.

"I can't let them see me," she said, started to try again. "They can't know. Please. Please don't tell them. Please, Jack. Please don't."

I put my hand on her shoulder.

"Stay still," I said. "I'll cover you up."

I went to the closet and took a blanket off the shelf. Standing over her, I partly unfolded it and laid it across her. There was a weird feeling of déjà vu, putting Sophie to bed one time when she had a fever. I brushed it away. Mandi was starting to shiver and I patted her shoulder again.

We heard a siren, whooping and approaching fast.

"Oh, no," she said.

"You've got to go to the hospital."

"But I—"

"Mandi," I said. "Do you have this guy's number?"

She looked at me, eyes wide.

"For me," I said.

"For you?"

"I'll take care of it," I said.

"My phone," Mandi said. "It would be on there."

"Where is it?"

"I don't know."

I stood, looked around the bedroom. There was nothing on the bedside table, nothing on the bureau except for cosmetics, some jewelry in an open box. The siren was louder. I went to the living room, saw beer cans on the trunk that served as a table in front of the couch.

A wine glass, half full. A bowl that had held potato chips, just crumbs now. Her bag on the floor in the corner by the boom box.

Outside the siren had stopped.

I went to the bag, opened it and rummaged. The phone was in the side pocket. I took it out, found the list of received calls. I had called that morning, twice. Someone had called at eight-thirty. Then nothing back to six p.m., last night.

I took out my notebook and copied the six o'clock number and the previous three, all received Sunday afternoon. I heard footsteps coming up the stairs. Dropping the phone back into the bag, I went to the door and opened it.

Two cops, a man and a woman, were coming up. The guy was first, his hand on his holstered gun. He looked at me hard. "You called?"

"There's a woman here," I said. "In the bedroom to the left. She's been assaulted."

He stepped up to me, pulled me out of the doorway and put me face-first up against the wall. He kicked my legs out and spread them.

"Stay right there, sir," he said, his big hand on the small of my back.

The other cop went inside, and I could see that she had her gun out as she passed me. I heard her say, "Oh, honey, it's okay now," and then louder into the radio, "We're gonna need that ambulance ASAP."

"What's your name?" the big cop said behind me.

"Jack McMorrow," I said.

"Got I.D.?"

"Back right pocket."

He fished my wallet from my jeans. I heard him flipping it open.

"Okay, Mr. McMorrow. Who's she?"

"Name's Mandi," I said. "With an 'i'."

"Mandi what?"

"I don't know."

He pressed harder on my back.

"You assault her?"

"No, I found her. She didn't answer her phone. I came by and the doors were open. Just a few minutes ago. She said a guy named Roger did it. Last night."

"You know this Roger?"

"No."

"What's your relationship with her?"

I hesitated. "It's kind of hard to explain."

"Why don't you just give it a try," the cop said.

"I'm a newspaper reporter. She's a source."

"Reporter? Writing what?"

"I can't tell you," I said.

I heard a jingle, and then he snapped on the cuffs, first the left wrist, then the right. He patted me down, found the pocketknife and took it.

"What kinda reporter are you?" he said, turning me to face him.

"Freelance," I said.

"On the floor, freelance," the cop said, putting his hand on my shoulder and pushing me down, slowly but firmly, until I sat, back against the wall.

9

Mandi went out first, her face gray, an IV in her arm. EMTs lifted the stretcher down the stairs, one of them giving me a dirty look on the way by. The cat started to follow and I said, "Hey," and it scurried back inside.

"Indoor cat," I said, and the woman cop reached back and closed the door.

"That right?" someone said, and I turned to see another cop coming up the stairs. Plainclothes.

He stood over me, glanced at the two patrol cops. "Cat doesn't go out?" he asked.

"She doesn't like it to," I said. "Name's Lulu."

He looked at me, then at the cops. Fortyish and fit, blocky build with big shoulders. Khakis and boat shoes, a dark blue polo shirt. Could have been a wrestling coach except for the 9 mm on his hip.

"Shoot," he said to the cops, and then to me, "Figure of speech."

"Called it in," the cop said. "Said he came by when she didn't answer the phone. Found her on the floor."

"So why the—"

"Was evasive about their relationship. Had a knife in his pocket."

"Swiss Army," I said. "It's Maine, for God's sake."

They looked down at me, all three of them. "Get him up," the detective said. "Get the shackles off."

They lifted me by my armpits, unlocking the cuffs. The detective held out his hand, looked me in the eye. I looked him right back.

"I'm Detective Raven," he said. "Belfast P.D."

I took his hand and gave it a hard squeeze.

"Jack McMorrow. Prosperity, Maine."

"Says he's a reporter," the cop said.

"Him and everybody else, all this blog crap," Raven said. "Reporter for what?"

"Mostly the *New York Times*," I said.

"Bought up the whole coast," Raven said. "Now they're bringing their own reporters, too?"

"I've lived here for ten years," I said.

"Married?"

"Yeah."

"Kids?"

"One."

"How do you know this young woman?"

"I interviewed her for a story I'm writing."

"About what?" Raven said.

I hesitated again. "I'm not at liberty to say."

The big cop looked at Raven, said, "See?"

Raven looked at me, said, "Let's walk over to the P.D. Make this official."

I nodded, said to the cops, "Don't forget the shoe."

We walked up the block, the skinny kid watching from the doorway of the pizza shop. When people passed us on the sidewalk, they looked at me warily, then nodded at Raven.

"Used to be I knew everybody in town, first-name basis," he said, strolling with his hands in his pockets. "Grew up here. Went to school and played ball here. There've been Ravens around here for six generations. Most of the families were like that. You knew the kids, their grandparents, the name of their long-dead dog. Now I know some people but it isn't the same. Like you, here ten years you feel like a long-timer."

"It's a good place to live," I said.

"Oh, yeah, but word's gotten out. People throw up a big house on the water, only use it three or four weeks. How you get to know somebody like that? Then there's the retirees, general transplants. People coming and going."

"Times change," I said.

We stopped at the corner and waited for the light even though there weren't cars coming. No jaywalking allowed.

"You remember the sardine factory?"

I shook my head.

"Kinda defined the town back then."

We crossed the street, went left up the block, past a yarn shop, a soup and sandwich place.

"Made a hell of a stink but you know what? We never noticed. What we did notice was when it closed down, jobs disappeared, and it didn't smell anymore. Now *that* stunk."

I'd known a lot of cops, and some were quiet, some were chatty. Raven was a chatty cop, going on like you were buddies, making you feel you could talk to him because the two of you were practically friends.

We were at the front door of the police station, a two-story brick building that looked like an elementary school. Raven held the door open for me and I went in. He put his hand on the inner glass door and someone inside buzzed it open.

He waved to the cop at the control desk, and we walked down the hall. There was a metal door on the right and he punched in a code and it clicked open. We stepped into another corridor, doors opening off of it. I saw detectives' offices, metal desks, cops in shirtsleeves drinking coffee and staring at computers.

Raven paused at a doorway, held his arm out. I stepped in ahead of him.

"Have a seat," he said.

There was a metal desk chair in front of the metal desk. The desk had a computer monitor, stacks of papers. I sat. He came around the desk, leaned toward the computer, tapped at the keyboard.

I scanned things quickly, a reporter's habit. A statement saying somebody had threatened somebody else, the words "blow his fucking head off" marked in yellow highlighter. An ad for a stun gun, a flyer for a conference in San Diego on Internet crime. On the wall was a framed certificate saying Brian Raven had completed an FBI course on crime scene inspection at Qantico, Virginia. Another one for a program in homicide investigation at the New England Police Academy, in Providence, R.I.

"Goddamn computers," he said, staring at the screen. "Control your life if you let 'em."

He looked away from the monitor and directly at me. "But at least now I know you really do write for the *New York Times.*"

"I guess that's why you're a detective," I said.

Raven smiled but only briefly and mostly with his mouth. His eyes stayed fixed on me. "Okay, I'd like to just shoot the shit some more, but we gotta take care of a certain amount of business."

"Go for it," I said.

"You say you didn't beat this girl, Mr. McMorrow. So who did?"

"She said it was a guy named Roger. Said he seemed nice and then he exploded."

"Where would she meet this Roger?"

"I don't know. A bar? Wherever young people meet each other, I guess."

"Or the Internet. These chatrooms. Can you believe young girls trust somebody and all they know is what they read on a computer? Impossible to really know somebody unless you look 'em in the eye, don't you think?"

I nodded.

"You must find that, as a newspaper reporter. I mean, you can tell when somebody is lying to you, right? You can see it in their eyes."

"Most of the time."

"Right. There's exceptions, the really pathological liars, they don't know they're lying half the time. But normal people."

"Right."

"Most people are terrible liars."

"Uh-huh."

"Like when you say you're a reporter and you got a wife and a kid, I know that's true from the way you say it. And when you say you don't know how 'Mandi with an i' would have met this guy, Roger, I know you're not being entirely truthful."

I didn't answer, but didn't look away, either.

"Which leaves me with only a couple of logical conclusions. Either you know how she met this Roger but you won't say; or you know there is no Roger."

"I don't know that."

"Maybe you beat the crap out of her, went home and got cleaned up, saw your wife and kid. Maybe just sobered up in your car and came back, see how bad you hurt her. She's still on the floor, you tell her to make up this story or else."

"Or else what?" I said.

Raven's radio squawked. He reached to his hip and turned it down. "Or else you'll beat her up some more. Or you won't sleep with her ever again. Or you won't someday leave your wife and kid so you and Mandi can get married and live happily ever after—take her to New York City, all the razzle dazzle; the restaurants, the shows."

"Or I can't tell you because it's something Mandi told me in confidence."

"This isn't the goddamn Iraq war we're talking about here, Mr. McMorrow," Raven said. "This is some poor girl got the crap beat out of her."

"I know that."

"You involved with this girl?"

"Not in the way you're thinking."

"You like her?"

"Yeah. She seems like a nice enough person."

"What's she do for work?"

"I'm not entirely sure."

"*Ehhh!*" Raven said, making a game-show-buzzer noise.

"Falsehood."

I didn't answer.

"She deals drugs? That's how you know her? Buy some coke off her? Just a few grams for a party? You and the missus like to have a few people over, get wired up? Lots of people do it. I know that. Some real respectable types, too."

I shook my head.

"The missus isn't like that," I said. "I'm not, either."

"Where the hell she come from anyway? Not from around here. No boyfriend. Pretty good looking girl to be living all by herself. You'd think somebody would'a scooped her up."

I looked at him and smiled.

"That's what I like about my work," he said. "Sometimes one little incident opens the door to a whole raft of interesting questions. And answers."

"That's what I like about my job, too," I said.

"Yeah, we've got a lot in common. Except I arrest people and you write about them."

"Right."

"Your wife know about Mandi?"

"Yes. She knows we met."

"She know you were gonna stop in at Mandi's today?"

"Yes. We talked about it this morning."

Raven looked at me.

"What do you do for fun, Mr. McMorrow?"

I hesitated.

"I don't know. Hang out with my daughter. She's almost four. I talk to my wife. I hike in the woods. I like birds. I read a lot of books. I drink beer, but only in moderation. You?"

"I don't drink. My father was an alcoholic. Hell of a nice guy, too, but it killed him."

"I'm sorry," I said.

He shrugged. "What I do is I build boats. Wooden boats."

"Really?"

"I build one, sell it. Start another one. Have a little space in a boat-shed, down by the harbor. I'm doing one now. It's sort of a rowboat called a Whitehall. It's oak and mahogany and I'm thinking of adding some teak."

"Good for you. I admire people who can do that," I said.

"You know what I like about it?"

"No," I said. "What?"

"You start with one piece and you add another and another. And eventually, if you keep adding the pieces, the whole thing comes together. And something you couldn't even see, something that was invisible before, is sitting right there in front of you."

He smiled. I smiled back, said nothing.

"When you leave here, where you gonna go, Mr. McMorrow?"

"Probably the hospital, see how Mandi is doing, then home."

"Nice of you. You always take such good care of people you interview for stories?"

"No," I said.

He looked at me. "I believe you," Raven said. "That one had truth written all over it."

10

The woman cop was named C. Lord, according to her nametag. She was standing by the reception window at the emergency room. She looked at me like I was dirt.

"How is she?" I said.

"Does Detective Raven know you were coming here?"

"Yes. We just talked about it. So how is she?"

The cop looked at me, then turned and left.

I was left with the television and an old woman sitting with her portable oxygen, a tank in a stand with wheels. She wheezed, a tube in her nose. We both stared at the television screen, where a young couple was arguing, the man shaking his manicured fist in the woman's made-up face. I thought of Mandi, wondered if there'd been time to argue or just a sudden blow to the face. Then another and another.

I stepped up to the reception window. The guy behind the glass looked up from a crossword book, pencil in one hand, mug of coffee in the other. He was red-nosed and thick and looked like an impostor, like he'd stuffed the regular receptionist under the desk.

I smiled. He slid the glass open.

"I'm here for Mandi," I said. "You know how long she'll be in there?"

He scowled. "I just told the officer," he said.

"Well, she's not here," I said.

"I can't divulge patient information."

"Okay. But could you tell me whether I'll be waiting for twenty minutes? Two hours? Two days?"

I leaned closer and smiled. His pencil was poised on the crossword, partway through ten letters, across—"Great Apes." He had C-H-I. With a weary sigh, he reached for a yellow Sticky-note. The pencil moved to it grudgingly.

"What's your name?" he said.

"Jack McMorrow."

"All I can do is let the staff know you're here."

"Thanks. I appreciate that."

"Jack what?"

I leaned closer.

"McMorrow."

He wrote that down.

"And you're here to see what patient?"

I wondered how many there were. Did the oxygen lady make two? "Mandi. It's the Mandi with the 'i'."

"Last name?"

I sighed, inwardly. "I don't know," I said.

His eyes glanced up, pink-rimmed and brimming with judgment.

"I can't confirm that we have a patient here by that name," he said.

"Fine. But if you do have one, could you let her know Jack McMorrow is here?"

He didn't acknowledge that, just said, "Relationship with the patient?"

Hard to keep secrets in this town, I thought. "Friend," I said.

He wrote that down, too. The Sticky-note was full. He looked up, this time his glance lingered. How was I connected to the young woman brought in beat up in black underwear. Exactly what sort of weirdo was I?

I tried to get back into his good graces.

"The word," I said. "It's not chimpanzee. It's orangutans."

He looked at the puzzle, counting the letters in his head.

"Thanks," he said.

"I'm a writer," I said, and smiled.

"Oh."

"So, two hours? Two days?"

"I'd guess closer to twenty minutes," he muttered softly, erasing carefully. "But you didn't hear it from me."

I sat alone after the oxygen woman was taken inside. I called Mary, who said Sophie was taking a nap, worn out from following the chickens. I tried calling Roxanne back, left a message at her office and on her cell. I was checking my voicemail when a side door opened and Officer Lord stepped out followed by an attendant pushing Mandi in a wheelchair. She saw me and smiled.

She was wearing green hospital scrubs and her right ankle was in a blue soft cast. Her right wrist, too. Her hair was pulled back and her face had been washed. Her nose was swollen and bruised and there were scratches on her face.

She looked exhausted, medicated.

I got up from my seat and Officer Lord gave me the cold stare, then strode out of the room, fiddling with the radio on her belt. The attendant, a middle-aged woman, pushed Mandi over. The door swung open again, and a doctor came out, stethoscope on her neck.

"Hey, Jack," Mandi said, sounding a little woozy.

"Hi, Mandi. How are you?" I said.

"Oh, okay," she said. "On the road to recovery."

The doctor, a fortyish woman, stood with her hands on her hips. She was tanned and fit, looked like a runner.

"Are you her caregiver?" she said.

I considered it. Mandi looked up at me, bruised and battered.

"Yes," I said.

"Well, then you should know, as I told Mandi, the ankle is a very bad sprain," she said, "but no fracture that we could see. A lot of soft tissue damage. We put it in a soft cast to protect it. The wrist is fractured, three different bones, including the trapezoid bone, which is a tough one to heal."

Mandi held her arm out, looked at it.

"You're not going to be able to do stairs for a couple of weeks, Mandi," the doc said. " And once you get a walking cast, crutches are still going to be difficult with the wrist."

Mandi smiled wanly. "Once I'm home I'll be—"

"You've got enough pain meds for a couple days. Prescription for more, and anti-inflammatories."

The doc looked to me. "We got her started on both but she's gonna need more by tomorrow."

"Right," I said, wondering what I'd gotten into, where she would stay.

"You're signed out for the wheelchair until next Friday," the doc said. "If you need to keep it longer, call patient services."

The doc looked down at Mandi, patted her shoulder.

"You take care of yourself now," she said. Her tone suggesting that was unlikely.

Then she looked at me. "And you take good care of her," she said. It wasn't a suggestion. It was an order. I nodded.

"Where can I reach you?" the doc said, like she was going to check up. She took a prescription pad out and I gave her my cell number and she scrawled it on the back of a page.

"I'm going to put this with the records," she said.

"Good idea," I said, and then off Mandi and I went, down the hall and out into the parking lot.

"So," I said, "where to?"

"Home," Mandi said.

I started wheeling her toward the truck.

"You can't get up those stairs."

"But I've got to take care of Lulu."

"You can't even walk. Or get in and out of bed."

"I'll be okay."

"You have friends in town?"

She hesitated.

"No."

"How 'bout another town? I can drive you there."

"No," Mandi said. "I'm pretty much on my own."

We were at the truck.

"You must have somebody," I said.

I moved around and bent toward her.

"Not here," she said softly.

"Where then? Family?"

She shook her head.

"Mandi," I said. "I can't be the only person you know."

She was looking away, a scowl settling over her, her face pale in the sun.

"You're the only person I trust."

"You barely know me."

"I'm a good judge of people," she said, then added, "Usually."

I looked around. A white-haired couple walked by carrying a pot of flowers wrapped in pink foil. The woman glanced at Mandi's bruised face, then at me, then quickly away. I opened the truck door, wheeled Mandi into position.

"In you go, then," I said, and I took hold of her under her arm and lifted her out of the chair. She stood on her good foot, reached for the door with her good hand. She hopped twice, started to lose her balance, and I caught her by the side, under the breast. I was instantly self-conscious and moved my hand to her shoulder, and eased her onto the truck seat.

"Thanks," Mandi said, and as I started to close the door she looked up at me. "I'm sorry. Just get me home. I'll be okay."

"We'll figure it out," I said, and closed the door, folded the wheelchair, and lifted it into the back of the truck. I came around and got in and started the motor. The Toyota's cab seemed very small.

I drove across town, sat at the red light at the corner of Mandi's block. She stared straight ahead, her eyes starting to droop. Noticing me looking at her, she said, "The drugs."

There was a space in front of her building and I pulled in and shut off the motor. We looked at the door, left wide open.

"You can't stay here," I said. "Not alone. He might come back."

I turned to her. "You know you should give the police that phone number."

"No," Mandi blurted, as though frightened at the thought. She added more calmly, "Maybe there's a shelter. Do you think they'd take cats?"

I hesitated, decided not to press it.

"I can take your cat," I said. "What else do you need from upstairs?"

She winced.

"Everything. Toothbrush and all of that. Clothes. Shoes. No, I'll be fine. Can you just get me up the—"

"I'll get enough for a day or two. You can make a list and we can come back."

She looked away. "Thanks," she said.

I got out, closed the truck door and locked her in. Shutting the entrance door behind me, I went up the stairs, pausing at the landing. I listened, heard a fly buzzing, nothing else.

I went to her door, turned the knob and the door swung open. The apartment was stuffy, the windows closed from the previous night. I crossed to the bedroom, which was as I had left it. The bed was rumpled. There was blood on the bedspread, droplets in a line. It seemed like the room should be sealed with crime-scene tape but it wasn't, so I walked over and looked again.

It looked like Mandi had first been beaten on the bed. Her nose bleeding, she'd rolled over and fallen. I wondered if the wrist and ankle had been done on the bed or on the floor. Had she been kicked? Stomped?

He could have killed her very easily. She was lucky to be—

Something fell in the living room and I whirled, walked to the door. Paused, then stepped out. The cat had knocked a picture off the windowsill. I walked across the living room and picked it up.

It was small, two frames connected by a hinge. One photo was of a young girl, maybe six, blonde and smiling, standing in a meadow. The other was a family, a couple with two kids walking on a beach.

I looked more closely at the smiling faces. These weren't Mandi's photos. They were generic ones, the kind that come with the frames. Photos of models of a happy family.

I put the frame down and turned back to the room. It seemed cold and bare. A couch. A small TV on a wooden box. A wooden beer crate stood on end to make a bookshelf. It was filled with paperbacks, all worn bestsellers, like you'd see at a book swap. On top of the crate was a Harry Potter. Next to the book was a ceramic bowl filled with Hershey's Kisses. Next to the bowl were several foil wrappers, rolled into tiny silver balls.

There were two wooden straight chairs, one by the window where Mandi could sit and look out. A couple of cheap art prints: a tropical sunset, a polar bear with cubs. It was like a dorm room but with nothing personal. It revealed nothing.

I went to the kitchen, opened the drawers. The bag of Hershey's Kisses, more balled up wrappers. Yard-sale silverware, a few cheap hand towels. Pots and pans in the cupboard by the sink; mismatched dishes on the shelf. Nothing on the refrigerator door except a menu from the pizza shop across the street. Inside, there was yogurt—all strawberry Dannon Light—and a plastic jug of cranberry juice. An unopened bottle of Chardonnay, two sticks of butter, and half a loaf of whole wheat bread.

It was like she was only staying a couple of nights.

I filled the cat's dish with dry cat food and added an extra water bowl. Then I went to the bedroom, where the cat was crouched on the bed. I reached to pat it and it bolted again, out of the room. I opened the middle bureau drawer, found gym shorts and T-shirts. I grabbed three of each, made a poor attempt to have them match. From the bottom drawer, I took a pair of nylon running pants and a pair of jeans. From the top drawer, I scooped out a fistful of underwear, in various colors.

And then I paused. Slid my hand under the bras and underpants and rummaged around. I felt something and pulled it out. Condoms. Reached back in and, at the back of the drawer, I felt a small box. I hesitated, then parted the clothes and took it out.

It was a small green jewelry box covered in crushed velvet, something a child would have. I flipped it open and inside was a heart-shaped locket, gold on a chain, the size of a pocket watch. I pried it open with my fingernail; inside there was a photograph of a baby.

The baby was nine months old, give or take. She had big dark eyes and soft-looking dark curls, and was wearing a pale-pink top with darker pink flowers appliqued on the front. There was a woman's hand under the baby's rump, but someone had cut the woman holding the baby out of the picture so that all you could see was a dismembered arm.

The baby's wide-set eyes, the mouth; it was Mandi. I looked at the picture for a moment and closed the locket. Put it back in the box and slid the box back into the drawer. I closed the drawer, went to a small closet and opened the door. Inside were dresses and skirts, shoes on the floor. I considered them, took flat leather sandals and black Nike flip-flops. I took the shoes and clothes to the kitchen and found a garbage bag in a cupboard. I placed everything in, looked around the apartment once more, and spotted Mandi's pocketbook, a gray leather bag.

I grabbed that, made sure her keys were inside. Went to the bathroom and scooped up the toothbrush, a few toiletries that were out on the counter. At the door, I tried the keys until I found the one to the apartment. I paused, dug out her wallet. It was black, shiny leather. I flipped it open and pulled out her I.D.

A Maine driver's license, Mandi's photo. It had been issued to Sybill M. Lasell, 14 Ellsworth St., Apt. 2, Portland. I stuck it back in the sleeve, opened the wallet and slipped out the cash. Counted it. $436, fifties and twenties. I shoved it back, dropped the wallet in the bag, locked the door behind me and left.

Mandi was in the truck, head back, dozing. I got in and she opened her eyes, looked at me.

"Find much?" she said.

"I got clothes and some shoes and your pocketbook. We can come back for the cat. I gave her food and water."

"That's not what I meant," Mandi said.

"What?" I said.

"It's okay. I'm sure you want to know who this girl is who just landed in your life."

I looked at her. "But I still don't think I do," I said. "Know who you are, I mean."

"No," she said. "Probably not."

And she closed her eyes again.

11

—∞—

There *was* a homeless shelter in Belfast. I called the police department and the dispatcher told me it was on Congress Street, a mile south of downtown. I drove there, Mandi quiet on the way, and pulled up in front of a shabby Victorian with a small hanging sign that said, "Refuge House."

There were four young guys standing outside smoking. I pulled up and they turned, all bad teeth and scraggly beards, their jeans hanging so low their boxers showed. They looked at Mandi. One of them, a guy in a sideways Yankees hat, said something and the others laughed and leered.

I frowned.

"I can handle them," Mandi said.

I left her in the truck and walked up to the house. The guys gave me the stare and I gave it back. The guy who had made the comment said, "Hey," and I looked at him, but didn't respond.

"Ain't too friendly, is he?" he said.

"Another time, chump," I said, brushing through them. I went inside, noting the steps. The door opened to a kitchen, a woman at the stove, her back to me. She was broad, strong-looking. I said hello. She turned to me, hands dripping dishwater.

"I'm sorry, we're full up," she said. She dabbed at her hair, left a spot of suds. "Might have a bed in a couple of days. Male?"

"No," I said. "It's not me. It's a friend. She's been in an accident and can't get up the stairs to her apartment."

"But she has an apartment?"

"Yes, but the stairs are steep and she broke her wrist and hurt her ankle and—"

"We're not equipped for that kind of care here," the woman said. "Sometimes it's just me. I volunteer. I mean, this isn't a rehab center."

"I see," I said.

"I'd say the best bet would be to stay with her in her apartment until she's up and around."

"I can't really do that," I said.

"Well, see if someone else can. Friends, family. Our mission is really for people who have no other safety net, no place to stay at all. It sounds like your friend, she has options."

"I suppose she does," I said, and I thanked her. She started to turn back to the sink, then stopped.

"Don't let the wise guys out there bother you," she said. "A couple of bad apples."

"Never do," I said, and went back out.

The bad apples were still there, smoking, standing, propping each other up. The mouthy one called over to Mandi, "Hey, honey, what the hell happened to you? Hope you got the number of that truck."

They all laughed. Saw me and stopped. I walked up to the mouthy one and said, "You think that's funny?"

"Dude," he said. "Chill."

I stepped into him, fast. His arms came up. I grabbed both wrists, twisted them, hooked his ankle and shoved with my shoulder. He went over backwards, his Yankee hat flying, cigarette, too. The others held back. The mouthy one tried to scramble to his feet, got tangled in his jeans, ended up on his knees.

"Now *that's* funny," I said, then turned and walked to the street while the guy told me what he oughta do to me.

I got in the truck. Mandy looked at me, interested but not wide-eyed. "What, you know karate or something?" she said.

"I know this guy named Clair," I said.

"He knows karate?"

"He knows all kinds of things," I said and I told her there was no room at the inn, put the truck in gear, and drove off.

I turned back toward town, drove on through. At the head of the bay, I swung west, out of town and into the country. After a couple of miles, I pulled over. "I've got to make some calls," I said.

Mandi nodded and smiled.

I got out and, standing by the side of the road near a dense bank of spruce woods, called Roxanne at work. Got her voicemail again and called her cell. She answered, road noise in the background.

"Hey," I said. "Where are you?"

"Going to see kids," she said. "Where are you?"

"On the way home. Did you get my messages?"

"I've been out of the office, and there's something wrong with my cell. Says my mailbox is full but won't let me in."

"I called," I said.

"Everything okay?" Roxanne said, on alert.

"With us, yeah. Sophie's fine. Taking a nap, Mary said."

There was a pause. A truck passed me and Roxanne said, "You sound like you're standing in the middle of the street."

"The side," I said.

"Why?"

"Mandi's in the truck," I said. "She's having kind of a bad time of it."

"Why?" Roxanne said, and I told her. When I finished, there was a very long pause.

"But her name isn't really Mandi. It's Sybill Lasell, according to her driver's license. Says she lives in Portland."

"So Mandi is her—"

"Stage name, I guess. I suppose you don't want people knowing who you really are."

"So you want to bring this Mandi-Sybill person—"

"Just until she can get around again. If it was the wrist *or* the ankle it would be one thing but—"

"Jack, you barely know this woman."

"What could I do with her? Leave her in a wheelchair on the sidewalk?"

"There's nobody else who could—"

"No. We went by the shelter and there were these dirtbag guys there."

"So—"

"So, she's alone."

"Not all the time," Roxanne said.

"No," I said. "But she says she has no friends around here. Her family is . . . I don't know where her family is."

"Jack, she's a prostitute. Or something close to it."

"I know. But she's nice. And smart. I mean—"

"We don't have room."

"Clair and Mary do."

"Have you called them yet?"

"No, I wanted to talk to you first."

The road noise subsided. Roxanne had pulled her car over and shut off the engine.

"And what if I say no?"

"I don't know. I don't really have a Plan B."

"Is this someone we want around Sophie?"

"She's not what you think, honey. She's, well, I can't quite figure her out, but she's not tough or loud. She's pretty normal and—" I paused as a pickup roared past.

"And what, Jack?" Roxanne said.

"If she were a kid, you'd want to help her," I said. "She is like a kid in some ways."

"But not in others."

A long pause.

"This is not normal, Jack."

"I know."

"She doesn't have a thing for you, does she?"

"No, she's like a kid. It's like I'm her father or her uncle or something. And honey, here's the other thing. What if this guy comes back? Now she really can't defend herself at all."

Roxanne didn't answer. I could picture her thinking, and then she said, "If Mary and Clair are okay with it."

"Right," I said.

"But you know they will be. She'll be another fawn with a broken leg, the owl with the broken wing."

"And they all went back to where they came from when they got better," I said. "As soon as Mandi can get around—"

"You don't even know where she came from, Jack," Roxanne said. "You don't really know anything about her."

I looked back at the truck, Mandi sitting there. She was turned toward the woods, and as I watched, she wiped her eyes. Once. Twice. Then a third time. Tears. After all she'd been through, it was the first time I'd seen her cry.

12

The phone was busy at the Varneys. As I got in the truck, Mandi gave her red-rimmed eyes a last wipe and mustered a semblance of a smile.

"I'd have you stay at my house but we only have two bedrooms," I said. "Clair and Mary, they're right on the road. A big house, their kids are grown. They watch Sophie when we're working."

"Nice people?"

"Nicest people in the world. I work with Clair in the woods sometimes. He was a career Marine, fought in Vietnam."

"That's where he learned karate?"

"He was in this thing called Force Recon. Kind of like Navy Seals."

"Huh."

The smartest, wisest man I know. Mary, she'll do anything for you. Rock solid. They both are."

Mandi looked away. "Then they're not gonna want *me* around."

"Sure they will."

"They don't even know me."

"They know me," I said. "And you're a—" I paused for an instant and she caught it.

"I'm a what, Jack?" she said, staring straight ahead.

"You're a friend of mine," I said.

"They won't believe that."

"Why not, Mandi?"

"Because it isn't true."

"Sure it is," I said, starting the motor and putting the truck in gear, giving her arm a gentle pat.

"Oh, but you shouldn't do this, Jack," she murmured as I pulled out onto the pavement. "You really shouldn't."

We drove north on the winding two-lane road, past the occasional house, miles of woods, a place where loggers were yarding logs by the roadside. Some of the houses were meager, handbuilt little places with sheds with blue tarps over leaking roofs. A few were big and new, set back with dug ponds and ski boats on trailers. There were pastures with the first crop of hay just cut, bales scattered like something left behind in a hurry.

Mandi looked away, out the window. She was silent, her good hand folded over her broken wrist on her lap. As I drove I tried Clair and Mary again, got the busy signal. I put the phone down, glanced at her, left her alone as we climbed the hills outside of Knox, dropped down into the valley with cows dotting the hillsides. We passed a big farm, a black-shuttered house with spreading silver maples facing the road.

As we passed, Mandi's gaze lingered on the place, her head turning, and then we climbed to the crest of Knox Ridge, saw the pastures and ridgelines rolling away to the east.

"Almost there," I said.

"This is beautiful," Mandi said. "You live here?"

I pointed to the ridges to the west.

"That way."

"Huh, with your wife and your little girl. Your wife's really pretty, I bet."

I nodded.

"What's she do? Stay home with your daughter?"

"No," I said. "She's a social worker. Takes care of abused and neglected kids."

I felt Mandi tighten up, saw her good hand clench.

"But you said—" She paused, looking out.

"You said you only had two bedrooms."

"Oh, no," I said. "I don't mean she takes care of kids in our house. She's a child protective worker. For the state."

"Oh," Mandi said.

"What's the matter?" I said.

"Nothing," she said. "Nothing at all."

We drove the rest of the way in silence, Mandi watching the woods slide past. We turned off the main road, drove south down a single-lane paved road, then swung west again, onto a dirt road that wound through tall maples and oaks. There were stone walls extending into the woods, dark lines slipping away into the undergrowth. As we came over a crest in the road, we came upon a flock of turkeys, crossing single file like hobbling old men.

"Sophie loves the turkeys," I said. "She calls them gobbles."

Mandi smiled, didn't comment.

A long bend, past a gnarly old oak, three apple trees that once grew in a dooryard but now were part of the forest. We passed my house, a shingled, steep-roofed place with a deck and a porch on the back, a shed attached to one side, a rope swing on the big maple out front.

"That's home," I said, and Mandi nodded. We continued on, drove five hundred yards and swung in beside a big white colonial, the shingled barn facing us. Clair's big Ford pickup was parked by the open barn door, from which the back end of a John Deere tractor extended.

I pulled the Toyota up and parked. "I'll be right back," I said. "Stay put."

"I thought I'd run for it," Mandi said, and she smiled, her game face back on.

I walked to the barn, squeezed by the big tractor tires. There was music playing inside, as always. Opera. My eyes adjusted to the dim light and I looked around for Clair, saw an oil drain pan on the floor. After a minute, I heard footsteps from the loft, and Clair appeared at the top of the stairs. He was carrying a case of motor oil and clomped his way down, turned and walked to the bench in the workshop. He put the case down. I walked over.

"Suppose you're here for that rotten daughter of yours," he said.

"Well—"

"She's a trial. Don't know how we put up with it."

"You're a saint."

Clair smiled.

"Last I saw, she and Mary had the girls' dolls out and were having a tea party."

"Great," I said. "I'll never get her to come home."

"Okay, she can stay," Clair said. "Twist my arm."

"Well, I might have to because I've got another favor to ask."

Clair looked at me, turned serious. I leaned on the bench beside him, told the story. He listened, arms crossed, Semper Fi tattoo stretched across his upper arm.

"I'll talk to Mary," he said.

"Okay," I said.

"But she'll say yes."

"I thought she might."

"How's a girl end up like that?" Clair said.

"Probably not easily," I said.

"Wouldn't be your first choice."

"No."

"When you're ten, dreaming about what you want to be when you grow up."

"I don't think she's grown up yet," I said. "There's still hope."

He picked up a radio from the bench, walkie-talkies they used to call between the house and barn.

"Hey," Clair said. "You there?"

She was, and Clair asked her to come out. She did, passing the young woman in the truck on the way. Mary came into the barn, said, "Yes, Sophie can stay."

She smiled. Then Clair retold the story, remembering all of it.

"She's not what you might think," I said. "She's sort of gentle."

"Well," Mary said. "Why don't you get this poor girl inside."

We stepped out of the barn and into the sunlight. Clair opened the truck door and smiled. His tanned face was framed by silver, short-cropped hair. His arms were big and muscled, your grandfather on steroids. Roger would have his hands full.

"I'm Clair, Miss," he said.

"And I'm Mary."

"I'm Mandi," she said, turning to them and smiling. "It's nice to meet you both. Jack told me lots about you."

"You've had a rough stretch, I hear," Clair said.

Mandi shrugged.

"How 'bout some lunch," he said, and he bent down and offered his hand. Mandi took it and Clair pulled and she slid out of the truck, got her good foot on the ground. I came around with the wheel chair and Clair said, "We don't need that. You get one side, I'll get the other."

We half-carried her to the back stairs, full-carried her up the stairs and in. The kitchen smelled of baking—muffins, bread?—and Mary already was standing by the big slate sink, arranging muffin tins in a baking pan. Sophie was stretched out on the floor, tongue sticking out in concentration as she drew. There were crayons scattered around her like fruit fallen from a tree.

"Daddy," she said, and hoisted herself to her hands and knees, then froze as Mandi hopped over the threshold, Clair following, holding her arm.

"Mandi, this is Sophie," I said.

Mandi said hello and smiled.

"Now get yourself into a chair there at the table and we'll get you some lunch," Mary said. "How 'bout a nice turkey sandwich. Sophie and I just made anadama bread."

"Sounds wonderful," Mandi said.

"I mushed the dough," Sophie said.

"I'll bet you're a good musher," Mandi said. "And an artist. Look at that picture. Is that a bird?"

"Two birds," Sophie said, turning back to the paper on the floor. "One is the baby bird and one is the momma bird. The momma bird is worried 'cause the baby fell out of the nest."

"Well, I hope she finds her way back home," Mandi said, her tone gentle and soothing. And then to Mary, she said, "This kitchen is so cozy. It smells so good. You must spend a lot of time in here, the fireplace in the winter."

"Home and hearth, as they say," Mary said. "Now, let's let you get yourself together. You brought clothes?"

"In the truck," I said. "I'll bring in the bag."

Sophie began her interrogation. "You got hurt. Were you in a accident?"

"Sort of," Mandi said. "I sure didn't mean to get hurt."

"You hurt your hand *and* your foot," Sophie said, moving closer, peering at the wrapping on Mandi's ankle. "How'd you do that?"

"I fell out of bed," Mandi said.

"I used to have a bed with sides," Sophie said. "Now I have a big-girl bed."

"Good for you," Mandi said.

"You should get a bed with sides and you couldn't fall anymore."

"Maybe I will, Sophie," Mandi said, glancing at me and flashing a smile. "Maybe I will."

I went out to the truck and Clair followed me. I hefted the bag out of the truck bed and we stood

"Thanks for doing this," I said.

Clair shrugged. Roxanne was right. A fawn with a broken leg. An owl with a bad wing. A young woman beaten by a john.

"Seems like a nice-enough person," he said.

"Yes."

"Something not right, though, doing what she's been doing. Drugs?"

"Not that I can tell. No sign of that at all. She does like chocolate, that's all I know."

"Musta been abused somehow when she was younger," Clair said.

"I don't know. She says almost nothing about her past, or about herself, for that matter."

"Seems kind."

"Yes," I said. "Sort of calm. Even when I found her, she wasn't hysterical or anything. Kind of like she expects this kind of thing."

"And puts herself in a position for it to happen," Clair said. "You know, in the war, the women, the ones who came to the American guys, it was like they didn't know they could expect any better."

"I don't know why Mandi would feel that way. But then I don't know—"

I paused. We both turned toward the road where a car was passing slowly. It was a beat-up Jeep, black, an old Cherokee lifted up over big off-road tires. A guy alone, dark beard, black baseball hat and a white arm hanging out the open window.

"Third time in the last few minutes," Clair said, "back and forth."

"Never seen it before," I said.

As the Jeep neared my house, it braked and continued on, but slowly.

"Roxanne home?" Clair said.

"Not yet," I said. "Guy was following her this morning. I warned him."

"What about Mandi?"

"Just said it was a guy named Roger."

"Cops pick him up?"

"I don't think she told them,"

"Let's check this guy out then," Clair said.

"I'll bring her bag in."

"We'll take my truck," Clair said, and he started for the big Ford. I dropped the bag in the kitchen, said we'd be right back. Sophie was showing Mandi a scab left from when she skinned her knee running up the stairs to the deck. I came back out and the truck was pointed toward the road, idling.

I got in. Glanced at the shotgun in the gun rack, Clair's Remington pump.

"Partridges," Clair said.

"When's the season start?" I said.

"October."

"Can't be too prepared," I said.

"Damn straight," Clair said, putting the truck in gear and accelerating hard out of the dooryard and onto the road.

13

We drove fast, a dust plume trailing behind us. When we got out onto the pavement of the main road, we paused, looked both ways but didn't see the Jeep.

"He could've taken off, soon as he passed my place," I said.

"Didn't seem to be in that kind of a hurry. Not any of the times he went by."

Clair looked up and down one more time, then turned the truck around and headed back. He didn't speak and I knew not to, not when he was hunting.

He drove slowly, the motor rumbling softly. I watched the trees on both sides, peering into the shadows where overgrown farmland cut into the woods. Clair was staring intently straight ahead and suddenly he hit the brakes. Stopped. Backed up.

"Here he is," he said, pointed to the road.

I didn't see anything at first, but then they emerged from the dust. Tire tracks curling across the road, headed for the remnant of a tractor path, now just two faint lines in dense grass and burdocks. Between the tracks, the growth was brushed back, like freshly combed hair.

"He's still in there," Clair said.

I nodded, opened the door and went to the front of the truck to lock the hubs on the front wheels. I heard a click as Clair put the truck in four-wheel drive. I got back in, easing the door shut. He turned off the road into the dappled shadows.

The path went straight in for thirty yards, then veered to the left and down. We'd both walked this land hunting deer and knew that the track went through the woods for about a quarter mile, eventually ending in an overgrown pasture. I tried to remember if there was a turnaround, picturing a place where the track widened under a stand of pines.

Clair eased the truck along and it lurched into a mud hole, out the other side. I could see the pines up ahead. No Jeep. We drove on, Clair keeping to the track, brush scraping the sides of the truck.

"There," I said.

Ahead to our right was a glint of metal. We drove closer, saw the front end of the Jeep protruding from the brush, fifty yards off the track. He'd backed in.

We stopped. There was no one in sight. Clair turned off and drove through the grass. He stopped fifty feet from the Jeep and shut off the motor. We sat for a minute and listened, watching the woods.

Nothing showed. Nothing moved.

We got out and walked to the Jeep and were about to look inside when there was a rustle in the brush, then a crash, a flash of white as the guy ran deeper into the woods.

Clair trotted to the truck, reached the shotgun from the rack.

"Flank him," he said. "Get up behind the stone wall. I'll drive him from this direction."

As I started through the trees, I heard the snick of shells being pumped into the gun.

The clearing under the pines gave way quickly to poplars and birches and I slipped between them looking for a deer trail that wove up into the pastures. I found it, just a faint impression in a grove of ferns and skunk cabbage, and I turned onto it and broke into a trot. The trail led through boggy bottomland and then back up. I slogged through mud, stumbled up an embankment, turned sideways to slip between the dense trunks of alders. The alders gave way to swamp maples and then I was into spruce and hemlock and finally into grass and burdocks and clumps of ash. I leapt the wall, and moved on the far side of it to my left, the general direction he had been heading.

After a hundred yards, I paused and listened. From the distance came the sound of someone breaking through brush. I crouched behind the wall, peered into the woods.

And there he was.

The arms showed first, disembodied in the shadows, brushing branches aside. Then the rest of him, emerging from the leaves and brambles. He was big, heavy, bearded. The hat and T-shirt were black and sweat-stained. As he approached, I could hear him panting.

I eased down lower, watching from the wall. He carried a small green bag, like Army surplus, slung over his shoulder.

He paused and stood fifty yards from me, listening. He switched the bag to his other shoulder, then suddenly turned west, bounding through the brush and quickly disappearing.

I jumped back over the wall, started after him, in a crouch, pushing branches aside. Then I stopped. Listened.

Heard nothing but birds.

He'd stopped, too, somewhere ahead of me. I began walking, freezing every ten feet to listen and peer into the trees.

A hundred feet. Two-hundred. I was in an opening now, hemlocks growing on the side of a steep ridge, trunks big enough for a man to hide behind.

I moved cautiously down the grade, sliding on the bed of needles. Caught the side of a trunk and, as I eased past it, he broke from the other side.

He was running but heavily, boots pounding as he slogged up the side of the ridge. I bolted after him, gaining quickly. When I was almost on him, he slipped, fell to his knees, came up and turned, a four-foot branch in his hand. He swung it like a sword and I jumped back, slid and started to fall. He came sliding after me, boot heels digging into the soil under the hemlock needles. As I raised myself up, the branch whipped at my head and I jerked back. His momentum spun him and he fell, tumbling past me.

I leapt and landed on him and we rolled down the hill, into a tree, and he was on top of me, a crushing weight, and I kneed him in the crotch and he gasped and fell back, scrambling backwards, grabbing for anything, coming up with a chunk of tree limb, a two-foot club.

He was on his feet, coming toward me, breathing heavily, teeth clenched behind the beard. He charged, the club raised.

And there was a blast.

He froze. On top of the ridge above us, Clair jacked another shell into the chamber.

"Next one puts you down," he said.

"Hey, I ain't doing—"

"Drop the stick," Clair said, the calm in his voice chilling as a scream.

The guy hesitated, then tossed the club and it slid and stopped. Clair started down the embankment, the shotgun slung under his arm.

"What are you doing here?" I said, moving closer, looking him over. He was in his thirties, big but out of shape.

"Nothin'."

Behind the black beard his eyes were small and dark. On his right arm was a tattoo of a bird, with tail feathers spread like a peacock. On his left wrist was a snake.

"Who are you?"

"Who are *you*?" he shot back.

"We can just run the plate on the Jeep," I said.

"You a cop? Game wardens undercover? 'Cause I—"

"Private property," I said, as Clair moved up to my right, out of range of a leap that would get the guy the gun.

"Hey, I just was looking for a place to smoke a joint, you know? I thought you guys was cops. What are you, some crazy farmers or something?"

"Something," I said.

"Well, I wasn't gonna hurt nothing. Smoke a joint, take a little walk in the woods, head for home."

"Where's home?" I said.

A pause.

"East Boothbay," he said.

"What are you doing here?"

"Driving down the main road, decided to have a smoke, you know? Kept driving until I found a good place."

"You've been up and down this road all day," Clair said.

"Just a coupla times. Once on the way, once on the way back."

"From where?"

"Waterville. My girlfriend lives there."

"Where's the bag?" I said.

"What bag?"

"The bag you had. The green Army thing."

"I don't have no goddamn bag."

"Not now you don't. But I saw it. You had it on your shoulder."

He shook his head.

"You musta been seeing things."

"No, I wasn't," I said. "You want to walk home? 'Cause we can blow the crap outta your car. A little target practice."

"That's against the law."

"Where's the bag?"

He hesitated.

"Okay. I tossed it."

"Where?"

He motioned toward the woods.

"Somewheres out there. It was just some dope. I thought you was cops."

I looked at Clair.

"He's lying," I said.

"You ain't cops," the guy said. "You can't hold me here."

"Because we ain't cops," I said, "we can do anything we want."

He stared at me, black eyes darting from me to Clair and back.

"I'm leaving now," he said. "I'm getting the fuck out of here."

"We can hold you until the authorities get here. You can explain why you were trespassing."

"You own this property?"

"Yeah," I said.

"What, you own the whole—"

He caught himself again.

"I'm going. Right now," he said. He looked at Clair. "So be careful with that thing, man. You could hurt somebody." And he put his hands up, started walking, moving away from us twenty feet before starting up the embankment.

Clair looked at me.

"Wilton had the same tattoo," I said. "The snake on his hand."

We watched him walk into the brush.

"You got the plate number?" I said.

"All set," Clair said.

"I think he knows who I am," I said.

"I caught that. The land thing."

"I'm gonna find that bag," I said.

I backtracked to the place where I'd watched him from behind the stone wall. At that point, he'd had the bag and had started running. I'd trailed him more or less directly, too close behind him for his to diverge far from the path I had taken.

I stood behind the wall again, then started walking. I tried to estimate how far he could fling the bag if he had thrown it. In the trees, it was unlikely it would travel more than forty or fifty feet before hitting something.

So every twenty feet along my path, I stopped and turned off. I walked slowly fifty feet into the brush, zigzagging to increase my coverage. I pushed alders aside, scuffed through patches of ferns. I looked up into the trees, in case the bag had hung up in the branches. When one pass was done, I did the same on the other side of my path. And then I walked twenty feet and started again.

The light was dim under the canopy of hardwoods and visibility was poor in the spruce thickets. Scuffling through the boggy stretches unleashed clouds of mosquitoes that swarmed around my head.

After an hour, I'd found a couple of mud-caked beer bottles. The remnant of a barbed wire fence, trees grown up and encasing the wire so the trunks looked impaled. Unidentifiable pieces of rusty metal, a single rotted work boot.

I was halfway to the ridge, where our friend had come out from behind the hemlock, when I heard someone coming through the trees. It was Clair, still carrying the shotgun, and he started to help, brushing blackberry bushes aside with the barrel of the gun.

We worked our way through the grid. Clair found old shotgun shells, a rusted hubcap from an ancient Ford. Clair flushed a snowshoe hare, in summer brown and gray. I found a horseshoe, wondered if it would bring me luck. Clair saw garter snakes, sent them slithering into the brush; I nearly walked face first into a paper wasp nest, hanging like a Chinese lantern from a birch branch.

I swatted at deer flies trying to burrow into my hair. Clair found a brassiere, disintegrating in a patch of grass. Then I saw a green canvas bag, the strap protruding from under a clump of ferns.

"I got it," I shouted, and Clair hurried over. When he got to me I was crouching in the ferns, oblivious to the mosquitoes biting my forearms and neck because I had the bag. I stood and held it out to Clair, pulling the top open wide. A pair of latex gloves, used. A pink pillowcase, wrapped up neatly. A roll of duct tape.

14

⁓

We slammed down the tote road, slowed as Clair scanned for tracks, and saw that the Jeep had taken a left, headed for the main road. We went left and at the first rise, I called the state police. It was hard to explain—a guy in the woods with duct tape, my wife working for the Department of Health and Human Services. The dispatcher asked how long the vehicle had been gone and I said ten minutes. She asked me to describe it and then asked if I knew its direction of travel. I told her what I knew and she took my name and number again, said a trooper would be in touch.

Then we were back at Clair's. Roxanne's car was in the driveway. I left the bag in the truck and went in. Clair went to put the shotgun away in the shop.

They were all in the kitchen: Mandi sitting at the table, her leg stretched out in front of her. Mary was at the sink, washing lettuce from the garden. Roxanne was leaning against the counter, talking to Mandi. Sophie was lying on her stomach in the middle of the floor, still drawing.

"Daddy," she said. "I drew Mandi but I made her all better."

She held up a paper, a figure of a woman in a dress, two legs, two arms, and a big smile.

"Hey, honey," Roxanne said. "Thought we'd lost you."

"Went down the road," I said, and smiled. "Clair will be right in."

I went to Roxanne, touched her arm. Mandi looked at me, grinned and said, "I feel like a princess here, being waited on like this."

"I'll make you a princess," Sophie said, and she started to draw a crown above the smiling face.

"Don't you worry," Mary said. "You get back on your feet, we'll put you right to work." She shook water out of a head of romaine. "You're all invited to dinner," she said. "Chicken on the grill. New potatoes, asparagus, and a nice salad."

"I'm sitting next to Mandi," Sophie said.

I looked to Roxanne and she nodded.

"Fine," she said. "We have some nice wine."

"Why don't we go get it then," I said, and turned, catching Roxanne's eye. She turned to follow me, stopped and glanced at Sophie.

Mary said, "Oh, she's fine right there."

I walked out to the drive, Roxanne behind me. I went to Clair's truck and took out the bag. I got into the Subaru and she climbed in, put the key in. She leaned over and kissed me, a glancing but affectionate peck.

"We have to talk," I said, the bag on my lap.

"It's okay," Roxanne said, starting the motor. "You're right. She seems nice. She's sweet with Sophie. I mean, I'm sure there's something pretty difficult in her past and she absolutely shouldn't go back to what she's been doing. I mean the health risks alone. But maybe we can—"

"Not that," I said.

We were turning around in front of the barn. Roxanne stopped the car in the middle of the barnyard. She saw Clair cross in front of the window above the workbench. He was carrying the shotgun.

"What?" she said.

I told her about the Jeep, the guy in the woods. I held up the bag. She looked at it like it might explode. I opened it and she peered inside, blanched.

"Oh, my God," Roxanne said.

"The Wiltons?" I said. "I don't know," she said. "You said you talked to him."

"A friend of his? A member of the coven or whatever the hell they call it?"

"It would be crazy. I mean, there's a good chance they could get their kids back. With counseling. A safety plan. But this—this would be the end."

"We're talking about a guy who takes his orders from Satan," I said.

"Did you call the police?"

"Yes," I said. "It was kind of hard to explain. The trooper is supposed to call back."

She looked away.

"I don't want to scare Sophie," Roxanne said.

"I know. But she should know not to talk to anyone on the road, or anyone coming into the yard. Not that she'll ever be alone."

"Not now," Roxanne said.

"No," I said.

"Clair will tell Mary. If Mandi's staying there, she should know, don't you think?"

"I guess. I mean, if she's in the house all day."

"I've got to call Richard at work," Roxanne said.

"The police will come here, I would think."

"We can meet them here. Sophie can stay at dinner."

The trooper called my cell as I half-heartedly opened the wine. We said Roxanne had to make a quick call for work, and I was going with her. Sophie was standing on a chair at the counter with Mary, arranging slices of cheese on a plate, eating every third one. She didn't look up, and we left and walked down the road. The trooper pulled into the yard as we got to our door.

Her name was Danielle Ricci and she was tall and strong, maybe twenty-five, serious, no small talk. We talked in the driveway by her cruiser, a maroon Crown Vic, no bar on the roof, lights in the grill. The radio chirped reassuringly. Ricci took notes on a legal pad in a blue plastic folder. The bag sat on the hood of the car.

"How far from where you encountered the subject to your property?" she said.

"A mile," I said. "Maybe a little more. But rough going, bushwacking your way."

"And your friend said he saw the car pass twice?"

"Three times.."

"So it could have been more but he might not have noticed?"

"He doesn't miss much," I said.

"This is the guy who fired the warning shot?"

"Yes."

"Clair—"

"Varney."

She wrote that down. Didn't look up. "Ms. Masterson. I know you said you're involved in this particular case right now, but are there others that might lead someone to want to harm your child?"

Roxanne was silent for a moment. Ricci looked up.

"In the last two months, I've pulled seven children from four different households. None of them were happy about it."

"Any of them threaten you personally?"

"You mean call me names? Sure. One woman said she hoped someday I'd know what it felt like, having my kids taken away."

"Did you report that?"

"No, she was drunk. Angry. You get that a lot but they don't usually act on it."

"That all? Threats, I mean?"

"A mom said she hoped I burned in hell. Her boyfriend said I was lucky I was a woman because if I was a man he'd put me in a coma."

Ricci looked up at that one. "But because you're a woman—"

"Chivalry is not dead," I said.

Ricci looked at me, then got it. "So the one with the burning in hell. Is that these Satan people?"

"No," Roxanne said.

"They don't believe in Hell like most people," I said. "They say Jews and Christians came up with it to keep the people in line."

"Worked for me," Ricci said. "Went to Catholic school."

"There you go," I said.

She scribbled a bit more, then closed the case and capped her pen. "We should be able to find the car," she said.

Roxanne and I nodded.

"And I'll see if we can get prints off the tape."

"Okay," Roxanne said.

"But on its own possession of duct tape isn't a criminal offense," she said.

"No, but—"

"You can ID the guy, Mr. McMorrow?" Ricci said.

"How many guys have peacock tattoos?" I said.

"The most important thing is to find him, talk to him, see if we can discern his intent."

"He knew I lived on this road," I said.

"Possibly," the trooper said.

"He wasn't picking berries back there."

"I know that."

"If I see him again, I'll stop him," I said.

Ricci looked at me.

"One way or the other," I said.

"Don't do anything stupid, Mr. McMorrow," she said. "You have a responsibility to your family."

"Exactly right," I said.

15

The Jeep had been reported stolen out of Rockland by a guy who'd left the keys in it in the parking lot of a bar on Thomaston Street. The guy was a construction worker, single, twenty-two, said he didn't know anything about any Satanists, had never had any contact with DHHS. He was upset about the Jeep being stolen because he'd just put in a transmission from a junkyard and it had cost him a grand.

The cops knew all that within twenty minutes of Trooper Ricci's leaving my house. Later that night they found the Jeep, burned to a crisp in a gravel pit in Montville Center, about twelve miles south of us. Someone had reported seeing the smoke. The Montville Volunteer Fire Department sent a truck but by the time the boys got there, there wasn't much left.

Ricci told me this in a phone message left on my cell a couple days later. She said they hadn't been able to pull prints off the duct tape, it was a brand sold at Wal-mart and Home Depot, which wasn't helpful, either. She said she was working on getting a list of the Wiltons' known associates, but the Wiltons weren't being helpful. She'd be in touch.

When I got the message I was on my way to Belfast to pick up Mandi's cat. It was Tuesday morning, raining in windblown squalls that were warm but stung like glass needles. Roxanne reluctantly had gone into the office after taking Monday off, was supposed to meet with her boss, Sophie was with Clair, Mary, and Mandi.

I called Roxanne's office, left a message saying everything was okay, nothing urgent, but to call me back.

She didn't call back. Was she in her meeting? Had she'd gotten to Rockland safe? Had anyone followed her? Would anyone follow her home? Sophie would be fine with Clair, wouldn't she? The questions cycled, running through my mind. Then I started replaying the conversation with the man in the woods. What were his exact words? "So you own all the way—"

More questions: If he torched the Jeep, how did he get away? Did someone pick him up? Harland Wilton? Someone else? How many people were in this group? More than I knew, Wilton had told me. How many more? Where were they? Did they meet for some sort of worship? Would they abduct a child? Or was it someone else entirely?

I was coming into Belfast, coasting down toward the harbor, where a chunk of bay showed between the downtown blocks. A rainy day on the main coast meant a trip to town for summer people and the main drag was busy, cars cruising for parking spaces. I drove slowly the length of Main Street, cars in front of me pulling in when a car backed out.

At the harbor, I pulled over into the loading zone, got out, and looked out over the railing. Boats bucked on their moorings, bows turned to the gusts. The water was dark gray, shrouded in rain, whitecaps showing faintly outside the harbor mouth. A lobster boat moved between the moorings, swung into the wind and eased up to the float to unload. The sternman, a big square-jawed guy in dirty yellow foul weather gear, stepped off and grabbed the bowline tossed by the guy at the helm. The sternman snugged the line to a cleat.

"Hey, Roger," the guy at the helm shouted, then added something unintelligible, the words whisked away by the wind. Roger looked up and caught my gaze, then turned away.

Could he be Mandi's Roger? How many Rogers were there around here, guys who would have come off a boat? An old-fashioned name. But would the guy use his real name going to see an escort?

I walked up the rail toward the restaurant then turned to see the lobster boat's stern. The boat was the *Mary Vic* out of Lincolnville. I walked back, leaned on the railing again. The helmsman was hefting red plastic crates of lobster over the side of the boat to Roger, on the dock.

"Little rough out there?" I called down.

Roger turned, lifting a crate. "She's kicking up a bit but nothing too serious."

"How far offshore you go?"

"Oh, in close, up around Seven Hundred Acre, little south of Islesboro, there."

I smiled down, the gabby tourist. "Me and my friend, we were having an argument. I said most lobsters were caught right on the coast because the lobsters hide in the rocks. My friend, her name's Mandi, she said the boats go way out so they can catch the big ones."

Roger looked at me. Her name didn't make him blink or flinch. "Well, I guess your friend is half right," he said, still swinging the crates. "Some boys go offshore. Need a bigger boat, a lot of gear to drop traps in deep water. Plus time and fuel to get out and back. Big investment."

He walked to the stern, undid the line. The helmsman fired up the motor, eased the boat forward to take off the slack on the bowline. Roger whipped it off the cleat, and stepped on board as the boat moved by. He waved.

What was it Mandi had said? He seemed like a nice guy.

I parked across from Mandi's building, looked up and down Main Street, all very Norman Rockwell. The woman standing on a stepladder outside the real estate office, watering geraniums in hanging pots. A portly cop walking up the street toward me, chalking tires. Two boys on bikes whizzing down the hill toward the harbor, fishing poles crossed over their handlebars, shiny mackerel jigs glinting in the sun.

The escort's cat sitting in the window.

She watched me as I took a cardboard box out of the back of the truck, and crossed the street. I used Mandi's key to open the door to the stairs. Closed the door behind me and listened. Faint television noise, a talk show. Voices from the clothes shop next door.

I went up the stairs, paused outside Mandi's door. There was no mail, no newspaper, nothing to indicate she lived here or that she was gone. I turned the key in the lock, pushed the door open, smelled the litter box. I heard the thump as the cat jumped down from the windowsill. She mewed as she crossed the living room, stopped short when she saw it was not her mistress.

"It's okay," I said, but she made a break for the door, still open behind me. I moved, headed her off, and she brushed my legs, scrambled for the bedroom. I stepped back to shut the door, felt it bump against something.

Someone.

The door pushed open.

"Mr. McMorrow," Detective Raven said. "What story you writing today for the *New York Times?*"

He stepped in, shut the door behind him. Held out his hand and smiled. We shook hands, and stood for a moment. He was in his detective's uniform: khakis, blue polo shirt, gun and badge on his belt. He said, "Let me guess. The cat."

"Right," I said. "I figured the food must be gone. Water, too."

"We would've taken it," he said, "before it died of thirst."

"Good to know you're looking after things," I said.

"Didn't know when Miss Lasell would be back," he said. "Matter of fact, we weren't really sure where she'd gone to."

"Staying with friends of mine. The stairs, what with her foot and her wrist—"

"Nice of you. Where might this be?"

"Prosperity," I said. "Right up the road from my house."

"So you'll be seeing her," Raven said, a half smile showing, hands in the pockets of his khakis.

I nodded. The cat poked its head out of the bedroom, pulled it back in.

"Tell her to call me. Been calling her cell phone yesterday, this morning. Leaving messages, but she never calls back."

"She may not even have it on," I said. "She's been a little distracted, settling in."

"She's doing okay?"

"As okay as you could expect, under the circumstances."

"Getting beat up, you mean," Raven said. "Having to go live with strangers."

"Yeah. I think her wrist really hurts. She's being a pretty good sport, all in all."

Raven smiled, said, "Good for her." He walked across the room, as if looking it over for something he'd missed. "How's the story coming?" he said, his back to me.

I hesitated, could feel him smile. "Still working on it," I said.

"I was thinking," he said. "What's the word for it when the writer has to say he has some connection to the thing he's writing about?"

"Disclosure?"

"That's it."

He was at the front window. Pushed the shade over with a finger and looked out.

"Was driving me crazy. You know how you have something on the tip of your brain but it won't come?"

"Yeah," I said.

Raven turned back. "Disclosure. You know I've been reading the *New York Times* a little since we were talking. I did a search of the archives, read some of your stories. Some interesting stuff in there. I liked the one on the Mexicans settling way Down East."

"Thanks," I said. "They were good people."

"You still see them? Go visit 'em or whatever?"

"No," I said.

"Okay, 'cause I was wondering. In your story, whatever it might be about, you're gonna have to say you helped Miss Lasell out? I mean, going to the hospital, finding her a place to stay."

"I guess I'll have to. Otherwise, it would be dishonest."

"Right. I mean, people who read these stories figure the reporter just wanders around, calls people up, writes the story. They don't figure the reporter took the girl home, came and got her cat."

"Unless you tell them in the story."

"Looking forward to that one," Raven said.

"Good," I said.

"Kind of like a mystery, not knowing what it's about."

"Yes," I said. "It is."

He paused, walked across the room, picked up one of the magazines. *People*. Lindsey Lohan on the cover, just out of rehab.

"You know, between us. What do they call it? Off the record?"

"Yeah."

"Off the record, that's what I figured Miss Lasell was up to. Drugs I mean. No job. Not on welfare, either. Pays the light bill. Pays her rent on time. Not living like a king, or a princess or whatever, but keeping up."

"It would appear so," I said.

"You know she paid everything in cash?"

"No, I didn't know that."

"Rent in an envelope, all twenties. Light bill, she paid down at the supermarket service window. Cash. Cash for groceries, too. Cash for gas."

"Some people don't believe in credit cards," I said.

"Or checks," Raven said, flipping through the magazine. "Or bank accounts."

"How do you know she doesn't have a bank account?"

"Nothing here to indicate it."

"Searched the place pretty good, considering she's a victim," I said. "Don't you need some sort of probable cause? A warrant?"

"Premise search is justified because we're investigating to try to apprehend her assailant. You don't see anything wrong with that, do you?"

"No. Catch him and lock him up."

"That's the idea. But anyway, I changed my mind about the drugs."

"Good."

"No evidence of anything here at all."

"She doesn't seem like a drug dealer," I said.

"People often aren't what they seem," Raven said. "But I bet you know that, doing what you do."

"Yes."

"You know what we did find? Off the record?"

"What?"

He put the magazine down.

"Prints. Lots of prints. I think the guys said it was something like a dozen distinct sets of prints."

I didn't answer.

"Haven't gotten anything back yet. It isn't like TV, two minutes after they dust a place, they're sitting down at a computer and the IDs are popping up. But I'm curious, because one of the neighbors, she said Miss Lasell was very quiet, a good tenant. But people did come and go, mostly at night. No noise or anything, just people visiting."

"Oh, really," I said.

"All men," Raven said.

"Huh," I said.

"You know what I'm thinking? And this might be totally crazy. And you can tell me if you think I am. But I'm thinking she's a hooker. Doing a nice little trade right here in the center of town. Don't have to walk up and down the sidewalk in hotpants anymore, not with the internet."

"Huh," I said again.

"Now, I know it's no biggie. Victimless crime and all that. But most women who do this are drug addicts. No evidence of that, though. No pills. No syringes. No spoons."

I didn't comment.

"But if she's a hooker, what does that make you, Mr. McMorrow?"

"I'm a reporter," I said.

"Writing about a small-town prostitute? Taking her home with you. Taking care of her after *somebody* beat her up?"

I didn't answer. Raven walked across the room, picked up the picture frame with the model's photos in it.

"You know, I should be working on other stuff. Chief's gonna get after me, I spend too much time on an assault case, especially one where the victim is less than cooperative. Closest thing to a witness isn't much better."

"I told you what I could."

"Right. Confidentiality and all that."

He put the frame down, turned to me.

"I've read all about these Washington reporters going to jail to protect their sources," Raven said. "You ever been to jail?"

"Yes," I said.

"I don't mean to visit or interview somebody. I mean to stay. Every night, every day, locked in that little place with all those people. Some of 'em are halfway normal. Some are totally insane. And you have to deal with 'em 'cause they're not going anywhere and you aren't either."

I didn't answer.

"I ran you, too, Mr. McMorrow. A couple of assault charges, both dismissed. A firearms charge. Concealing a weapon without a permit."

"That was filed," I said.

"Play it pretty close to the line, don't you? What do they think of that at the *New York Times*?"

I didn't answer. He smiled, like this was so much fun. "You know what?" he said.

"No, what?" I said.

"Stuff I know doesn't bother me as much as stuff I don't know. The stuff I don't know drives me crazy. I've always been like that. When I was a kid, I was always looking stuff up. And this was when you had to go to the encyclopedia. The row of books, not the internet."

He looked around the room. "Just bugs me, not knowing things, like who this young woman really is. I mean, I ran her license."

"Sybill Lasell," I said.

"Right. Portland address. But the record of Sybill Lasell begins four years ago, when she got that license. I can't find that name anywhere else. Nowhere."

"So she stayed out of trouble."

"Could be."

We were quiet. Raven was looking away, thinking. I was staring at him, waiting. "Another thing," he said, and he turned to me. "You're not gonna believe this, the way her face was all bruised and cut."

He paused. "But you know, she looks familiar to me. Like I've seen her before."

"She's been here for a few months," I said.

"No, not here. I'd remember that. This goes back a ways. I'll keep thinking about it, see if it comes to me. It wasn't her in person as much as it was when I looked at the picture on her license, something started to click. Then it stopped."

He smiled. "Showed a few of the other officers and one of them had the same feeling. He's from out of state. Massachusetts."

"I don't know," I said.

"Oh, well, it'll come. Sometimes it's best if you put it aside, don't try too hard. Just let it flow. That's my experience, anyway."

He started for the door. Stopped. "Tell her I called," he said. Started again, stopped again, held up one hand. "Hey, you know that boat I was telling you about? The one I'm building?"

"Yeah," I said. "How's it going?"

"Good," Raven said, with a slow smile. "It's coming together, piece by piece."

16

I yanked the cat out from its hiding place under the bed, squeezed her tight and stuffed her into the box, and folded the top closed. The box went on the floor of the truck on the passenger side. The cat cried nonstop. Every few minutes, a black paw darted out of the crack, like a hand poking out of a coffin.

I took a circuitous route across the ridges, between the hills. Four miles outside of town, I took a right on a dirt road that turned to a track through dense poplar and around brush-filled bogs. The road was rutted and mud-holed and I put the truck in four-wheel-drive, pounded my way through. When I emerged on the paved road, three miles later, I took a left and a right and wove my way northwest. The cat cried but we weren't followed.

It was after ten when I pulled up to Clair's barn. His pickup was out front, the woods truck pulled into the barn door. I heard the clank of tools, the faint strains of Mozart. As I opened the door, Clair stepped out, wiping his hands with a rag. I came around to the passenger side, opened it and picked up the cat in the box. A paw darted through the top.

"She wants out," Clair said.

"I know. Been crying for half an hour straight."

"No, not the cat. Mandi."

I stood, looked at him.

"Where is she?"

"Last time I looked, in the kitchen. Wanted to call a cab but Mary told her to wait for you."

"A cab to where?"

"Don't know. Don't think she knows."

"Sophie?"

"She's in there with 'em."

I went to the door, knocked. Mary came across, peeked through the glass window, opened the door.

"Hey, Jack," she said. "You have a little girl who's been missing you."

She moved aside and I stepped in. Mandi was sitting at the table, her face purple and yellow. Sophie was sitting on a stool by the stove, eyes puffy.

"Hey, honey," I said. "What's the matter? You been crying?"

She pursed her lips, started to cry, dry sobs like all the tears had drained out. "Mandi. She—she wants to go away."

"Oh, but honey," Mandi said. "I'll come back and see you. Really, I will."

"You can't 'cause you can't walk."

"I'll come back when I get better."

"You'll forget," Sophie said.

I knelt by Sophie, put the box on the floor. "You want to see something?"

She leaned toward the box. I opened the top flap and the cat lifted its head, then leapt out, darted out of the kitchen and into the house.

"A kitty," Sophie said, and started after it.

"Her name is Lulu," Mandi said, and Sophie began calling. "Lulu. Come here, Lulu."

They were gone. Mary started after them, saying, "Honey, don't pick her up yet. She's nervous."

I stood, looked at Mandi, her bare leg in gym shorts, stretched out in front of her. "So what is it?" I said.

"I can't be here, Jack," she said.

"Why not?"

"I just can't."

"Where will you go?"

"I've got friends."

"Where?"

"Portland. They'll take care of me for a while."

"Okay. I'll drive you."

"You don't have to."

"A cab to Portland will cost you a fortune. I'll run you down there, make sure you're all set."

"No, that's okay."

"Have you talked to them yet? You know they can put you up?"

"No, but they'll be there," Mandi said.

"But what if they're—"

"I gotta go," she blurted. "I just gotta go."

She took a breath. "I can't be here, okay? You guys, you've been great. Mary and Clair are so nice, and Sophie she's just adorable. But I can't be here."

Drugs, I thought. She *was* an addict. She was going into withdrawal, the painkillers wearing off.

"Clair told me about the guy in the woods."

"Roxanne, she's having some trouble with a family," I said. "The police are—"

"How do you know he wasn't after me?"

"Roger?" I said. "Beat you up and now he's coming back to kidnap you? Doesn't make sense. The two things are very different. A drunken rage and this other thing."

"It's control," Mandi said.

"What'd Roger look like?"

"Your size, blondish brown hair, cut short with these little flipped-up bangs in the front, kind of like a little kid."

"This guy was big and heavy with a thick black beard."

"Could be a friend of his—"

"Some control freak gets his friend to control you, too? And what's with this control stuff?"

For a long time, Mandi didn't answer. Leaned forward over her legs, ran her hands through her hair. From deep in the house we could hear Sophie calling the cat.

"I saw him five times," Mandi said, looking up at me.

"Over what period of time?"

"A month."

"And?"

"And he was like the guys I was telling you about. It was like each time he was asking me on a date. He'd say what we were going to do. The first time we went to this place across the bridge, you drive down you can sit on the rocks. We take his truck and—"

"What kind of truck?"

"I don't know. A black truck. A big one, bigger than yours."

"Ford? Chevy?"

"Um, I don't know. What's an F-50?"

"F-150?"

"Right. It said that on the side."

"That's a Ford. Go ahead with the story, then."

"Okay. Well, he had a bottle of wine and we drank the wine out of paper cups and looked out at the water, the boats and everything."

"And he paid you?"

"Yeah. Then he asked me if he could call me again. I said, 'Sure.'"

"So he did?"

"Yeah. The next time we went out to dinner. This place on the water in Lincolnville. He had on dress pants and a shirt with a collar."

"What did he talk about?"

"He told me he liked the Baltimore Orioles. I got him talking about that for a while. You could tell he was really into it, knew all the names and stuff."

"Were you into it?"

"No."

"But he didn't get that?"

"He was kinda clueless, in a way. Like a guy who never had a girlfriend before. Wasn't sure how to go about it."

"So did he—"

"Pay me? Yeah. Two hundred bucks each time. Cash in an envelope with a card with roses on it. Like it was my birthday."

I didn't ask the obvious question.

"No, he didn't sleep with me or anything. The second time he kissed me goodbye. Third date, we went bowling in Rockland. He kissed me more after that. I mean, it was like high school or something. With a shy guy."

We heard a distant shriek of delight from Sophie.

"Fourth time, he brought a picnic. Crackers and cheese and fruit and wine. Even had it in a little basket."

"What'd you talk about then?" I said.

"Oh, more baseball. Boats. He's been fixing up his boat. He told me about his parents, how they had a real lot of money, how they liked his sister more because she was really smart in school. He was the dumb one."

"What did he do for work?"

"I don't think he did. He never talked about that."

"Was he from Belfast?"

"Seemed to know his way around but I don't know."

"You didn't ask where he lived?"

She frowned, making her purpled-eyes squint.

"You gotta understand. First of all, I don't ask. They won't tell, not the truth. And Roger, it was different right from the start. He was acting like we'd met at work or someplace and he'd asked me out. I was, I don't know, going along. He could be kind of annoying, explaining simple things like I'm dumb. But he wasn't ugly or smelly and he brought me stuff and, I don't know, it was kinda fun to be on a sort of date. But still, it was—"

"Business," I said.

"Yeah. If he wanted to have this fantasy that we were dating, I mean, so what? The money was good. Get him talking about sports and boats and pretend to be interested. Beats—"

I didn't want to know what it beats. "And then what?"

"The last time, we went to dinner, this fancy place down in Camden. He called and asked me to get dressed up, so I wore a dress, my new shoes. Dinner cost like three-hundred bucks, eighty something dollars just for the wine. One little bottle."

She shook her head. "It was like I was in a movie or something. I just had to remember my lines and he played his part fine. This kind of doofy guy with money."

Mandi sighed. Ran her hands up and down her thighs, over the bruises. She sighed again. "So after dinner, we came back to town, went for a walk down on the harbor. Looked at the lights, then came back to the apartment. He put the card on the table, you know, the card with the money. And we sat on the couch and things were, I don't know, progressing. More than before. And I figure, well, he's gonna want to do more than kiss goodnight this time.

"So I got up, went and got my nice dress off, put on this nightgown, kinda slinky. I kept the shoes on, the heels. Some guys like that, you know? But then he—"

She paused. Turned to listen for Sophie and Mary. Their voices were distant and Mandi continued. "But then he didn't like jump my bones. He just sat on the edge of the bed and he held my hand and he—"

She swallowed, like the words couldn't come.

"He asked you to marry him," I said.

Mandi nodded, eyes tearing. "It was awful," she said.

"Why?"

"Because I couldn't marry him. And he didn't know that. But how could he not know that?"

"He was serious?"

"He had a ring," Mandi said. "A diamond. In a little box. Velvet on it. And he opened it and he started this speech, like he'd been rehearsing. How he knows we've only known each other for a few weeks but when he met me, right away it was like he'd known me his whole life."

She swallowed.

"He said we were soul mates."

"Yikes," I said.

Mandi closed her eyes. "So he's looking at me and I'm looking at him and I'm, like, totally shocked. And he's going on about how wonderful I am and beautiful and I felt like saying, 'Stop. I am not this person you think I am.' "

I waited.

"And then he, like, slowly starts to get it. I could see it in his eyes. It was horrible. I mean, I didn't even have to say anything. He could just see it. He could see that I didn't care for him, really. It was just—"

"Business," I said.

"Right. And the guy has just said he wants to spend the rest of his life with me. I'll never forget that look. It was like he'd just seen somebody die or something. He looked, I don't know, crushed. Slowly crushed, like one of those big snakes in the jungle was squeezing him."

"And then angry?"

"Like a light switch. Like a little kid having a temper tantrum. He flung me back and just started swinging. He was making this screaming, sound, no words, just like this bellowing, you know?"

"And he knocked you off the bed?"

"And then he jumped down and landed on my leg and kicked me and punched me and I thought he was gonna kill me. I thought, well, isn't this a weird way to go? Killed by the only guy who ever asked you to marry him. I remember thinking, how bizarre."

"But you didn't."

"No. I passed out. And then you were there."

We didn't speak. Mandi looked down at her leg. I stared at the wall behind her, the bulletin board with a John Deere pin, pictures of Clair and Mary's grandchildren, smiling towheads in their green yard in North Carolina.

"Tell me something, Mandi," I said, dropping my gaze to her eyes. She looked up.

"Why is it you don't think you're good enough?"

She continued to stare at me but I saw a hardness form, like she was made of glue and it had just set.

I waited. I waited some more. "You're nice," I said. "And you're attractive. Why wouldn't some guy want to marry you? Take you on dates? Why did you say—what was it? 'I'm not the person you think I am.'"

I watched her. Her eyes narrowed. Her jaw clenched. Her attention turned away from me, like she had moved deep inside herself. "Jack, you don't know me," she said.

"I feel like I know you some," I said.

She shook her head. "I'm a stranger. I don't belong here, in this house with your pretty little girl and these nice people. Mary brought me breakfast in my room. She washed my clothes. Clair rigged up a chair in the shower. Mary asked me if I was a vegetarian 'cause if I was, they wouldn't have pork chops."

"And Sophie thinks you're just great," I said.

"I'm not, Jack," Mandi said. "Look at me."

"I am looking."

"You know what I do."

"I don't know why," I said. "You could do anything."

She looked past me, past the house, past the woods and away to some distant place. "I'm damaged," she said softly. "Damaged goods."

"Damaged by what?" I said.

She smiled, shook her head at some irony only she was aware of. "Long story," she said.

"I have time."

"No," Mandi said. "This story, it lasts a lifetime." She smiled. And then she chuckled, an odd sound that wavered, a half cry.

"Roxanne knows people you could talk to," I said.

"Oh, God, I've talked. But you know what? The talk goes in circles and always ends up in the same place. Right back where you started."

She looked at me. "You know what," she said. "It's people like you. Like all of you."

"People like us what?"

"That I have to get away from."

"Why?"

"Call me a cab."

"There are no cabs out here."

"Sure there are. There are cabs in Belfast."

"Where would you go?"

"I don't know," Mandi said. "Portland. Like I told you, I have friends."

"Then I'll drive you."

"No."

"Because there aren't any friends," I said.

"Sure there are. I used to live there."

"Then let's go. You can call them on the way, tell them you're coming."

"No," Mandi said, agitated now, picking at the cast on her wrist.

"I'm not going to let some cabbie dump you on a street corner. You can't even walk."

She started to cry. "Why, Jack?" she said. "Why not?"

"Because it wouldn't be right," I said.

"Right?" she said, sobbing. "Nothing's right. Nothing will ever be right."

She rocked forward and back. I put my hand on her shoulder and patted and she felt small, more like Sophie than Roxanne, a sad, sad, child. "I'm sorry, Jack," Mandi said. "I'm so sorry."

"For what?" I said.

"I'm so sorry," she whispered, and she rocked and I patted, and the cat dashed into the room, skidding to a halt. There was a flurry of footsteps and Sophie followed, stopped in her tracks and looked at Mandi, tears streaking her cheeks, blackened eyes even more swollen.

"What's the matter?" Sophie said.

"Oh, nothing, honey," Mandi said.

"When I'm crying, Mommy and Daddy hold me," Sophie said. Mandi smiled.

"Where are your mommy and daddy?" Sophie said.

I looked to Mandi and waited but I knew she wouldn't answer.

17

Mandi stayed. I took Sophie home and she asked when she could go back to see the cat. I said maybe after her nap and she got her blanket and a stack of books and I read to her on her bed, a story about a dog, a cat, and a goat who were best friends.

"Mandi and Lulu are my best friends," Sophie said, and two pages later she fell asleep.

I went downstairs to the study, did some work. There was a story in the Belfast paper about a young woman in Rockland arrested for dealing crack. She was nineteen. Her four-month-old baby was in the back of the car when the police picked her up. In her mugshot, she was pretty and blonde. The story said she'd been a high school cheerleader.

I called Myra at the *Times*, sold her on the story of the infiltration of crack and heroin to mid-coast Maine. Six-hundred words for six-hundred bucks. I called the police chief in Rockland, got his dire assessment of the situation. Called a county detective who specialized in drug investigations. He said the drugs were coming through from Canada, so I called the INS office in Boston, got a quote from an agent there who said they were seizing more heroin on the northern border than ever. And they knew the vast majority of it got through.

An hour on the phone. An hour to write it. The story still seemed flat so I got the phone book out, called six people in Rockland with the same last name as the young woman: Beech. In fifteen minutes, I had her mother on the phone. She cried.

Sometimes you get lucky.

She said drugs had taken her daughter away but now she hoped she'd get her back. "Police arresting her, that might've saved her life," the mother said.

That was how I ended it. I e-mailed the story as Sophie stirred upstairs, a book falling out of the bed onto the floor. As I got up from my desk to get her, I wondered what had taken Mandi away, and if there was anyone out there who wanted her back.

The Wilton kids were causing trouble. It wasn't that they meant to, but their talk about Satan and the false Christian god was giving the foster parents the willies.

"The foster said she's been having nightmares, feels like she should lock the bedroom door at night," Roxanne said. "She's actually afraid of them."

"How old?"

"Eight and four. Jeremy and Luc. With a 'c.'"

"Short for Lucifer?" I said.

"I don't ask," Roxanne said. "It's hard. We don't want to discriminate against them because of their religion."

"They complain, you can just tell them to go to the devil."

Roxanne smiled, but barely.

We were sitting on the deck having a drink. It was a little after five and Roxanne had changed into shorts and a tank top, her bare feet were up on the table. Sophie was playing with a Fisher-Price barn that Clair and Mary had gotten down from their attic. The toy cows were grazing on the lawn.

"Are they happy?" I said, holding my beer glass.

"The boys? Seem pretty well adjusted. I mean, they eat like there's no tomorrow. The doctor said they were really malnourished."

"Making up for lost time."

"Right. But I've got to find somebody else to take them, ASAP."

"No Satanists on your list?"

"Just deluded Christians and Jews," Roxanne said.

"Just find a nice agnostic."

"I suppose."

She sipped her wine. I took a swallow of Ballantine. Bright goldfinches swarmed around the bird feeder. Sophie chattered, made a mooing sound, the cows talking to each other.

Roxanne, lost in thought, didn't notice.

"I read as much as I could about it online," she said. "It says there are tens of thousands of people who believe this, that Satanism is the first religion, the real one. The rest are all fakes, invented in this sort of power grab."

"Muslims, too?"

"Yup."

"Well, makes some sense, I guess," I said. "First thing you do when you conquer someone is take away their religion and give them yours. Think of the Aztecs and the Mayans and all of the other Native Americans. Converted them right off."

"It also said Satanists don't push their religion on other people. Don't advocate violence. Obey the law. Believe in separation of church and state."

"Your guy must be on the Satanist fringe," I said.

"I know he's gotten increasingly isolated. Probably paranoid. I mean, when you think Christian food will poison your kids. But he swears he wouldn't stalk me. Doesn't know anyone who would."

"What does he swear on?"

"Presumably not the Bible," Roxanne said. She sighed. "How do I get into these things?"

"How do we get into these things?" I said.

Roxanne turned her glass in her hand. Sophie was whinnying, galloping a toy horse. I waited, then began. "Mandi wanted to leave today," I said softly. "Said she didn't belong here. Wanted me to call her a cab."

"Why didn't you?" Roxanne said.

"To take her where? She can't even walk."

"Where did she say she wanted to go?"

"She said she could go to Portland. Said she has friends there."

"So let her go."

"I don't believe her, the part about the friends," I said. "I told her as much."

"Everybody has somebody," Roxanne said. "Unless they choose not to."

"Why would she—"

"She's run away from something, Jack. Maybe she was assaulted."

"She seems to have taken this one in stride," I said.

"Well, maybe somebody betrayed her in a terrible way. But clearly something happened."

Sophie clucked and quacked, little sandals tucked up underneath her. She leaned down to peer inside the barn.

"She doesn't think she deserves to be here," I said. "It weirds her out to be liked, to be on the receiving end of kindness."

"Why?" Roxanne said.

"I don't know."

We sat. Sipped. Sophie started packing all of the animals into the barn. She shut the doors and locked them. "It's a big thunderer," we heard her say. "You must stay inside."

"How did you get home today?" I said.

"Took 17 to Union, then I went up toward Appleton but I cut off on 105, did a little detour onto the North Union Road, circled back, went back up until I caught 220. When I got to Liberty, I stopped at the top of this hill and I looked back. There was nobody."

I nodded. Sipped my beer. We were quiet for a moment. "So the Wiltons have no idea where their kids are?"

"No. If and when we establish visitation, it'll be at the office," Roxanne said.

"What do you do? Beam them back and forth?"

"We pick them up."

"Easy enough to follow you back," I said.

"If they do that, they really lose them."

"If you know."

"We keep the parents in the office, gives us time to get the kids on their way."

"More than the parents to worry about," I said. "There's the rest of the coven."

"Covens are witches and all that. It's different."

"How?"

"I'm not sure. It's just that Satanists go way, way back. Witches are more recent."

"Huh," I said. "Well, maybe you'll be staying home by then."

Roxanne shrugged.

"I made six hundred today. The crack-heads-on-the-Maine-coast story for the Times."

"That's a start."

"As long as the tragedy and calamity keeps coming, we're home free," I said.

On the grass, Sophie was unloading the barn, shaking it upside down to get the animals out. "They're stuck," she said.

"I'll help you," Roxanne said, and she swung her legs down, fished for her sandals and went down the steps. I got up and was about to follow when the phone rang. I went inside, grabbed it off the counter. Said hello.

"Mr. McMorrow?"

"Yes."

"Listen, I'm a friend of Mandi's."

18

I didn't reply. Checked the caller ID. Didn't recognize the number.

"Well, I heard she got hurt and I just wanted to talk to her, see how's she's doing."

"Who is this?"

A hesitation, just a millisecond. "This is Alex Warren."

"How did you get this number, Alex?"

"The hospital. I went over there, 'cause I heard she had this accident, you know what I mean? I got worried. Hadn't seen her around town, hadn't been at the apartment, she wasn't answering her cell."

"The hospital gave you this number?"

"I said I was Mandi's cousin."

"But you're not."

"They wouldn't tell me anything if I said I was just a friend."

I didn't say anything.

"I was in town and somebody said this ambulance came and everything and then I really started to be concerned. I mean, an ambulance. That could be a lot of things, you know what I'm saying?"

"Yeah, Alex," I said. "I think I do."

He wanted me to pass along a message. Standing there in the kitchen, I said, "Hey, Alex, I've got to run. Listen, buddy, I'm sure she'll be glad to hear from you. I'm gonna be in Belfast tomorrow. How 'bout we meet up, you can give me your card or whatever. I'll get it to her. She's a little under the weather, probably not up for visitors."

"But she's okay?"

"Well, okay is probably generous. She's fair."

"Well, what happened? She get sick?"

"How 'bout I tell you about it tomorrow. I've got to drop by the apartment, get some stuff for her. Eight o'clock, I'll be there."

"How will I know you?" he said.

"I'll be the one waiting for you," I said.

I hung up and went outside, down to the lawn where Roxanne and Sophie were setting up the farmyard. "It's sunny now," Sophie said, putting the horses inside a paddock made of plastic fences.

"Good, honey," I said.

"Who was on the phone?" Roxanne said.

"Friend of Mandi's," I said.

"I'm Mandi's friend," Sophie said.

"I know," I said. "But I guess she has another one."

"Was he a boy or a girl," Sophie said.

"A boy," I said, and met Roxanne's eyes, looking up from the pigs and goats. "What was his name?" she said.

"He said his name was Alex Warren. He wants to come see Mandi. He said he was worried about her."

"Does he know where she is?" Roxanne said.

"No, that's why he called."

"Is he going to bring Mandi some flowers?" Sophie said.

"I don't know, honey. I'm going to meet him and we'll talk about it."

"When?" Roxanne said.

"Tomorrow morning."

"Maybe someone else should meet him," Roxanne said. "Maybe Detective Raven."

"I know what a raven is," Sophie said, putting a cow in the hayloft. "It's a big black bird. Daddy and I see them flying when we go for our hikes. They say, 'cronk, cronk.'"

"Yes, they do," I said.

"Maybe Detective Raven should talk to Mandi's friend," Roxanne said again.

"I'll think about it," I said.

"His name is Alice? That's a silly name for a boy," Sophie said.

"He said that was his name, honey," I said. "But maybe it isn't."

After dinner, while Roxanne was giving Sophie her bath, I left the house, locking the door behind me. I walked down the road a quarter mile, watching the woods, listening for cars. Then I turned around and walked back up the road to Clair's, saw the lights on in the barn. I stepped in and heard Vivaldi, "The Four Seasons," the summer part. Clair saw me from the workshop and came out. We walked back out to the road, turned under the big silver maples that marked the entrance to his farm and started toward my house.

I told Clair about the call. I told him about my conversation with Mandi, the marriage proposal. Clair and I had no secrets.

He didn't answer for a minute, processing the way he did. As we walked, a chipmunk dashed across the road in front of us and disappeared into the brush. A shadow passed and I looked up, saw a kestrel. The hunter and the hunted. I knew which one I wanted to be.

"Lots of people say that, 'know what I mean.' They say 'like' all the time, too. Could be a coincidence," Clair said.

"Wasn't his name, either," I said. "I could tell by the way he pronounced it. It wasn't something he'd been saying his whole life."

"Her line of work, she probably meets a lot of guys don't use their real names."

"Yup."

"How you gonna know if this is Roger?"

"Instinct," I said.

"Now there's a plan."

"Wait until I tell you Plan B."

"Why not have the police meet you there, too?"

"Blows her cover," I said. "She could go to jail, if he decides to testify."

"To get even," he said.

"The suitor scorned."

"Interesting how closely love and violence are intertwined," Clair said.

"All about control," I said.

"Can't back you up," Clair said. "Would leave the flank unprotected."

"I know. You stay with Mandi and Sophie."

"Supposed to rain the next three days. Won't be cutting wood, not that you need inclement weather to keep you out of the woods."

"I've been busy," I said.

"Collecting strays," Clair said.

'You're the one with a house like Dr. Doolittle."

Clair smiled. We walked, coming up on my house, the car and truck parked in front of the garage, the shades on the road side drawn.

"Thanks for taking her in," I said.

He shrugged.

"No problem."

"What do you think of her?" I said.

"Very likeable, the part you can see," Clair said.

"And the part you can't?"

"Hard to tell, Jack. It's dark in there. Very dark."

Roxanne didn't want me to go. I said I'd just get a look at him, see if he fit Roger's description. If he was five-three and blond, I'd know he was some other stalker.

"What if it is him?" Roxanne said, the two of us in bed, legs intertwined, her hand on my chest.

"Then I'll have a choice."

"Call the police—"

"—or give him a stern lecture."

Roxanne was quiet, her chest rising and falling with her breath. The miracle of her every breath. "They still have a case if she won't testify," she said. "Domestic assault doesn't require the victim's testimony."

"I know."

"And you still won't just turn him in?"

I didn't answer for a moment. I could see her staring up at the skylight, the falling dusk.

"She said she might want to stay in Belfast, stop moving around."

"And she'd have to leave?" Roxanne said.

"If she's arrested for prostitution. How could she stay if she's known as the town whore?"

"But Jack, how can she stay if this guy is loose?"

"It's a tough one," I said.

"I'm beginning to wonder what isn't," Roxanne said. "The little Wilton boy started asking for his mother. Last night he cried for three hours, wanting to go home."

"To be starved and beaten with a belt."

"The devil you know," Roxanne said.

In the half light, I felt her thinking. "I want you to promise me something, Jack," she said.

"What?"

"I want you to wait for him outside, on the sidewalk. I want you to talk to him in public, a restaurant. I want you to come home in one piece."

"I promise," I said.

She turned her head. "All of it?" she said.

"Every bit."

She looked at me closely, like it could be a trick.

"I promise," I said. "Cross your heart."

I ran my finger across her chest, the flat part between her breasts. She took my hand in hers and held it tight. I smiled. I knew she didn't.

I was there at 7:30. It was raw, the way it often is on the coast, the cool ocean rising to meet the falling rain and mixing into something that just hangs, a dense and pervading dampness like the clouds have fallen to earth. I drove past Mandi's apartment, circled at the landing. The bay was out there behind the wall of rain and fog, but the boats at the far end of the moorings barely showed through the gray. From the truck, I looked out, made the circle and came slowly back up the street.

There were two guys sitting in a pickup outside the pizza shop talking and smoking, flicking ashes through the open window tops.

There was a gray-haired man sitting in a Volvo with Pennsylvania plates parked outside the Rexall. The old guy was reading a paper. I pulled into a space in front of Mandi's door and looked in the rearview. I waited and watched. He turned the pages only occasionally, reading thoroughly, not flipping through.

I got out. The old guy didn't turn around. I stood on the sidewalk by the door and he didn't look. I watched the street, and nobody seemed to notice me. At 7:45 I unlocked the entrance door and went upstairs. At the landing, I stopped and listened. Jiggled the knob. It was locked.

I knocked twice, stepped to the side and flattened myself against the wall. I waited. Listened for any sound from inside the apartment. Nothing.

I unlocked the door and eased inside, closing the door behind me. The apartment was stuffy, smelled faintly of cat. I looked around. The place was disassembled, but not trashed. I ran a finger over a wooden box that served as an end table.

Dust. Raven and his forensics.

I went to the window and eased the shade open. I looked up and down the street. Watched and waited some more. Nobody. It was 7:55.

I went to the door and let myself out. Promises to keep. I waited a minute with the door open before stepping into the hallway. Listened.

No breathing. No shuffle. No rubbing of clothing. Nothing but the sound of rain dripping from the roof.

I walked slowly down the stairs and back outside. The rain was steadier now, and dense, cars passed with their lights and wipers on. There was no shelter and I pulled up the hood of my rain jacket, put my hands in my pockets. Felt my knife in one, the cold chisel from Clair's barn in the other.

I stood there against the brick wall, my feet dry in Bean boots but the water running off my jacket and onto my jeans. At eight-fifteen, I walked down the block, scanning the cars. Most were unoccupied. A black SUV pulled out and drove down the block toward the water as I approached. A new Mercedes convertible took its place, a young guy inside, New York plates.

Did Roger have that kind of money? How big was his boat? I walked past, looked him over. He was thirtyish, tanned and neatly shaved, handsome in a cologne sort of way. He was on the phone. He didn't look shy.

I crossed the street. The guy in the Volvo was reading the classified ads. The personals? Companions? I kept going, didn't see much more. Crossed back and got in the truck. Backed out and started up the block. I stopped at the red light, watched the cars pull up behind me. Four in line: a little Ford pickup, the color of rust. A minivan, white with a headlight out. The Volvo, the older man finished with his paper. The black SUV, which had looped back from the dead-end at the harbor.

The light changed. I took a right, started out of town past the big Victorians, the captains' houses, relics survived to see the new money come in. The pickup followed closely, a young kid alone. The minivan behind him. The Volvo took the right, too, but then turned and parked again. The SUV brought up the rear.

I did the speed limit out of town, following Route 137 to the east. The coast money quickly fell away, the houses merely serviceable, the boats, not in the harbor, but sitting on trailers, waiting for the weekend.

The pickup turned into a driveway. The van followed me but in no hurry, the SUV in the distance behind it. I sped up and the van did, too. I slowed and it caught up, the SUV behind it. I braked, trying to draw the van in closer but it stayed back.

We drove on, the three of us, prudently spaced. And then, three miles out of town, where the road climbed a grade and there were oak woods on both sides, I signaled and swung left onto a two-lane back road. A hundred yards in, there was a dirt road to the left. I slowed, signaled again, waited, and turned.

The van was gone. The SUV had stayed with me. Another hundred yards into the woods, the dirt road started to narrow. I braked hard, put the truck in reverse, turned and slammed it into the grass and brush.

I sat and waited. Waited some more.

The SUV rolled slowly by. A black Tahoe, pretty new, with Massachusetts plates. The guy at the wheel wore a gray sweatshirt, the hood up. I counted to twenty and pulled out. Went left and followed.

I saw him up ahead, brake lights flashing in the rain. The road turned, dipped to a ravine and crossed a culvert. I drove across, started up the other side, the truck's tires grabbing in the mud. At the top of the rise, the road widened.

And there he was.

The road had ended with a rough turnaround, a chain slung between two pine trees blocking entrance to the remaining path. A sign wired to the chain said "No Trespasing" in orange spray paint. The SUV was backing up, jockeying to turn around. I stopped the truck. He saw me and stopped, too. I swung the truck sideways to block the road.

I got out. The SUV's brake lights went out and the door opened. A man swung down from the seat. Tall, long-limbed, wearing jeans and running shoes. I walked toward him, hands in my jacket pockets, in the right, the chisel, in the left my phone and Swiss-Army knife. Blade out.

He was wearing sunglasses in the rain. The hood stayed up. When we were forty feet apart, he slowly pulled his sweatshirt zipper down.

I smiled. "Looks like we ran out of road," I said.

"Looks like it," he said.

We were still walking. I could see his face clearly. Ruddy cheeks, not quite a smile, but a relaxed expression like he'd expected this all along. Older than me by five years, maybe more.

Not Roger.

"Thought this road went all the way through," I said.

"Probably did at one time," he said. "Guess somebody decided they didn't want it open to the public."

"Good speller, too," I said.

"Makes it clear enough."

We were five feet apart now. I could see red spider lines on his cheeks. The glasses were very dark and I couldn't see his eyes. Very hard to read somebody if you can't see their eyes.

"If I'd known it was a dead end, I wouldn't have led you in here," I said.

His mouth flattened almost imperceptibly. Even without the eyes, I could feel him tense.

"What do you mean?" he said.

"Followed me all the way out from Mandi's."

He didn't answer for a moment, just stared. "Don't know what you're talking about," he said.

"You called last night."

He shook his head. I could see some gray at his temples. The sweatshirt was darkening as the rain soaked in. "Got the wrong guy, my friend. I was just looking for a shortcut."

I took out my phone, saw his hand move to the opening in the front of his sweatshirt. I pressed the button. Waited. The black glasses stared. I smiled again. And from somewhere on him came the sound of a cell phone ringing.

"Can you hear me now?" I said.

He reached behind him and under the sweatshirt, took the phone off his belt. Flicked it open, pressed a button, and the ringing stopped.

"You're Alex," I said.

"Maybe," he said.

"Or maybe not. You should practice saying a name a few times. It came out like you were reading it."

He ran a hand over his chin, dropped it down again. I thought I could see a bulge under the sweatshirt just in front of his left hip.

"Is that a gun?" I said.

He looked at me, gave a cold, hard stare. "Kinda nosey, aren't you?"

"I'm a reporter," I said. "We're trained to be observant."

"That right? Well, there's something heavy in your right pocket. What you got there, a roll of quarters?"

I didn't reply.

"I've known lotsa reporters. Cocky bastards, even the ladies."

"At least we're not liars," I said.

He stared. There were raindrops on the lenses of the glasses, made them seem like windows. "What's with you and Mandi?" I said.

"I could ask you the same question."

"That's easy. I met her in passing. When she couldn't go home because she was hurt, I helped her out."

I paused. The rain fell. "Your turn," I said.

"She's good in the sack," he said.

I flinched, felt an urge to take his head off. Choked it down. Smiled instead. "That's not what she says about you."

He didn't answer. The mouth was a blue-white line.

"What were you gonna do? Follow me, hope I'd lead you right to her?"

"Wanted to see that she's okay," he said, both of us keeping it under control. "What I hear, she's in kinda rough shape. Could be pretty vulnerable, wrong guy picked her up."

"She's fine. Love to find the guy who beat her."

He snorted. "Real knight in shining armor, huh?"

"I don't know about that."

"You know what I heard," he said. "I heard she won't even cooperate with the cops."

"No kidding."

He smiled and it was jarring, like an ape baring its teeth.

"Happens in friggin' domestics, eight out of ten times. Some dirtbag beats the crap out of his girlfriend, cops lock him up. Trial comes, she says she can't remember nothin', just wants Daddy home."

"You're a cop," I said.

He shook his head. "Nope."

"Ex-cop, then. Retired. Twenty and out in Mass."

He didn't answer. Behind him, the SUV idled, spewing clouds of steam. Every few seconds the wipers gave one swipe, like the truck was trying to see.

"Guy who beat her up," I said. "Name's supposed to be Roger. Know him?"

He shook his head, slowly. "You know nobody tells a hooker their real name."

"What's yours, when it's not Alex?"

"Marty."

"What is it when it isn't Marty?"

He didn't answer. "What brings you up here, Marty?" I said.

"Fresh air," he said. "Get away, some peace and quiet. Wish I'd bought something here twenty years ago. Coulda made a killing."

He seemed to linger on the last word. He smiled.

"Yeah, well," I said. "You know what they say about hindsight."

We stood. He ran a long finger over his glasses, wiping away raindrops. He wore a pinky ring and a gold bracelet, like a Jersey mobster. Crooked, I thought. A crooked cop. Marty belonged in Atlantic City, not Belfast, Maine.

"I'll tell her we met," I said. "What name should I say?"

"Marty's fine," he said. "Tell her I was asking for her."

"Will she be glad to hear that?"

"I don't know. Mandi and me, her and I, we do have a sort of bond." He leered. I felt something well up. Anger? Jealousy? Took a deep breath and choked it down again.

"Doesn't talk much about her past," I said.

"You ever met a hooker who does? Don't want to remind themselves that they didn't used to be like this."

"Before drugs," I said.

"Or something," he said. "Always something."

I started to turn away. Turned back. "Don't follow me," I said.

"No need," he said, flashing the leer again. "I can tell she's in good hands. Taking real good care of her. A lot to be said for a sweet young piece, don't you think?"

"You're a pig, you know that?"

He smiled again. "Real tough guy, for a reporter. You're lucky I've mellowed out, up here in Maine. Old days, I mighta just kicked your ass."

I just looked at him. "Old days, I would have hoped you'd try."

He looked at me, sizing me up.

"Well, another day. But you know what? You're playing with fire, McMorrow." He turned and started walking back to his truck.

"So are you," I said to his back. "Not a good time to come poking around my house. Word to the wise, that's all."

He stopped, turned back to me. "The fire, it ain't me, my friend. It's your little lady friend. And I don't mean in the goddamn sack."

He started walking away, said over his shoulder, "You've got a tiger by the tail, pal. You have no fucking idea."

19

Mandi was in the kitchen. Mary and Sophie were at the counter, making cookies. Sophie was standing on a chair, wearing one of Mary's aprons like a dress, the ties around her neck. Mandi had on gym shorts and socks and a sleeveless T-shirt that said MAINE on the front, the word spelled out in seashells.

She was standing with the help of a single crutch.

"Watch, Jack," she said, and she half-hopped across the room toward me. As she reached me, she started to turn, teetered toward me. I steadied her, holding her by her upper arms. It struck me that she was bigger than Roxanne, felt more substantial. I fought off an image of her with Marty, but not quite in time.

"No," she said, "I can do it."

"Mandi's doing the bunny hop," Sophie said, spooning dough onto a cookie pan.

"I just go left, right, left," Mandi said, and she crossed the room in a rocking, halting sort of gait.

She turned to me and smiled.

"I'll be able to go home," she said.

"I don't want you to go," Sophie said.

"There's still stairs to negotiate," Mary said.

"I think I can go up and down on my butt," Mandi said. "I'll go try it."

She crutched her way out of the kitchen, into the living room, with its antiques and photos. I followed. The crutch caught on the lip of the carpet and she started to fall forward and I lunged and caught her by the arm, held her up. She shook me loose, said, "No, I can do it," and hopped her way across the room and out into the hallway. She stopped, put one hand on the railing, sat down hard. "Ouch," she said.

She pressed the crutch under her bad arm, pushed herself up with her good arm and the heel of her good foot. The heel slipped, the sock providing no leverage against the wood of the stair treads.

"My stairs at the apartment have rubber," she said.

"Or you could wear a shoe," I said.

She took off her white sock and tried again.

Slipped. "Hold my foot," she said.

I hesitated, then took her bare foot in my hand. I was aware of her legs, bare and long in the shorts.

"Cinderella," she said, pushing against my hand. "See if the glass slipper fits."

"Mandi," I said. "Stop for a second. Just hold it."

She eased herself back down. I let go of her foot. "What? I can do this. And then I can get out of your hair. You can go back to your life, write your stories, forget you ever—"

"Just listen," I said. "I stopped at your apartment this morning."

I told her about the call from "Alex." I told her about the car that followed me out of Belfast. I told her about the black SUV. I watched her as she listened passively, no expression, like she'd tuned out. And then I told her about Marty.

She blanched, caught herself and tried to smile. Looked away, a bad attempt at nonchalance. "What did he say?" she asked, still looking away.

"He said he knew you. He said he heard you were hurt."

"I wonder from who?"

"He said he knew you weren't cooperating with the police."

"Oh," Mandi said. "So he talked to that detective."

"I'd say so. He was a cop himself, right?"

Mandi didn't answer. I watched her closely. "Was it Marty who beat you up? Is this whole Roger thing made up?"

"No," she said, shaking her head, looking into my eyes now. "It wasn't him, it *was* Roger. It was just like I said. Really it was. He must have told you he didn't have anything to do with it, right? What did he tell you?" There was something faintly frantic in her tone. The beginning of panic.

"Mandi," I said. "Why are you so afraid of him?"

"I'm not. It's just that—" She paused.

"Just that what?"

She didn't answer.

"You're more afraid of this guy than you are of the guy who beat you up, aren't you? Does this Marty guy hurt you, Mandi?"

She looked at the stairs. "No," she said, her voice barely audible.

"He said—" I began. Then it was my turn to pause.

"He said what?" she asked.

"He said the two of you had a bond," I said.

"Yeah, well, whatever."

I hesitated, then said, "You don't have to do this, you know."

"Please, Jack. Don't—"

"I can help get you a job. Roxanne can. She knows a lot of people. Not a lot of money, maybe, but you wouldn't have to—"

"No," Mandi said. "Please don't."

"Don't what? Don't try to help you?"

"No, you've done enough. Too much. I don't—" She had her arms wrapped around her chest, was starting to rock.

"You don't what, Mandi?" I said.

"I don't deserve *this*," she said, tears starting to flow. "I don't deserve any of it. I don't deserve to be here. I don't deserve to be in this big house with these nice people and your pretty little girl and your beautiful wife. I wouldn't blame her if she said, 'Get this filthy slut out of here. Don't let her near my kid.'"

The words came fast, the tears, too. Mandi wiped her eyes with the back of her hand, started to sob. I patted her shoulder. "Don't you see?" she said. "Don't you know this is why I keep moving? I don't want people like you in my life. I don't want anybody. I don't. I just don't."

"But why do you say that? Everybody makes bad decisions sometimes. Gets in the wrong situation with the wrong people. I'm not an angel. I've done things I—"

"You don't know, Jack," she said, slashing at the tears running down her cheeks. "You don't need to know. Just let me get my stuff. Get me back to town. I'm okay now. I don't need you anymore. Thanks for everything. You've all been great. So thanks. Catch you around."

She hoisted herself up on her hand, scooched up a step.

"Mandi. You don't have to—"

"Let me go," she snapped. "Just let me get the hell outta here. I'll leave in the morning. You don't let me go, I'll call the cops."

"Easy. Just calm—"

Footsteps crossing the living room. Sophie ran into the hallway, holding a plate with cookies. "The first ones," she said, and she held one out to me. I smiled and took it.

"Here's yours, Mandi," Sophie said, and she climbed a step, held out a cookie. "They're still hot so the chocolate chips are melty," she said. "You can have two if you—"

She looked up at Mandi, who, still wiping her eyes, attempted a smile. "You sad again?" Sophie said.

"I'm okay, honey," Mandi said.

"Eat a cookie," Sophie said. "A cookie will make you happy."

Mandi took a bite.

20

Clair was in the barn, the carburetor for one of his tractors disassembled on the workbench. Rain pattered on the roof and some sort of Celtic music was playing. Acoustic. Instrumental. Harp. "Can't hold her here against her will," he said, picking up a tiny spring.

"I know. I just hope that whoever beat her up doesn't come back to finish the job. And this guy from Mass., he seems like he had a real mean streak. She's afraid to death of him."

"Kind of life she leads, it's a fine line she's always walking."

"He has some hold on her or something. The way he talked, it was like he was in control. I wonder if he's taking a percentage or something."

"Or not paying his way," Clair said.

"Jesus," I said. "I don't know why she has to do this."

"Well, you know it's something put in motion a long time ago. Something made her what she is."

"Yeah, well, I like her," I said.

Clair looked up, screwdriver in hand.

"Not that way," I said.

"Careful," Clair said. "Women like her, a lot of times they only know one way to relate to men. Can't believe anyone would care for them for any other reason."

"I know that. I just think she could do so much better."

"In a perfect world," Clair said, peering inside the carburetor, poking with his forefinger. "But it isn't. It's a big, jumbled chaotic mess. All this tragedy, it hits like God looks down on the map and sticks in the pins. A flood here. A mudslide there. How 'bout a civil war? Let's kill a few thousand women and children."

"You believe in God?" I said.

"Sometimes," Clair said. "You?"

"Yeah, I just don't think he or she has everything under control."

Clair picked up a spring, hooked onto a piece of metal.

"These Satanists," I said, "they say their boy is the real deal."

"Believe it," Clair said. "I've seen some of his work." He put the piece of metal down. Reached for his coffee. "Our young friend reminded me of things. Vietnam. Thailand. Women doing whatever it took to survive. Slap in the face on top of it all was most of 'em didn't get anything for it, just handed the money over to some criminal. Made a fuss, they got a beating. Or worse."

"There's somebody deserves to burn in Hell," I said.

There was a moment of quiet and then Clair said, "Couple of 'em are." He held his coffee. "This poor Vietnamese girl, sweet little thing, worked in a massage house at China Beach. A prostitute and a nice kid. Supported her whole family. Eight of 'em or some goddamn thing. She'd fallen in love with one of my soldiers. Latino kid from San Diego. They called him Chico. Real name was Arthur. Arturo."

I listened, had never heard this one.

"He was shipping out in a week. Ly, her name was. Chico tells Ly he'll take her home with him and they'll get married, live in a ranch house. And he was serious, not playing some cruel joke. I remember he took her to dinner at this real restaurant so all the GIs could see she was a lady. Nice guy. Moved really well in the jungle, too. Grew up in the city, but turned out to be a great tracker. Some people just have a gift. Anyway, she tells the boss man at the massage house she doesn't need to go with Americans for money anymore. Gonna marry one so the boss man, he can piss off."

"Don't tell me. He can't have that."

"Hell, no. So the boss man, older South Vietnamese mafiosi, real puke, decides to make an example of her. Cut her face all up with a razor. To ribbons. Woulda been scarred for life, but she bled to death."

"God."

"Or evidence of the lack of one," Clair said. "Well, Chico finds out, goes ballistic, gonna go kill the guy, burn the place down, get himself in a bucketload of trouble just before he was supposed to get out of that hellhole."

"You persuaded him not to?"

"No. I told him to take him for a ride instead of making a big public scene, end up in the brig for twenty years."

"So he did?"

Clair paused. Picked up the carburetor. "We did," he said. "I drove."

"He killed him?"

Clair didn't answer. The Celtic music played, some suitably sad lament. The rain fell. "I don't tell that story much," Clair said.

"No," I said.

"You know, as I get older, I have less tolerance for cruelty, the strong preying on the weak."

"I didn't think you had much to begin with," I said.

"Probably not," Clair said. "Always thought there was good and there was evil."

"And nothing in between?"

"You're the exception," he said.

"Thanks," I said.

"So if it turns out this guy who followed you—"

"Marty."

"Right. If it turns out Marty is forcing Mandi to do this, coercing her in some way, I'd feel an obligation to stop him," Clair said.

I looked at him.

"Not kill him?" I said.

"No, just persuade him."

"To leave her alone?"

"Last night, we heard her crying out," Clair said, "like she was having a terrible dream. I mean, it gave you chills."

"She definitely has her demons," I said.

"Doesn't need any more," Clair said.

Roxanne got home at 5:30. I was in the kitchen, cutting vegetables for chicken pie. Sophie was asking if the chicken in the pie was like the chickens at Clair's and Mary's. I said it was but it had died of old age. Roxanne put her briefcase down, kicked off her shoes, kissed me once, and swung Sophie up in to her arms.

"Hey," I said.

"How's my little chick?" Roxanne said to Sophie, hugging her, and clucking into her neck. Sophie guffawed, said, "Do it again."

Roxanne did and I watched her, saw the relief in her expression, something you could see in her eyes. I knew it was the look that came after a difficult day, helping families you knew you probably couldn't save. Home was her respite. Sophie was her joy.

"What the heck?" Roxanne said, peering at Sophie's head.

She picked something out of Sophie's hair and said, "What's this?"

"Cookie dough," Sophie said. "Me and Mary made chocolate chips."

"You are a messy cook, little girl," Roxanne said. "Into the tub."

She put Sophie down and gave her bottom a pat. She trotted out of the kitchen, started up the stairs. Roxanne turned to me.

"You are, too."

"What?"

"A messy cook."

"The tub?"

"Maybe the shower." She smiled, and her eyebrows twitched, a come-hither flick. "Later," she said.

"Just say the word," I said. "How was your day?"

"Long," she said, and started for stairs. I could see her pull herself up.

Some days Roxanne was like that. She'd shake off the weight of her work as she came in the door, throw herself into the rest of her life. Hold Sophie tightly, and tell her crazy, funny stories. Kiss me so hard it knocked me off balance. Open a bottle of the best wine for no other reason than it was time to celebrate. Make love with me with a fierce intensity that left both of us breathless.

Then there were other days, when the burden was too much to throw off, when the sadness clung to her, when all we could do was hold her close and wait for the clouds to lift.

This wasn't one of those days.

I heard the water running, Sophie chattering. Then there was the sound of toys splashing into the tub: one, two, three. Roxanne said, "Hey, there won't be any room for you."

I smiled, cut chicken into pieces and tossed them into the pan to brown. Then onions, put the pie crust into the plate and spooned in the vegetables. I was mixing the sauce, holding the measuring cup up to the light, when it rang.

Roxanne's cell phone, in her bag. I walked over and took it out, looking at the number.

"Damn," I said. The office, never good.

I loped up the stairs, the phone still ringing. Roxanne was on her knees, in her skirt and bare feet, arms over the tub, lathering Sophie's hair. I saw Roxanne's shoulders fall. Sophie scowled, suds on her face.

"Mommy has to go?" she said.

I grabbed a towel, handed it to Roxanne. She sighed as she wiped her hands. Took the phone and, with weary resignation, said, "Hello."

She listened, concentrating. Sophie was making a plastic frog swim through the soapsuds. I remembered the chicken, hurried back down to the kitchen. The chicken had stuck to the pan, so I scraped it loose, turned down the flame.

"Damn," I said again.

"Jack," Roxanne called, urgency in her voice.

I took the stairs two at a time. She was standing in the bathroom, wiping her hands and arms.

"I've got to go," she said.

"No, Mommy," Sophie said. "We have to play games."

"When I get home," Roxanne said. "Promise."

Sophie smacked the frog into the water, splashing the floor and the wall. Roxanne tossed the towel down onto the puddle, moved into the hallway. "The Wiltons found the foster home," she said. "They called them."

"How did they find them?

"I don't know. Followed me, maybe. I was there this morning."

"So why do you have to go? Can't the foster parents just hang up? Take the phone off the hook?"

"He said Satan would kill them if they didn't let the kids go."

"Uh-oh," I said.

"Except he didn't say kill. He said smite."

"Close enough," I said. "What are you supposed to do?"

"The parents are afraid, it wasn't a good fit from the beginning. They want them out. We're moving them tonight."

"I'll go with you," I said.

"No, Jack. You stay with Sophie."

"I'll call Mary and Clair. They'll come over."

"You can't be with me, Jack."

"Then I'll follow you."

"There'll be another worker. I'll be okay."

"Not with this guy," I said. "No way."

The foster parents lived in an in-town ranch house in Belfast a block up from the city park. The street was just a quarter mile from the courthouse, where Wilton's wife had made her appearance and Wilton had started to tail Roxanne.

It was almost seven, still light, but the foster parents had put all of the outside lights on. Lamps by the front door, spotlights over the garage. I followed Roxanne until she pulled her Subaru into the driveway and parked next to a minivan, close to the side door. She got out and a tall gray-haired man opened the door and waited for her. He looked grim, a do-gooder who had gotten more than he'd bargained for. Roxanne hurried over, and he held door as she went inside.

I drove to the end of the street, eyeing every car. There was an entrance to the park, which fronted the bay. I drove in, made a loop past the playground, the swimming pool. There were a few kids in the pool, parents sitting on folding chairs watching them. A few teenage guys were playing pickup soccer on the lawn beside the pool. A woman pushed a little boy on the swings.

There was a man in a small silver car, parked down by the water. I drove up, slowed. He was parked facing the bay, which was gray and monotonously calm. I went past the silver car once, circled back, looked him over as I passed.

The car was a new Toyota, Maine plates. He was fiftyish, smoking a cigarette, one arm out the window. He turned and looked over at me, hopefully. He wasn't there for the Wilton kids.

I drove back up the street. An official-looking white Taurus sedan had parked behind Roxanne's Subaru. I drove up to the main street, made a loop around the block. I saw a young couple, the guy pushing a baby in a stroller; a boy on a skateboard; an old white-haired woman slowly walking an old white dog.

There were cars parked but nobody inside them. A van, a white Ford with a painted-over contractor's sign on the back doors pulled out as I passed. I drove a block north, took a left on a side street, and the van continued on. I saw a woman at the wheel but little else. I drove back and parked at the corner, with the house in view, lit up like a riverboat casino.

Cars passed. None of them passed twice. Nobody turned onto the street. Every ten minutes, I drove two blocks up, two blocks back. I looped through the side streets. I was thinking of going back to the park when someone came out the side door of the foster home and walked to the Taurus.

It was a small guy, dark slacks and a white polo shirt, a deputy's summer uniform. He got something out of the car and went back in the house. Five minutes later, he and Roxanne emerged, the two kids with them: a boy about eleven, in baggy shorts and big sneakers, a smaller boy, in shorts and a T-shirt, too. The guy had his hand on the older boy's shoulder. Roxanne was holding the smaller boy's hand. In the other hand, the boy was carrying a drink.

They walked to the driveway, then the kids got in the back seat of Roxanne's car. The younger one waved the drink back at the foster parents, who were standing in the doorway. They waved back.

Roxanne shut the car door and then got in herself. The guy got in the Taurus and pulled out into the street. He waited for Roxanne to back out and then followed her up the block toward me.

Both cars turned left. I sat and waited, counted to ten slowly. When I was sure nobody else was following them, I pulled out, punching the throttle to catch up.

We drove south on Route 1, through Northport and Lincolnville, into the shadow of the mountains north of Camden. On the edge of town, we took a left, and Roxanne and the cop drove down to the end, by the water, and pulled into a driveway.

Another house, this one pretty grand: a big split-level overlooking the bay. I saw the kids staring up as they walked to the door, like it was the castle at Disneyland. They wouldn't go hungry here.

I was just down the street, pulled over to the side of the road. Roxanne and the detective followed the kids inside. There was a BMW in the driveway, parked alongside a new Suburban. People with money who had decided to give back.

Sitting there in the truck, I was thinking that this was the silver lining in this sad story. I made a mental note to look into it. Were they retired, looking for something more meaningful than golf and a sailboat? A lead emerged: *John and Jane Smith worked hard to be able to retire to Maine, in a big house overlooking Penobscot Bay—with lots of room for the foster kids they take in.*

Maybe it was a trend. I could find a few examples, pitch it to the *Times*. My pledge to make more money to give Roxanne a break had been interrupted by Mandi, and no story had come of that, either. Maybe I could find a few new companion ads, see if I could do the same story without her. Or maybe use a very real pseudonym—Mandi, not her real name.

And then there was that park in Belfast. Maybe a story on how few places there were for the public to have access to the ocean, how the Maine coast was becoming more and more the property of the prosperous. I smiled at the alliteration, reached for a notebook to write that phrase—

My cell phone rang. I picked it up, answered. "Jack," Clair said. "Everything's okay but you'd better get back here, ASAP."

There was a knock on the door, and Mary answered. A woman was there, in her thirties, poor looking. Sunglasses and odd hair that looked like a wig. Just down the road was a beat-up white van, its hood up.

The woman asked to use the phone, said her cell phone didn't get reception there. They needed a wrecker. The van had broken down, overheated. Her husband thought it was the water pump.

Mary turned to get the phone and the woman waited at the door. When Mary came back, the woman said it was a nice house. Mary said she didn't live there, she was babysitting. The woman said they'd been visiting her sister on the Horseback Road, decided to take a shortcut, head back to Albion. And here they were.

Mandi was in the kitchen, immersed in *Newsweek*. Clair was reading to Sophie upstairs. He heard the voices, told Sophie to finish the story, about a family of squirrels, one who is afraid of heights. Sophie said she would read it to her animals.

Clair eased down the stairs. He heard the woman in the hallway by the side door, talking about the water pump. At the bottom of the stairs, he turned toward the kitchen, went out the back through the sliding door. He circled the house, moved along the edge of the woods to the road. The van was pulled over on the far side of the house; the front doors were open.

Clair crossed to the far side of the road, walked slowly in the shadow of the trees. Approaching the truck, he noticed there was no rear license plate. The hood was up. Someone was sitting in the driver's seat. The van was an old Econoline, the motor covered by a canopy between the front seats. The water pump was under there, but the canopy still was in place.

Clair moved up on the driver's side. "Hey," he said.

The guy turned. "Hey."

He was tall, thin, almost gaunt, a stretched-leather face out of the Depression. Clair looked inside, saw the engine cover in place, three coffee cups on top of it. A can of Skoal, an empty Pepsi bottle for the spit.

"Water pump?" Clair said.

"Yeah," the man said, turning and facing front. "Shit the bed."

"Overheated?"

"Needle went right off the chart"

Clair sniffed silently. There was no smell of coolant. He took a step back and looked at the ground under the truck. There was no puddle of anti-freeze.

"Yeah, old lady went into that house there, use the phone," the man said. "Figure it's better to have it hauled than have the motor seize up. She's been pretty reliable, too."

He patted the steering wheel. On the top of his left wrist was a tattoo. A snake. Clair looked at it. The three cups. He turned and ran.

He was too late.

A second guy, wearing a red ski mask, had approached the house from the back, come up onto the deck. The sliding glass door was locked but he slipped a screwdriver into the crack and, after a minute, popped the lock.

He eased the door open. Stepped inside, the screwdriver held low against his leg.

And Mandi, pressed against the wall, pivoted on her good foot and stabbed him with a paring knife.

Clair heard the scream as he ran from the truck. He dashed across the lawn, past the woman peering into the open door.

"What's the matter?" she said, as he pushed her aside.

The man had run back out the door, Mandi said. Clair followed, running toward the woods. And then he heard the van start, a scrabble of tires clawing at the gravel. By the time he got back out front, the van and the woman were gone.

He ran back to the house, where Mary had called 911. Mandi said the guy had fled with the knife still stuck up to the wooden handle in his right upper arm. Sophie had come down the stairs with her bear in her arms.

"I want Mommy and Daddy," she said.

21

~w~

That was the story, told to me as I sat at the kitchen table, Sophie on my lap, her arms wrapped tightly around my neck. I got up and eased her off of me, made a plate of crackers and cheese and fruit, set her up in the den with *The Jungle Book* on television. And then, with Mowgli and Ballou singing in the background, Roxanne on her way home, they told the story again.

This time the audience was Trooper Ricci, who arrived and told us an BOLO was out on the Wiltons and the van. I told her to check the gravel pit. She looked at me and said, "Right." Then Ricci took off her trooper hat and put it on the table, took out a notebook and a pen.

Clair leaned against the counter and Mary sat on the arm of the big chair by the woodstove. Mandi was perched in the chair, rocking slowly, arms wrapped around herself protectively. Mary kept patting Mandi's hand, the right hand, the one that had plunged the knife in.

"So he gained entry by breaking the lock on the sliding door?"

We all waited. Mandi didn't seem to have heard the question but then she said, in an exhausted voice, "Yes." She nodded, eyes half closed.

"And then what happened?"

Another long pause. "He had a screwdriver," Mandi said. "It was long and it had a yellow and black handle. Stripes."

"How was he holding it?" Ricci said, looking up from her pad.

"Low but sticking out, like it was a knife."

"And you—"

"When I heard the glass door rattle I got over to the counter and there was a knife. It was just there."

This time Ricci just waited.

"So I kinda leaned against the wall right there, next to the bird picture."

She looked to the wall in front of her, an Audubon print of a great blue heron hung there.

"And then what?" Ricci said.

"I couldn't let him hurt Sophie. I couldn't let him touch her."

"So you—"

"I just—"

Her voice trailed off and her eyes were focused on something inside her. "I stabbed him," she whispered. And she started to cry, the tears welling, then spilling over and running down her cheeks. Mary handed her a tissue but Mandi just held it and rocked and didn't wipe her face. A tear crossed the bruise on her chin and dripped onto her leg.

"It's okay," Mary said.

"But just once," Mandi said. "It was only once." She said it defensively, like she had done something wrong.

"Don't worry," I said. "You did the right thing."

"Did he attack you or attempt to defend himself?" Ricci said.

"No. He just yelled. When you see it, when you see the knife go in you, it's more like shock than real pain. It's just—"

She paused. "—the way it works."

Mandi suddenly wiped her eyes, like she'd looked down and realized she was holding the tissue. Clair was studying her, Mary watching her closely as she patted Mandi's hand.

"And he just left?"

"I let—" Mandi paused and swallowed. She ran her hands up and down her thigh. "I let go. And I tried to back up and he just stood there, looking at it."

"At what?" Ricci said.

"At the knife sticking out," Mandi said. "And then it started to bleed, running down his arm and . . . and dripping."

We looked to the blood spots on the pine floor. "And he just turned and ran," Mandi said.

"Would you recognize him?" Ricci said. "I know he had the mask on but the tattoo?"

"A snake," Mandi said. "Coiled up but the head raised like it was going to bite."

"It's the guy from the woods," I said. "You catch him and you can take blood out of him, compare the DNA to those blood spots, lock him up for attempted kidnapping, attempted robbery."

"The district attorney will decide on charges, Mr. McMorrow. What we have now is an attempted burglary."

"To hurt or abduct my daughter," I said. "He wasn't busting in here to steal the goddamn microwave."

She looked at me. "We don't know that," she said. "There's been a rash of burglaries in this area in the past few weeks. They knock on a door, if nobody answers, they break in. In this case, they may have thought Mrs. Varney was sufficiently distracted to—"

"Get a picture of Wilton and show it to Clair here."

"I don't know that we have a photo immediately available."

"No mug shot?"

"Mr. Wilton hasn't been charged criminally that I know of," Ricci said.

"Just beats his kids and starves them. You don't get your picture taken for that?"

"Thus far, that's been a civil matter. So there's been no reason for law enforcement to have a photo of him."

"So get one," I said.

"We're working on it, sir," Ricci said, bristling.

"Yeah, well, while you're working on it, this nut case is cruising around on some vendetta for my wife. Says she'll be destroyed, it's Satan's will. Says she's a Jew bitch and—"

"We'll find him, Mr. McMorrow. This isn't television. Things don't just happen when you snap your fingers."

"On television, they catch people," I said.

"We will locate Mr. Wilton. But it may take time."

"Then I'll find him, and it won't be eventually," I said.

"Jack," Clair said.

"And when I do, you won't need—"

"Jack," Clair barked. "Easy."

Ricci looked at me, then at Mandi, who had the balled-up tissue pressed to her mouth. "Detectives are going to want to talk to you at some point, Mr. and Mrs. Varney," she said. "And you, too, Ms. Lasell. You seem quite upset. If you need to talk to someone, we do have counselors who can be helpful in these situations."

At first Mandi didn't acknowledge that she'd heard. And then, like the words had been slowed, traveling through syrup, she turned and looked at Ricci. "Too late for that," she said.

22

Roxanne pulled in as Ricci was pulling out. Ricci pulled her cruiser back in and waited as Roxanne ran inside, swept Sophie up in her arms. I walked into the room as Roxanne was squeezing her, Sophie watching the television over her mom's shoulder.

"This is a funny part," Sophie said. "The monkeys' house, it all falls down."

Roxanne held her for a long time, then gently placed her back on the floor. Sophie held onto Roxanne's hand and said, "Sit and watch with me," but Roxanne said, in a few minutes, she had to talk to the police officer.

We walked outside, and I embraced her, held her, and Roxanne said, "I feel like my house is falling down, Jack. All around me. People coming here, my God. It never happens. Maybe I'll take Sophie and go away. Go to New York. Take her to the zoo and Central Park, stay in a hotel."

"I know. But we'll fix it. It's just these Wilton people. We'll take care of it."

"It'll be okay."

"It's not, Jack. It's crazy, out of control. And it's not just this. It's this Mandi. Oh, Jack. I want my life back. I just do."

She paused, fell away from me. "This officer. What'd she say?"

"She thinks it might just be a random break-in."

"Bullshit," Roxanne snapped, and she marched to the cruiser, opened the passenger's side front door and got in. "Who do I have to call," I heard her say, "to make you take this seriously?" And then she slammed the car door shut.

Mandi was quiet, sitting at the table as we all had a late dinner at our house: pasta and salad from the garden and red wine from Spain—the chicken pot pie forgotten and unmade. Clair and Mary tried to make conversation but there was a weariness to it, only Sophie chattering away, telling us the whole *Jungle Book* story, roaring like the scary tiger.

"I have that book," Clair said. "When you're a little older, I'll read it to you."

"Read it to me now," Sophie said.

"I used to love being read to," Mary said. "I can remember my mother, sitting with me on the swing on the veranda." She smiled. "I don't think you ever outgrow it," and she turned to Mandi beside her. "Did your parents read to you?"

"No," Mandi said. "They never did."

She looked away, then back at Mary and seemed to catch herself. She smiled and said, "When Clair reads to Sophie, I'll sit in."

Roxanne got up abruptly, set her plate on the counter. I could see Mandi watching her, and I said to Sophie, "Hey, little girl, time for you to go to bed."

"No, I'm not tired," Sophie said, but then she yawned and I said, "ah-ha," and tossed her over my shoulder. We said goodnight and Sophie grabbed Clair's earlobe as she passed him and he pretended to not know who had done it.

"It's only me," she said, and laughed that pretty little-girl laugh, and then we were headed up the stairs. I put her in her nightgown, helped her brush her teeth, walked back with her to her room. "I want to sleep with you and mommy," Sophie said, and this night of all nights, it seemed okay.

I grabbed some books from her shelf and she took her bear, hugging him close. We went to our room and I tucked her in the middle of the big bed, sat beside her to read. I read about farm animals and a spider named Sparky and a brother and sister who lived in a treehouse deep in the woods.

"Can we still go in the woods, Daddy?" Sophie asked.

"Sure," I said.

"But what about the bad man?"

"He ran home to his house and it's far, far away," I said.

"How do you know?" Sophie said.

"I just do," I said. "Daddy knows these things."

"Will he come back? What if he does and Mandi isn't here?"

"Mommy and Daddy will be here," I said.

"But Mandi saved us," Sophie said.

"Yes, she was brave," I said.

"And then it made her sad. It made her sad to be brave."

We read more, and then I felt Sophie head loll against my shoulder. Her eyes were closed, lids pale as a baby bird's, and I eased out from beside her and laid her head on the pillow. Her bear stood guard.

I eased out of the room, crossed the hall, paused at the top of the stairs. Listened.

It was Roxanne and Mandi, in the kitchen. Clair and Mary doing dishes, plates dropping into the dishwasher. I heard a chair slide and clatter, then Roxanne her voice low and solemn. "Thank you for what you did," she said.

There was no reply. "I appreciate it," Roxanne said. "For Sophie. For all of us."

"It was nothing. I didn't even think about it," Mandi said. "It just happened."

"But still, it took courage to do that, not just scream and run away."

"I couldn't run," Mandi said. I pictured her smiling.

"Well, thank you."

There was a pause and Mandi said, "I know you don't want me here."

This time it was Roxanne who didn't answer.

"I didn't have much choice, at the time," Mandi said. "I'll go tomorrow."

"It's up to you," Roxanne said. "And Clair and Mary."

"No, I'll go back. I can hop around now. And the hospital called. I have to see a doctor in town at eleven."

"Okay," Roxanne said.

Another pause, and then Mandi said, "You know, I don't blame you. Not wanting me around your daughter."

No answer. "But I hope you know, your husband, he's been nothing but kind to me."

"I know that," Roxanne said.

"And I mean, that's all. Nothing else."

"I know that, too."

"I didn't want you to think—"

"I don't. I wouldn't."

"Some guys, they—"

"He's not some guy," Roxanne said.

"You're lucky."

"Yes, I am."

"And he's lucky. You and him, you're totally together. And Sophie and this house. It's like this dream life, you know?"

A pause. I stood and waited.

"It doesn't have to be a dream," Roxanne said. "A lot of people live just like this."

"I know."

"You don't have to be alone."

"But I do," Mandi said.

"Why?" Roxanne said. "And why do you—"

"Do what I do?"

A pause. The sound of water running. Silverware clinking. "Yes," Roxanne said. "You don't have to do that."

"Jack already gave me that lecture. Said he could find me a job."

"And?"

"They wouldn't want me," Mandi said.

"You don't know that."

"Oh, yes, I do," Mandi said, and then Clair called over, "the uptown bus is leaving."

I came down the stairs, around into the hallway. Mandi was crutching her way across the kitchen. Roxanne was sitting at the table, had made no attempt to help her. Clair came over and took Mandi by the arm. Mary picked up her bag.

"We'll see you in the morning," Clair said to us.

"If you're going to town and need someone here, you let me know," Mary said.

"I can get a taxi," Mandi said.

"We'll talk about it," Clair told her.

"I'll call you early," I said.

"I'll be fine," Mandi said, but fine was the one thing she wasn't.

Some nights we moved Sophie from our bed, carried her into her room. Tonight we left her there, curled up like a cat against the pillows. I slid in on one side of her and Roxanne slid in on the other.

We both stared at the skylight, listened to the summer rain, the soft puff of Sophie's breathing. "I don't care about anyone else," Roxanne said.

"Like who?" I said.

"Like Mandi. Like the Wilton kids. Like the other forty-eight kids I have and the forty-eight who will come after them. I don't care anymore, not like I did. Like I should."

"Who do you care about?" I said.

"I care about our little girl. And I care about you."

"And I care about you both," I said.

"I'm calling in tomorrow," Roxanne said. "I'm not leaving her until this thing is settled, and Mandi's—"

"Gone?" I said.

"Yes."

I didn't answer. I turned so I could see her face. It was motionless and taut, her eyes shining in the dim light.

"I'm scared, Jack," she said. "And I'm never scared. Think of the people I've dealt with. Crazy people, bad people, people who do terrible things."

"Yes."

"And I've never been afraid. Never."

"I know," I said.

"But these people," she said. "They scare me. They scare the heck out of me."

"I'll take care of you," I said. "I'll take care of them. Clair and I, we'll take care of it. You know he told me something—"

"It's not just them," Roxanne said. "It's her, Jack. It's Mandi."

"What about her?"

She turned to me, Sophie sleeping between us.

"I don't know why, Jack, but she scares me, too."

At first light, Roxanne called her office, said she wouldn't be in, would call later. She climbed back in bed, on my side, snuggling up against me. I held her, her head in the crook of my arm, my other arm across her hip. Sophie was snoring softly.

"I think she's getting a cold," Roxanne whispered.

"You can take it easy today, both of you."

"What are you going to do? After you take Mandi into town."

I smiled. "I'll just go down to Clair's, see what they're doing."

"You won't let her take a taxi, Jack. Just tell me what time you'll be home."

"By lunchtime."

"Where are you going?"

"To find a story," I said. "Make some money."

"And what else?" Roxanne said.

"Talk to that Belfast cop."

"About—"

"The Wiltons. And this Marty guy."

"You can't keep her secret for her, you know. It's a small town."

"Then I'd rather let somebody else let it out."

Roxanne didn't answer for a moment. I waited.

"Jack."

"Yeah."

"She told me you didn't have a thing for her."

"Huh," I said. "Were you worried?"

"Not really. I just—I don't know. She's attractive."

"Not now, all beat up."

"She wouldn't have said that if it hadn't occurred to her. And it wouldn't have occurred to her if she hadn't thought of you in that way."

"I don't know about that," I said.

"I'm a woman, and I do," Roxanne said.

"Well, you don't have to worry."

"I'm not. Except that she's pretty and young and she's a stray. I know how you have a weakness for strays."

"Not this one, not in that way."

"She's broken, Jack. There's something wrong. It's like—"

"—she's grieving," I said. "But I don't know why."

Roxanne didn't answer. I could feel her thinking. And then she squeezed my wrist. "I want you to let her go, Jack."

"I will. I'll drop her off."

"No, honey. I want you to really let her go. Drop her off. Wish her luck. Tell her to call social services or the town if she has a problem."

I didn't answer.

"Cut it off right here, Jack. Please."

Sophie stirred. We waited. Her breathing lapsed into a regular huff and puff.

"For me, honey. For Sophie."

"She can't even get groceries. I suppose they deliver; she could just—"

"She'll survive."

"I know but—"

"I don't want her connected to our family. I don't want her connected to you."

"But honey," I said. "I've known all kinds of people. Criminals and cops and Rocky and Tammy in Bangor and—"

"We didn't have a daughter then," Roxanne said. "I don't bring my kids here. I don't think you should bring yours."

"She had no place to go."

"A wall, Jack. I want a wall between our work lives and our home."

I hesitated. "Okay," I said.

"And Clair. We can go down there until you get back. But he'll be home today, right?"

"Wild horses," I said, "couldn't drag him away."

We left at eight. The rain still fell, a steady drizzle that smelled like the woods. Clair carried Mandi's bag and the cat in a cardboard box. Mary held Mandi's arm as she crow-hopped to my truck. I put the crutches in the back of the truck and her bag behind the seat and they helped her in. She slid across, her shorts sliding down and her sweater riding up, baring her lower back, showing her underpants.

I looked away. She pulled her bad foot in and straightened herself. Clair gave her the box and she held it on her lap, her bandaged right hand against her belly.

The cat cried. I noticed Mandi's bruises had yellowed more.

"Thank you, both," she said to Mary and Clair. "You've been so nice."

Mary told her to take good care of herself. Clair just smiled and closed the truck door. I waved and started to pull out, as Roxanne and Sophie pulled in. Roxanne swung left of the truck, and Sophie waved excitedly as we passed. Mandi waved back.

We pulled out onto the road and I looked over at her. She was staring straight ahead. "You okay?" I said.

"I'll never see her again, will I?" Mandi said.

"You never know."

"I'm sure she'll grow up into a really great person."

"I sure hope so," I said.

The conversation stopped there. The cat cried and the muddy gravel slapped the bottom of the truck. I sped up, feeling an awkward silence settle over us, wanting to shorten the drive to Belfast.

Except for the cat, we were quiet all the way to town. Mandi seemed lost in her thoughts, moving only to reach back with her good left hand to tighten the scrunchy that held her hair back. The woods were green and lush in the rain and the traffic moved steadily.

Finally, after a half-hour, we drove down the hill into Belfast, hit both traffic lights, and eased up in front of the apartment. Two older women were getting into a BMW from Connecticut, arms laden with shopping bags. We waited as they loaded the stuff in the back seat. They got in the car and we waited for them to pull out, but they didn't. A car pulled up behind me and honked. I looked in the mirror. Waited. The guy leaned on the horn.

I put the truck in gear and drove down Main Street to the harbor. "We'll try again," I said.

As we circled by the landing, Mandi looked out at the boats on their moorings. Anxiously, I thought.

"You alright?" I said, watching her.

"Yeah," she said, but she still peered out at the boats.

"Somebody you know out there?"

She shook her head. "No."

Inside the box, the cat had cried itself hoarse. I continued on, back up the street. The women in the BMW were talking.

"Go left," Mandi said, and I turned at the left, and she pointed and I went left again and we drove past the rear of the block, a hodgepodge of decks and balconies, tacked on for the harbor view. She looked closely at the parking lot.

"Car still here?" I said.

She nodded, still pensive. "Which one is it?" I said.

She pointed in the general direction of the building and said, "Back there."

Back to the harbor, up the front side of the block again. This time the BMW women were leaving and I cut across and into the space.

"You don't have to come up," Mandi said.

"I'll help you," I said, and I got out, came around, and opened her door. As she eased her legs out, I looked up and down the street. No black SUV in sight. No cops, that I could see.

She looked up at me. "All clear?" she said.

"For now," I said. "But Marty's going to figure out that you're back."

"I'll keep the curtains closed."

I took the cat box from her, Lulu's cries weak but still incessant. Mandi stood and I started to hand her the crutch but the cushion part was soaked from the rain. I put the cat back in the truck and closed the door. Took Mandi by the arm and helped her up onto the sidewalk.

We walked to the door and I opened it and held it for her. She stepped in and took a breath and we started up. I held her by her right upper arm and she gripped the railing with her left hand, leaning to take the weight off her left foot and half-hopping up each stair.

It was slow going, like holding Sophie's hand when she had just begun to walk. We made it to the first landing, paused to rest.

"All set?" I said.

"No problem," Mandi said.

We did the next set of stairs, and I stood beside her as she fished in the pocket of her shorts and took out a key. She unlocked the door and pushed it open. There was a rush of stale air, a faint smell of trash.

"Uck," Mandi said, and I helped her in. We shuffled into the living room, crossed to the couch and she turned and fell back, holding her right hand in front of her, reaching back with her left.

She sighed, smiled at me. "Thanks," she said. "Sorry to be such a poop."

"You're getting stronger," I said. "You should still go to the orthopedic doctor."

"I'll call this morning."

"I'll get your stuff," I said.

I started for the door, looking toward the bedroom. I stopped, listened. Walked to the bedroom door and peered in. The bed still was unmade, blood on the sheet. She'd need help with that. Turning back, I said, "You have clean sheets and stuff?"

"Yes, in the closet," Mandi said from the couch.

"And you'll need groceries, right?"

"I'll call. They deliver for ten bucks."

"Is your phone dead?"

"The charger is on the counter in the kitchen."

"I'll plug it in for you, somewhere out here."

I left, leaving the door ajar behind me. It was one trip, the cat, the bag, the crutches. I paused, opened the glove box, and took out a can of pepper spray. Went back upstairs.

Mandi was on her feet, using the back of the couch to make her way toward the kitchen. I handed her a crutch, still wet, but she took it and hopped across the room. I put the stuff down, opened the box and the cat leapt out. It froze, scurried into the bedroom. After a moment, it scurried back out, claws skittering on the wooden floor, headed for the kitchen.

"Hey," Mandi said. "Easy."

I walked to the kitchen entryway. Mandi was in front of the refrigerator, pulling out stuff and tossing it into the sink.

"I can take a bag of trash," I said, and she said, "Okay." I took the bag from the trash can, put the stuff from the sink—brown grapes, wilted lettuce—into it. I pulled the drawstring tight.

"I'm gonna go," I said.

Mandi turned, hopped to the counter and leaned.

"Thanks," she said. "For everything."

"No, thank you," I said.

"I'll worry about you guys."

"We'll be okay. They'll take care of it."

"If you want to do that story, let me know."

"Right," I said. "Seems like years ago."

"Doesn't it," she said, and she smiled.

"What are your plans?" I said.

"A nap," Mandi said.

"You staying around here? For a while?"

"I don't know."

I took the pepper spray from my jeans pocket. "I had this in the truck. It might come in handy."

I handed it to her and she looked at the label. "Oh. I'd probably spray myself."

"Spray and run," I said. "It won't drop somebody but it'll give you a chance to get away."

"Maybe," Mandi said, looking down at her foot.

"Right," I said.

There was an awkward pause, like we were saying goodnight after a first date. There was traffic noise from outside, flies buzzing in the window, rain dripping into a gutter, the cries of gulls.

"Well," I said.

"Yeah," Mandi said.

"I'll head out."

"Right."

She looked away, watched the cat sniffing around the floor in front of the refrigerator. Looked back at me.

"I'm glad I met you," she said, "but in some ways, I'm not."

"Why is that?"

"It's hard," Mandi said. "Kind of one of those what-might-have-been things, you know?"

"You can make a new life," I said.

"Not really," she said. "And not with you, Jack."

So there it was. Roxanne's instincts on target, as usual.

"A lot of guys out there, Mandi," I said.

"I know that, me of all people." She smiled.

"But the good ones are all taken. And even if they weren't—" The sentence ended. Her expression changed, some sort of veil falling over her. "Take care," she said.

"I will," I said, and she held out her hand. I took it and gave it a quick squeeze and let it fall. Turned and walked out of the kitchen, out of the apartment, down the stairs.

Outside, I got in the truck, gave the apartment windows another look. The cat had found its place on the sill, was crouched there. I pulled out, drove down the street, all the way down to the harbor. I looked out where Mandi had, saw boats riding moorings in the rain. Bare masts. Canvas up. A gray haze over the distant bay. What was out there? What had she been thinking?

I circled around and started back up the street. As I approached Mandi's block, I slowed. I wondered if there was something else I could do, get her mail or bring her some magazines. I pulled into a parking space across the street. Got out and headed for the newsstand. As I walked, I glanced over.

The cat was gone. The curtains in the right window moved. A hand came through and eased one side of the curtain open. She was looking out. I wonder if she'd see me. I wondered if I could still do that story, if she were one of three or four women who—

It was the curtain on the right side. It was a right hand.

No bandage. Not Mandi.

23

I bolted across the street, dodging cars. Slammed the door open, bounded up the stairs. As I neared the landing, I heard voices. A woman. A man. Mandi saying, "No, don't."

I kicked the door in, the jamb shattering, the door rattling back. Mandi was on the couch, a man in front of her, his back to me. She had her hands over her mouth, was screaming into them. He had a gun pressed to the side of his head.

He whirled, had two hands on it as he came around, fired once as I dove for the floor, the shot over my head. The recoil jerked the gun up and it was coming back down when I came off the floor, hitting him in the legs, shoulders first.

Mandi was trying to get to her feet, rolling to the side. He went down against the couch, tangling with her legs, the gun in his right hand. He was trying to bring it around.

It was a .45, big and heavy, and I got my hand on his right forearm, driving my fingers in. He was grunting, teeth clenched, and I punched him over and over.

Mandi was screaming, "Oh my God, oh my God."

I hit his mouth, nose, eyes, blood spurted from his lip. He got his left forearm up, blocking me, and I lunged, got both hands on his right wrist, the gun hand, squeezing, twisting, turning my head as he punched my neck, the side of my face.

We rolled onto the floor, the gun underneath us, the butt in my belly. Another shot, deafening, a pulse of heat, missing everyone, and I slammed his arm against the floor, dug my fingers into the tendons of his wrist.

"Get out," I bellowed at Mandi.

She rolled and crawled toward the door, dragging a crutch, then out of sight. He was tearing at my ear, scraping my neck with his nails. And then his left arm came around me and he passed the gun to his left hand, the side of the hot barrel pressed against my face. I grabbed for his left wrist but he pulled it away, tried to bring the gun to bear on my head.

I could see the muzzle, the black hole, and he shifted, bent his wrist so the gun was nearly pointed at my face. His finger was outside of the trigger guard and he tried to pull it back, and I grabbed for his hand, got his wrist but the finger was in now.

The finger on the trigger—

The muzzle moving—

There was a clang. Then another. And another. His wrist went limp, and the gun fell to the floor. I shoved it away as the clangs kept coming and I saw Mandi, on her knees behind him, swinging the crutch at his head.

He rolled off of me, came to rest on his back, facing her, and the crutch came down again, splitting his forehead. Again, it raked the side of his face, then his head. Again, and again.

I got to my knees, grabbed her arms in mid-swing and pushed her backward, landed on top of her. I could feel her breathing hard, moaning, then squirming to get loose. I let her go and she rolled to her knees again, and the crutch came up and then down.

"You'll kill him," I shouted, and she was swinging the crutch again and I blocked it with my shoulder, felt a jab of pain. I wrenched the crutch away from her and flung it aside.

"Mandi," I said. "It's okay."

She panted, then seemed to calm. And then she looked at me like she was someone else, like she didn't know me, like she'd just been jarred awake from a nightmare.

"You can stop," I said.

There was blood on her arms, blood on her shirt. His blood, my blood, maybe hers. She wiped at her mouth and left a streak of dark red. Looked at it and fell back on her haunches.

I turned to him. He was unconscious, blood streaming from his forehead down his temple, running out of his mouth and nose, which was flattened. I could see white where the flesh had split at his hairline.

"We need an ambulance," I said. I was digging in my pocket for my phone when I heard the sirens. "Who is he, Mandi?" I said.

She looked down at him, like she didn't know how he had gotten there. "That's Roger," she said. "He said he wanted me to forgive him."

There were cops with guns drawn, one with a shotgun, everyone barking orders, telling us to show our hands, stay on the floor. A big buzzcut kid kneeled beside me, his hand pressing down on my neck. Mandi said she was thirsty and an older cop went and got her a glass of water. He took the glass back. Held it and waited. When they finally told us to get up, Mandi said she couldn't, not without some help.

And then there were medics, calm and efficient, sticking an IV in Roger's arm, strapping him to a board, his head immobilized in a big collar thing. He was taken out first, the medics calling ahead to the hospital, saying they were coming in with a patient with a possible skull fracture.

Mandi and I sat against opposite walls, medics crouched beside us. They put big bandages on my neck and ear, so I looked like I should be playing a fife in the Revolutionary War band. Mandi told them her wrist and ankle hurt and they started to examine them all over again, not understanding that she'd brought those injuries to the fight, though swinging the crutch hadn't helped.

A cop picked up the .45 with a pen and dropped it in a plastic zip-lock bag. Then he looked around the room for the slugs in the walls.

"There should be three," I told him. "They might have gone out into the hall."

The first two had, one in the wall, one through a window in the stairwell. The third slug had gone through the ceiling and lodged in the floor of the apartment upstairs.

Raven told me that a while later as we sat in his cruiser out front.

"You know how I told you a case like this was like building a boat," he said.

I nodded.

"Well, I gotta tell you. I feel like we keep adding pieces to this boat but instead of getting done, it just gets bigger."

I thought about that, concluded that the boat metaphor didn't quite fit. "I'm not sure it gets bigger," I said. "It's just that it isn't what you thought it was when you started."

"Me? I don't know what it is now," Raven said. "A young woman beat up, who has no obvious means of support. So I start from there and every time it seems like the fog is lifting, it settles back in."

He dug for a package of gum, in the console between the seats. Offered a piece to me and I shook my head. Peeled it out of the foil and popped it in his mouth. The car filled with the scent of mint.

"Let's hear it," Raven said.

I told him about coming in, Roger with the gun, Mandi on the couch, the shots, Mandi crawling away, then coming back

"So she saved your butt," Raven said.

"In the nick of time, as they say."

"Tough little lady.

"In a strange way, yeah."

He chewed. The gawkers milled, walking up and down the sidewalk, looking to get a glimpse of Mandi in the other car, turning and coming back to get a look at me.

"Beats television," Raven said.

"Yup."

"Don't often get excitement like this."

"Glad to keep the populace entertained."

"I guess you are. Heard about the incident at your house, up there in Prosperity."

"Figured you had."

"You're a regular crime magnet," Raven said.

"A tough stretch," I said. "Hard on my wife."

"I'll bet. Bad enough doing that job without having it follow you home."

"Yes," I said.

The woman cop was turned to Mandi, and seemed to be doing all the talking.

"Heard our lady friend here stuck a guy with a kitchen knife."

"A paring knife, actually. Three-inch blade."

"Still impressive," Raven said. "And now she beats this guy over the head with a crutch, busts his skull."

"I think he was gonna kill her, then kill himself."

"Lot of that going around. Control freaks. I think they're basically kind of spoiled. You know a lot of 'em are real momma's boys, when you dig into it?"

"Is that right?" I said.

"Can't accept it when things don't go their way."

"Huh," I said.

"Hey, good thing you showed up. The hand and the curtain and all that—quick thinking."

"Lucky," I said.

"Pretty tough yourself. For a reporter, I mean," Raven said. "Take that big gun off the guy—nice gun, by the way, Sig P220. Guy's got good taste in firearms."

"Yeah when you have the money," I said.

So you hold him down while your girlfriend beats the crap out of him."

"That's not what happened. And she's not my girlfriend. Like you said, she saved my life. If she hadn't hit him, who knows what would have happened."

He shrugged. Chewed. Blew a tiny bubble and stuck his tongue threw it. Chewed some more. "You know, for one young woman, awful lot of guys around. You. Roger, with his head busted."

"A guy named Marty, too," I said. "I think he's an ex-cop from Mass."

"Oh, yeah. Ran into him. Not the kind of cop we usually see around here."

"The cologne," I said.

"Yeah," Raven said. "We're not much into that around here. But things are changing. Maybe cologne is coming. I mean, we got sushi now? Three hundred years of cooking fish, all of a sudden we start eating it raw."

I waited. Raven did, too. He chewed, watched the ambulance pull away, a second one, not needed. With the ambulance gone, we could see the other cruiser, Mandi in the front seat talking to the woman cop.

"I think they're all set here," he said. "Let's go for a ride. You okay for that? Cuts aren't bothering you?"

"I'm fine," I said

"Don't want to keep you from anything," Raven said, but he'd already pulled away from the curb.

We drove down Main Street to the harbor, swung right at the circle by the town landing and the boat launch. A steady drizzle fell, and in the distance on the bay, the sea and sky melded so there was no horizon, just different shades of gray.

A big sailboat was motoring into the harbor, figures in yellow raingear on the foredeck and cockpit.

"Pretty boat," Raven said. "Older wooden ketch. Like a piece of sculpture, don't you think?"

"I guess."

"More and more big sailboats in the harbor every year, fewer lobstermen. Turning into a theme park, a place for rich people to play."

We were driving along the shore, winding between metal buildings, boats on stands beside them, lobster traps in stacks. Raven suddenly pulled in beside an old garage, gray and sided with asphalt shingles. He parked by a big rolling door, got out and I followed. He unlocked a padlock, rolled the door sideways just enough for us to fit through.

He reached to his left, hit a switch and overhead lights glowed dimly. There was a half-painted lobster boat, a ladder leaning against it, a lift of lumber, some blue steel drums. Raven led the way and at the end of the room he stopped and unlocked another door. It was a small space, smelled of wood. There were hand tools on a bench, lumber scattered. In the center was the shell of a boat, the ribs showing where the planking was unfinished.

"Here she is," Raven said.

He stood by the boat, ran a hand over the gunwale. Picked up a piece of sandpaper and started to rub it.

"Nice," I said.

"Thanks. Awful pretty, don't you think?"

"Yeah," I said. "Very graceful."

"Glad you can see that, Mr. McMorrow. Some people just see a pile of wood nailed together. Look at the stern here. Isn't that lovely?"

I said it was.

"When I look at this, I see it all done," Raven said. "I can picture it in my mind. Painted, with seven coats of varnish, all the brass fittings."

He ran a hand over the ribs on the inside. Turned and looked at me. "And that's what's really been bothering me about you, Mr. McMorrow. I couldn't picture it. But it's starting to come to me."

He looked back at the boat. "I think she's is a prostitute, like I guessed. I think this guy today, this Roger, he got obsessed with her or whatever. She put up with him for a while but then he wouldn't go away."

"Have to ask him, I guess," I said.

"When he wakes up."

"Who is he, anyway?"

"Who is she?" Raven said.

"Are we trading information?"

"Yeah. You give me information, you stay out of jail."

He turned to me, eyes cold. No more boat talk. The room was damp and silent.

"Jail for what?" I said.

"I prove she's a prostitute, then maybe you're in cahoots with her. Maybe *you* busted the guy's skull. Maybe it's a love triangle. Fighting over Miss Lasell. You know you really can die when somebody stoves your head in like that. All those sharp bones squished into your brain tissue."

"It was self-defense."

"That's for me to decide, after I conclude my investigation. And the ADA. And the judge and jury," Raven said. "In the meantime, you and Miss Mandi will be on the front page of the local paper, the Bangor Daily, too. Got a good relationship with the local press. I give 'em stories and they print 'em. And a hooker in a love triangle, that's big news around here. Should I choose to tell them about it."

"So you're asking me to rat her out, assuming she's done something wrong."

"I'm asking you to stop jerking me around, sir. I'm gonna find out eventually."

I looked at him. "You're gonna pull a print?" I said.

He shrugged.

"The glass from the apartment?"

Raven looked at me.

"FBI doesn't see any urgency on something, they can take weeks. Trick is convincing them this is an urgent matter. Like somebody might get killed, we don't find out who she is."

I didn't answer, my mind replaying the scene: the big barrel of the .45 pressing toward my face, Roger's finger moving toward the trigger, the gun-oil smell. Mandi, who could have been on her way down the stairs, slamming the crutch into his head.

"You're right," I said. "It's a nice boat."

24

—⁂—

I walked back, winding my way back through the boat sheds, along the waterfront. Gulls were hunched on pilings and they leapt into the air, then circled back and plunked down, webbed feet on spatters of droppings. I made my way toward Main Street on a diagonal, ending up behind Mandi's block. The people next to her had wind chimes hanging on a little tacked-on balcony. Mandi had the shot-out window. From a distance, the pattern looked like a flower.

I approached, looking up, then at the cars in the gravel lot. There were a half dozen parked there. A VW Jetta with a ski carrier, the kind that looks like a capsule; two pickups, a Toyota like mine with kayaks on a rack, and a four-wheel drive Chevy, a Harley sticker in the back window; an old hippie Volvo, with a bumper sticker that said "No Iraq War;" A plain green Toyota sedan, drab and anonymous.

Glancing up at the hallway window, I slipped between the trucks and moved to the car. I passed by once, like I was looking for a doorway. Backed away and stopped, peered in. The Toyota was clean inside, nothing in the front seats, nothing hanging from the mirror. I took another step, peered into the back seat. On the floor there was a bag of cat litter and a bowl. The bowl was white and fluted, matched the dishes in Mandi's apartment.

I looked the car over more closely: an oil-change tag from a place called Bobby's Auto in South Portland. It was from January, six months back. A parking sticker, half scraped off. It was from Maine Medical Center in Portland, the rest illegible. I checked the hallway window again. Nobody behind the bullet hole. I leaned over the windshield, slipped a notebook from my pocket. Wrote down the VIN, and with a last glance upward, walked away, up the street, and around the block.

On Main Street, tourists were going into the quaint five & dime, buying the *Times* at the quaint newsstand. The cafes were filling, people in Gore-Tex slickers sitting in the fogged-up windows watching other people in Gore-Tex slickers walking up and down, peering into the windows of the quaint shops. The unquaint cops were gone. The illusion was restored. I went to Mandi's doorway, tried the knob. This time the door was locked.

I stepped back and looked up. Lulu stared down at me like a vulture. I took my phone out and called. Mandi's cell phone rang. A robot voice told me the number I had reached, said I could leave a message.

There was a beep. "This is Jack," I said. "Thanks. Call me when you can."

I walked to the truck, got in and looked up. The curtain moved but it could have been the cat, which had left its perch on the sill. I backed out and headed for home, twelve miles to hash and rehash, trying to winnow the truth from the lies, and both of those from the stuff that fell somewhere in between.

Roxanne's car was in the yard. I parked beside it, went to the door and found it locked. I knocked. Waited. There was a rush of footsteps, Sophie's voice, then Roxanne's steps and the sound of the locks being undone. The deadbolt, then the keylock. The door opened.

"Daddy," Sophie cried, jumping up into my arms. Roxanne glared at me and turned away. I carried Sophie inside, followed Roxanne to the kitchen. Clair was putting on his rainjacket; he looked at me closely and said, "Everything okay?"

"More or less," I said.

"Call," he said. "When you have a chance."

"Thank you, Clair," Roxanne said, strain in her voice, holding something back. "Tell Mary to let me know if she's making jam."

"Surely will," Clair said, and he slid the glass door open, stepped out onto the deck and into the rain.

Roxanne closed the door, locked it, and closed the curtains. She smiled at Sophie and said, "Honey, can you go watch Jungle Book for a few minutes? Mommy and Daddy have to have a grown-up talk."

Sophie dropped down, ran for the den. I heard the click of the television, a rush of music. I took off my jacket, draped it on a chair. Roxanne walked to the counter, picked up a mug of coffee.

"Was it too much to ask?" she said.

"Why?"

"A reporter just called."

"How'd he get our number?"

"I don't know. He was from the Bangor paper. Wanted to talk to Jack McMorrow. I said, 'About what?' He said, 'The shooting on Main Street.'"

"Oh, lord," I said.

"My heart stopped, Jack. I said, 'Is everyone okay?' He said, 'Yeah, except for this guy got his head bashed in.' My heart stopped again. I said, 'Who was that?' He told me some name. All I know is it wasn't you."

"Somebody was waiting in Mandi's apartment," I said. "He had a gun."

Roxanne stared at me. "I thought you were going to just drop her off," she said.

"Had to get her stuff in. I looked around and left. When I was walking to the truck, I looked up, saw somebody move the curtains. I could tell it wasn't her."

"So you—"

"Went back," I said.

"He tried to shoot you?"

"Yes, but he missed."

"So you hit him in the head?"

"No," I said. "Mandi did. With her crutch."

Roxanne looked at me, then looked away. Her face was pale and hard, an angry statue of herself. "What if he hadn't missed?" she said, her jaw clenched.

I shrugged. "Well, he did. I don't think he'd spent a lot of time with guns."

Roxanne closed her eyes. Took a long breath. "You can't do this, Jack. You're a father. You have responsibilities."

"If I hadn't gone back, he might have killed her."

"So you saved her?"

"I guess. Maybe. Who knows? And then she saved me."

Roxanne opened her eyes.

"He still had the gun when she hit him," I said.

"So if she hadn't—"

My turn to look away. "I don't know," I said.

Roxanne sipped her coffee, held the mug on her chest with two hands.

"I'm grateful to her. I am. But are you done with her now?" she said.

I didn't answer.

"Jack, this can't be one of those things where she saved your life and now you owe her."

"She could have gotten away," I said, "but she didn't. She stayed. If she hadn't—"

"If you hadn't gotten involved in the first place, you never would have been there at all."

"It was a story," I said. "That's all."

"It's always a story," Roxanne snapped. "That's how it always starts." 'It's what I do.'

"Other reporters don't get shot at. Other reporters don't have their lives saved by prostitutes."

"Some do, I'm sure," I said. "If you were in Russia or something, or Thailand. Places like that where—"

"Goddamn it Jack, this is Maine. Why can't you just write about something normal? Something nice?"

"I don't do those stories."

"Well, you've got a daughter. A family."

"So do you, honey. Why don't you work in a gift shop? A law office? Why do you have a job that has you snatching kids from wackos and drug addicts?"

"You know I can't let those kids just rot."

"And I can't not write what I write."

"Why not? Does the world really need to know that there are call girls in Belfast, Maine?"

"Yes."

"Why?" Roxanne said.

"Because it's true," I said.

"Oh, God," she said, and the tears began to flow. I took her in my arms, the coffee mug hard between us. Roxanne slid it out and put it on the counter and wrapped her arms around me, pulled me close. "Oh, Jack," she whispered, her tears on my cheek. "Oh, my baby. What would I do if something happened—"

"I'm fine," I said. "We're fine."

"Hugs," Sophie said from behind us and she ran into the room, wormed her way between us, and I lifted her up as Roxanne wiped her eyes.

"It's a mommy and daddy samwich," Sophie said.

"And you're the peanut butter," I said.

"I'm hungry," Sophie said. "Can I have a sandwich now?"

"Sure," Roxanne said, and she peeled away from us, turned toward the cupboard. She opened the door, was reaching for the peanut butter when the phone rang. She picked it up from the counter, said, "Hello."

I saw her face tense. "You can't call here," she said.

Still holding Sophie I went to the caller ID box and looked. An area code I didn't recognize.

"Mr. Wilton," Roxanne said. "Nobody is holding your children hostage. We are—"

I heard a man's voice, shouting from the phone. I put Sophie down and said, "I'll bring your sandwich. Mommy has to do some work."

Sophie looked at her mother curiously, then skipped from the room.

"I'm going to hang up now, Mr. Wilton," Roxanne said. "Don't ever call here again. If you do, you could be prosecuted—"

There was more shouting from the phone. Roxanne's expression was hard. "This isn't going to help you get your children back," she said. "I wish you would try to understand—"

Louder shouting, a string of obscenities. Roxanne started to hang up the phone but I moved and took it from her. "Listen, you crazy son of a bitch," I said, my hand guarding the receiver. "If you ever come here again, I'll kill you. If you ever call here again, I'll come and find you. That's a promise. I will track you down. Got it?"

I paused, listened, and then Roxanne grabbed the phone from me. Hung it up. "Jack," she said.

"Sorry."

"You don't have to be," Roxanne said. "You don't. He was going on about a conspiracy and Christians and how Satanists have been persecuted for thousands of years and he wasn't going to take it any more. And what did he say to you?"

"An eye for an eye," I said.

We heard music from the den, then Sophie's twinkling laugh.

25

Roxanne talked to Trooper Ricci by phone. Ricci said she'd been to the Wilton compound but he wasn't there, or at least didn't show himself. She'd talked to a woman who wasn't Mrs. Wilton and had told her to tell Wilton the state police wanted to talk to him.

We were still talking about it in bed that night.

"What about a tracking dog?" I said. "Flush him out."

"She said they were doing everything in their power," Roxanne said.

We tried to sleep, listened to each other's breathing, felt the bed shift as we turned one way, then the other. Finally, I took Roxanne's hand in mine and held it, waiting for her to fall away.

She did, settling slowly. I counted her breaths up to a hundred, then started again. And then I slept, but fitfully, dreams waking me. I was awake again when, at a little after three that morning he called. "An eye for an eye," he said, when I answered, then hung up.

He called at 6:10, three hours later, and said, "This will not stand."

At 7:34 he said, "Satan will not let you keep my children."

When he called at eight-thirty, Roxanne said, "I'm out of here. I'm taking Sophie."

The state said they'd put her up in a hotel in Portland or wherever. Roxanne picked wherever, said she'd call when she could. This was Friday. She said she'd let them know if she was going to be in on Monday.

We left the house in staggered order. It was a sunny morning after the rain and the trees were dripping, the road still puddled. I drove to the first intersection, stopped at the pavement. Roxanne left in the Subaru ten minutes later, with Sophie playing hide and seek in the back seat. Sophie hid first, on the floor.

Clair was a hundred yards behind her, in his big Ford. When Roxanne reached the intersection, he went ahead, waited at the main road. I let her go, sat and watched to see if anyone followed. There was one car, an old man from the Freedom side of Prosperity, his beagle on the seat beside him.

He waved. I followed.

We did it four times, leapfrogging our way to Waterville. At the interstate, Clair peeled off. I followed Roxanne down the highway to Augusta, pulled over to the breakdown lane as she got off the exit. I watched to see who followed. A tractor trailer from Quebec, loaded with lumber. Two young women in an SUV from Maryland, a Colby College sticker on the back window. A Willie Nelson lookalike on a Harley, who, at the bottom of the ramp, took a right and headed west.

Roxanne waited in the parking lot of a seafood restaurant. When I called, she got back on the highway.

We did that in Brunswick, too. Nobody followed. When we got off the interstate in Portland, we made a loop through the back streets of Munjoy Hill. Pulled over and parked and waited to see if anyone showed.

Did it one more time, Roxanne calling to say Sophie had to go the bathroom. We drove into the Old Port, swung into the Regency Hotel drive, and Roxanne and Sophie left the car with the valet and went in, Sophie skipping with her backpack on.

I made a loop, sat in the truck at the corner.

Watched. Waited.

I called. "What name?" I said.

"Allison Parker," she said.

"I love you," I said.

"We love you, too," Roxanne said.

Away from the phone, she said, "Want to say hi to Daddy?"

"We're going in the swimming pool," Sophie said. "Good thing I brought my swimming suit." I smiled, put the phone down and headed for home—or at least in that general direction.

Ellsworth Street ran from Congress down toward the bay. It was a neighborhood I remembered for its criminals, but now they were gone—in jail or dead—and the streets were full of twenty-somethings with good looks and college degrees.

Number 14 was on the Congress Street end, a square tenement with shingles painted dark red and white Christmas candles in the windows on the second floor. There was a mountain bike locked to a tree out front; an older BMW motorcycle parked on the walk to the side door, a Ford pickup in the driveway.

I pulled in by a hydrant and waited, hoping someone would come or go. After five minutes a man appeared from the side door dragging a heavy trash bag behind him. He was 60 or close to it, short and stocky, wearing dirty jeans and a black T-shirt. I got out and started up the walk, saw sweat stains on the shirt, a tape rule in a leather case on his belt. The landlord.

I walked toward him, tucked my notebook in my pocket. "Hello there," I said.

"You looking for a place, I got nothing here," he said, his accent Spanish. He crossed the driveway, heaved the trashbag into the truck. "But something coming open on Munjoy Street, end of the month. One-bedroom, real nice."

"No, I'm not looking for an apartment," I said. "I'm looking for one of your tenants. Ex-tenant."

He was walking back to the house but he stopped, turned to me. "You the police?"

"No," I said. "A reporter."

His eyes narrowed and he put his hands on his hips. "One of my people in the newspaper?"

"No," I said. "Just someone I met a few months back, wondering if she's still around."

"Who's that?"

"Sybill Lasell."

He hesitated, eyed me more closely. "Nice girl, Sybill," he said carefully. "She left, maybe six months ago. How you know her?"

"I interviewed her once."

"About what?" He watched me, waited.

"How Portland was a good city to live in. It had just made one of those lists."

He seemed to relax. "Oh, yeah. Great city. Great for the young people. They love it here."

"Right. Sybill loved it, didn't she?"

"Well, she was a quiet girl," the guy said, guarded again. "She gave me no trouble. No trouble at all."

"You know where she went?"

"Never said a word. Paid the rent on time, then one day I come by, she's gone. Key is on the floor inside the door. No note, no nothing. Never asked for her security, neither. Just poof. She's gone. You tell her, you see her, I still got her money. Six-hundred bucks."

"Huh," I said. "Leave her things behind?"

"Hey, she barely got any. Girls usually got all kinds a stuff, you know? She got a bed, a chair, a little TV. No cable, just the antenna. Looked like a jail cell, you know what I'm saying? Nice rooms, too, you fix 'em up. You should see it now. Girl in there, she got the place looking so nice."

"I'm sure."

"Hey, I was shocked. Nice girl, has the guys starting to come around. One of 'em, he's got serious money. Mercedes Benz, clothes right outta some magazine. He really likes her, too, I can tell. Bringing her flowers."

"So she dumped him and left," I said.

"Hell, no. Day after she's gone, he's standing at the door, bottle of wine and some roses in his hand. He says, 'Where is she?' I says, 'Gone with the wind, just like the movie.' I thought he was gonna cry, right there on the doorstep." He pointed to the front door.

"Yeah, I can see she could be a real heartbreaker," I said.

He looked at my hand, at my wedding band.

"I'm married," I said. "My heart's fine."

"Me, too. But I'll tell you, if I was twenty-five and not married."

He shook his head, recalling her. "Nice-looking girl."

"Yeah," I said.

"Sweet, too, you know. I talked to her sometimes, working around the place. Thought about things. Worried, you know?"

"What kinda things?"

"Oh, about people, why they do what they do. Had these people next door. Not my building, don't think that. Man and a lady. Fight? Oh, Jesus, did they fight. I always kinda thought that might've been the reason Sybill left. Screaming and yelling, and the cops coming. And then—"

He paused, looked around like somebody might be listening. "You know what happened?"

"Remind me," I said.

"You work for the paper here, right?"

I didn't answer. It didn't matter.

"Then you know that house right there, that's where the guy got killed. Lady had moved out, she'd had enough. But somebody, they decided this bastard had it coming. You remember."

"Oh, yeah," I said. "Hey, refresh my memory. How'd he get killed?"

"Big goddamn butcher knife, right off his own counter. Said it was some artery got cut, why it sprayed all over the place. Artery in his neck."

He felt his neck. I felt mine.

"Goddamn mess, I heard. Hey, I don't mind cleaning up food, drinks spilled. But blood, no thanks. All over the wall. Man, does that stain, you don't get it off right away. You gotta seal it and seal it again or it bleeds right through."

"Musta been cops all over the place."

"Big police van, place all taped off. Detectives talked to everybody, what did they hear, see anything that night? Houses so close together, you know."

I looked at the house next door, thirty feet between the buildings. "Sybill know this guy?"

"Nah, she kept to herself. Her job, it kept her out a lot."

"What job was that?" I said.

"She worked in some fitness club, one for ladies. I know that 'cause I asked her where it is. She said, 'Hector, you can't go. You're a guy.' Felt like a creep, you know, like I wanted to see her in her little outfit or something. I was just being friendly."

"I understand."

"But she was funny, you know. You get too close, she'd just shut the door."

"Huh," I said. "Probably right."

He took a deep breath. "Well, probably oughta get going. Just hate to go back in that cellar."

"Right. Hey, listen, this guy who got killed. How long before Sybill left did that happen?"

"Like, two days," he said. "It freaked her out, you know? I said, 'It's still a safe neighborhood. Hey, these things happen.'"

"Yes, they do," I said.

"But she wasn't having any of it. Still, I thought she'd give her notice, take her deposit. Not just pack up and disappear in the middle of the night. Hey, still got a storage box of hers down in the cellar. Keep it in the back of the closet, blanket on top of it. Figure I throw it out, the next day she'll show up looking for it."

"Isn't that always the way," I said.

"Hey, I gotta get some breakfast," he said, turning toward the truck, then back. "I don't eat enough, I get weak in the knees. Sorry I couldn't help you."

"That's okay," I said. "It was a shot in the dark anyway."

He looked at me, flashed a conspiratorial smile. "Yeah, right. Hey listen, I'm gonna give you some advice."

"Go for it," I said.

"You got a good lady at home?"

"Yes," I said. "I do."

"Then you stick by her. Grass ain't always greener, lemme tell ya. A word to the wise, my friend."

"Gotcha," I said.

He nodded, got in the truck, backed out. Drove off slowly toward Congress. I started for my truck, watched as he turned at the first stop sign. I stood by the driver's door and waited. Counted to thirty. Tossed in another twenty for good measure. I drove down the block and parked out of sight. Walking back to the house, I took a last look down the street, then walked up the driveway, neither slowly nor quickly.

The cellar door pushed open. The light switch was on the left.

26

The far half of the cellar was divided into five sections, wood-framed stalls separated by chicken wire. There was a number on the two-by-four on each stall, 1 to 5. The stalls weren't locked. Inside were jumbles of skis, bikes, microwaves, a mattress with a brown stain.

If apartment 2 had been rented, that meant Mandi's stuff didn't get a stall. I looked around for anything loose. Along one wall was a workbench, a few tools scattered on top, and a toilet plunger. I circled the cellar. There was a roll of insulation in one corner, sitting on a wooden pallet. Along the wall there were mouse traps, the box kind that catch the mouse when he steps on sticky paper.

I came back to the door, which was half open. I pulled it shut— and there was a plastic box on the floor behind it.

It had a blanket on top, covered with dirt and dust. I listened at the door for a moment, then bent down and popped the lid off. It was partly filled with papers, maybe an inch deep at the bottom, the top yellowed with faded handwriting. On top of the papers was a small toy dog, a Valentine heart hanging from his collar.

I took the dog out, lifted a sheaf of papers and held them up to the light.

A faded meatloaf recipe from a newspaper, stapled to a piece of loose leaf. A drawing of a woman with wings, an odd sort of angel, angry, as though Lucifer had a sister. A poem, handwritten on a page of yellow legal pad, in a girl's careful script.

You and me, we go way back,
  back to the beginning when there was just
One of us, not two,
when you stayed out of sight,
let me fight my own fights.
I lost most of them, but not all
If I'd lost more, maybe they wouldn't have noticed,
wouldn't have come with their serious, sad voices,
Trying to tell me they were so concerned.
But they did notice, came and cornered the girl who won,
  the girl who wouldn't take it lying down, or if she did,
  absolutely wouldn't cry out, wouldn't make a sound,
until you came out of your hiding place and you told them,
leave her alone. Leave her alone.
  Leave her alone, alone, alone.
So they did.

I turned to the next page. Another drawing, this one of a woman kneeling by a chopping block, a sword raised in one hand, her other arm across the block.

The scars on Mandi's wrists.

The page after that was a clipping from the *Portland Press Herald*, a story about a family that went on a ski vacation, smiling blonde kids, handsome parents, mountains in the background. Then another poem, written on the same legal paper as the first.

If you have no memories
Are you still alive?
If you have no family,
Are you close to death?

If loneliness is pain, then I am hurting.
so don't let them tell you the first cut
is the deepest, because it isn't,
it is just the first
of many.

I heard a truck pull in.

The papers in my arms, I pressed against the wall behind the door. The truck motor idled for a minute and then shut off. I heard muffled country western music, and then the truck door must have opened because the music got louder, then the door slammed shut.

There were bootsteps and then the door was pushed open wider until it touched my knees and chest. I flattened myself, saw just the edge of him as he crossed the cellar. The landlord. Whistling, he picked up a carton of something, turned and walked back out to the truck. There was a thud as he put the carton down, and then he whistled his way back.

He crossed the cellar again, this time crouching to open a carton and rattle the contents. "Who saves this shit?" he said, and picked up the box, started to turn toward me. Stopped.

He looked to the far corner and put the box down. He walked to the back of the cellar, bent to inspect a mousetrap. Holding the pile of Mandi's papers, I stepped around the door and out. I switched off the light and pulled the door shut behind me. "Hey," the landlord said, and I walked quickly down the driveway and up the street.

Back in the truck, I circled over to the Eastern Prom, cut back on Congress Street, then down the hill past crapped-out tenements with gangbangers on the stoops, the gentrification not there yet. I jumped on the interstate, drove north, moving slowly in the convoy of out-of-staters. There were trucks pulling boats, trucks pulling campers, Saabs carrying kayaks, and motor homes the size of apartments. Everybody happy and healthy, nobody drawing pictures of themselves cutting off their hand.

Every few minutes, I reached over, pulled a few pages off the pile. More poems, some sort of journal. A diagram of a room. I glanced up at the New York Volvo in front of me, looked back down. A bed. A chair. A dresser and a desk. A hotel room? A homeless shelter? Where had Mandi been?

An hour out of Portland, I swung off the highway, cut through Augusta and headed east. The traffic was lighter, still mostly tourists, bound like lemmings for the coast. I passed them on the hills, called Roxanne from the crest of a ridge in the town of Palermo. The number rang once, and then went to voice mail.

I glanced at the papers. Felt the words forming: *I stopped at Mandi's old apartment. I got some of her stuff. She was one unhappy young woman.*

I heard Roxanne's response. *I thought you were through with her.*

I left a message: "Just checking on you. Call me when you can." And then it was down into a valley with green ridges to the west, wooded hills to the east. There was no phone reception for the next ten miles, and I sped up, racing through the black hole.

And then I turned off, tracked through the back roads in North Searsmont and Morrill. There were old farms, orchards overgrown with poplar, trailers parked next to fallen-in houses. It wasn't that they didn't value sentiment in these parts; it was just that they couldn't afford it.

To the tourists, bound for Belfast and beyond, it was the heart of darkness, dirt roads leading to nowhere, traveled by people who lived odd, inexplicable, and presumably dull lives somewhere in those deep woods.

I wondered where Mandi would land next. Would she head for the woods? And why?

And then I was turning onto my road, Clair's end. His truck was in the yard in front of the barn but I kept going, slowed and passed my house, turned around in the trees three hundred yards beyond, and came back. I pulled in, parked, shut off the motor. It was a little after noon and the place was still. The sun had come out and the air was warming and humid. Bugs buzzed in the trees and hornets moved to and from a nest in the eaves.

I got out of the truck. Walked to the side door and looked back. Nothing showed on the road. I felt for my knife, took it out and flicked open a blade. I started to put a key in the lock but when I pushed it in, the door just swung open.

I listened. Nothing.

I took a step inside. Listened again. Looked down and saw a dark splotch on the wood floor. I crouched slightly, peered down. There were red-brown droplets leading into the house. Blood. I held the knife low in front of me, wished it were bigger. My rifle was on the high shelf in the hall closet and when I got there, I eased the door open. Listened. Reached onto the shelf, felt the stock of the rifle.

I slipped it out, reached above the closet door to the shelf. All the way back was a box of 30-06 shells. I got it down, opened it. Levered five shells into the chamber I put the knife away, followed the trail.

In the kitchen, there were flies. They landed and tasted the blood, buzzed away and circled as I passed. I looked to the study, saw the sliding door open, the screen, too. The blood trail went to the right and up the stairs. A bumblebee droned into the room from outside, then droned back out. I started up.

There was a drop on every other tread, then, at the top of the stairs, a spatter on the white paint of the landing. No footprints in the blood, nobody walking through it.

I continued down the hall, the doors to both bedrooms closed. The droplets stopped at Sophie's door and I had to remind myself I'd just left her in Portland, eighty miles away. But then who was—

I tried the latch, lifted it with the top of my forefinger. The door opened an inch. I pressed it with the barrel of the rifle. It creaked. Opened.

I pushed it wide.

Felt the breath fall out of me.

There was blood on Sophie's bed, a red splotch at the center of the white bedspread. I took a step, whirled around, and covered myself. There was no one there.

I turned back. Stepped closer, saw there was something under the blankets. The shape of a small child. Droplets of blood on the blankets. I swallowed. Held the rifle under the crook of my arm, finger on the trigger. Eased the blankets back.

Nearly gasped.

Blonde hair.

I forced myself to look. It was Twinnie, Sophie's doll, a hunting knife driven through her pink chest. Her blue eyes stared at the ceiling, as if in death. The blood was from a dead chicken, torn open, staring up at me with a glass eye from bloodied sheets. There was a paper at the doll's pink plastic feet.

I took it by the edge and opened it gingerly. Read it and swallowed hard again.

Sophie Masterson
RIP

Wilton, who knew Roxanne's last name but maybe not mine. I let the paper fall back.

Turned slowly, the gun ready. I looked around the room. Stuffed animals, books, drawings pinned to her bulletin board. Nothing disturbed. I went to her closet. Counted three and yanked the door open, falling back with the rifle trained.

Little dresses. Her pink winter jacket, hanging on a hook.

I walked slowly from the bedroom, across the hall. Listened at our door. Eased it open. The room was as we'd left it. Everything had been directed at Sophie. Anger, frustration, whatever twisted need he had for revenge.

I walked slowly downstairs and went to the phone. The red light was flashing like something on a monitor. If it stopped, I thought, I was dead. I pressed the button. The machine beeped and hissed.

"Love you," Roxanne said. "Call us."

Another beep: "This is Sarah at the Rockland office calling for Roxanne. If you get this, call me, honey. Thinking of you, Rox."

One more: "It's out of my hands. I await his next orders. And you know, there is no way to hide from him. He is all-seeing, almighty. The false prophets kneel at his feet and beg forgiveness. And you will, too."

I swallowed, looked at the time of the call: 10:42. Pressed the button and listened again.

Wilton's voice was calm and content now that it was out of his hands. I concentrated on the spaces between the words. Closed my eyes. I heard a humming sound that started partway through. A refrigerator.

I heard a creak, like he'd leaned back in an old chair. Then another creak. A rhythm to it. A rocking chair.

Wilton was home.

Holding the rifle in the crook of my arm, I called Roxanne's cell phone. Got a message. I called the desk at the Regency and asked them to ring Allison Parker's room. I left a message, said call me when you can.

I dialed the state police. I asked for Trooper Ricci and the dispatcher said she was off duty until Saturday, 0600. He asked if I wanted to talk to the trooper on duty for that area. I said, yes. He said the officer was tied up, a car accident with multiple injuries. Then his shift was over at 4. It might be tomorrow.

"What is this regarding?" he said, radio traffic crackling in the background.

"Somebody came into my house and stabbed my daughter's doll," I said.

"Uh-huh," he said. "Is the intruder in the residence?"

"No. It happened this morning. It has to do with a DHHS case."

"Right."

I knew what he was thinking. A DHHS mess. Even worse.

"Listen, sir, we're kinda busy here right now. Can I get your name, sir?"

I told him. "I'll get the message to the on-duty trooper."

"And Ricci, too," I said.

"Okay, but like I said, we've got a serious car accident transpiring so I wouldn't expect a call very soon. There's no imminent danger?"

"No," I said. "I guess not."

I put the phone down. Closed the sliding door with the barrel of the gun. It looked like he—or they—had come in the side door, exited at the back. Maybe they knocked to see if anybody answered, if Mary was there again. I watched the woods for a minute, but nothing stirred, no glint of metal or flash of color.

Turning away from the door, I went to the study and Roxanne's desk. I opened the binder in the top drawer, flipped through until I found July, then I found her mileage log.

Two trips to the Hatchet Mountain Road, North Appleton, a crossroads ten miles and a few light years west of ritzy Camden. I closed the binder, put it back in the drawer. Rifle in my arms, I headed for the side door. On the way by, I reached into the closet and took the rest of the shells.

27

I pulled into the barnyard, slid the truck to a stop. I could hear the music—piano, Duke Ellington—and I went to the barn door and pushed it open. Clair was coming out of a storeroom with a bag of chicken feed on his shoulder. He saw me and put it down. "What?" he said.

"He was here," I said. "This morning, after we left."

"Where?"

I told him: the doll, the knife, the blood, the call.

"Your knife?"

"No, he brought it with him."

"That's not good," Clair said.

"No. Pre-meditation. He had a plan."

"What's yours?"

"Go talk to him."

"Can you do that? With Roxanne and the job? I'm sure there are rules."

"There were," I said. "Not anymore."

"Gonna talk to him?"

"Can't wait for the cops. Trooper Ricci is off until tomorrow. I left a message for somebody else."

"I'll go, watch your back."

"Okay."

"'Cause you've got a daughter. You don't want to watch her grow up from a prison visiting room."

"I'm just gonna talk to him," I said. "I can't just sit there, wait for him to do something. Next time, it might not be—" I didn't finish the thought.

"What are you bringing?" Clair said.

"The Remington."

"I'll bring a shotgun," Clair said.

"For self-defense," I said.

"Just in case."

"Because we don't know what Satan is gonna tell him."

"No," Clair said. "That's hard to predict."

We drove south on Route 131. I knew Hatchet Mountain was south of the intersection and cemetery that marked North Appleton. The woods of Appleton Ridge were on our right, rugged country that dropped down to a stream and swampland. We cut to the east on 105, were almost to the town of Hope when we saw the road sign, bullet holes through the word Hatchet.

I turned to Clair. "Think that means anything?"

"I've been counting," he said. "Passed eleven road signs, eight of them shot up."

"Yeah. And so far he's been a knife and club kinda guy."

"I wouldn't count on it," Clair said.

"No," I said. As I turned off, Clair started slipping shells into the shotgun.

The road was gravel, a lane and a half, in need of ditching. There were puddles in the low spots, ruts from heavy trucks. "Somebody's been cutting in here," Clair said.

I eased the truck through one deep pool, heard the water against the skid plate underneath me.

The shotgun was loaded. Clair rested the butt on his thigh. I could feel him focus, the way he did before we did something like this. He grew calm, quiet, hyper-aware. "Roxanne say anything about the house?"

"Dark. Home-built. A rough road in."

"Straight or curved?"

"She didn't say."

"How far off this road?"

"A few hundred yards."

"If it isn't in sight of the house, you can drop me partway."

I nodded. "How long you want?"

"Ten minutes," Clair said.

The road climbed, gradually at first, then more steeply. A half-mile in there was an opening cut in the spruce on the right, logs and tops rotting in the ditch. A rusty chain hung from a tree on one side of the road. There was an eyebolt screwed into a tree on the opposite side but the chain wasn't up. The Wilton welcome mat was out.

I slowed, peered up the road. It curved gradually and there was no house in sight. I drove for a hundred yards, veering around potholes and mud. Clair rolled his window down and raised the shotgun slightly, the butt under his arm. In the distance I saw a no-trespassing sign on a tree.

I pulled up. "I'll come in from the back," he said.

I nodded and Clair got out, glanced up the road and crossed into the woods. In a minute, he was gone. He was moving through the trees but I couldn't see him. I listened and heard only chickadees, and a tufted titmouse.

I put the truck in four-wheel-drive and eased into the ditch on the left side. I got out and slipped the rifle from the scabbard behind the seat. I laid it across the driver's seat and stood and waited.

Watched. Listened.

Red squirrels chattered. A pileated woodpecker called in the distance. Mosquitoes rose from the brush and buzzed around my head. I looked up and saw a red-tailed hawk slip past. Then turkey vultures circling over the trees, a pair of ravens rising from the woods behind the house.

Carrion.

I watched the vultures for a minute, then looked down and saw an empty jug in the grass: coffee brandy. Was Wilton a drunk? I recalled my conversation with him in Camden, his calm certainty. How would that combine with alcohol? What would I say if I faced him again?

Tell him I'd shoot him on sight if he came near my property. Tell him it was his only warning.

What would Roxanne say when I told her I'd been here? Would she understand that I couldn't sit and wait for him to harm our daughter. That I couldn't sit on my hands while this cop played it strictly by the book.

And then a darker thought intruded: shoot Wilton now and be done with it. I chased it away, but it was followed by another: if he fired first, we'd have no choice.

Nine minutes gone. I got back in the truck, propped the rifle on the passenger seat. Drove out of the ditch, jounced onto the road, and eased my way along. Fifty yards in, the driveway veered left. I stopped and looked.

The brush had been cleared and the trees were bare, as though the place had been ravaged by goats. Through the trees I saw a small, low house. It was sided with rough boards and had mismatched windows on the front. The homemade door was topped by an unshingled plywood roof. There were gardens hacked out of the woods, now ringed with broken down chicken wire fencing and overgrown—broccoli in yellow flower showing in the grass and weeds. By the door there was an old Isuzu SUV. White with rust.

I turned in, drove part way and stopped. I listened. No barking. Where were the dogs Roxanne had talked about? Had the clan moved on? Who was inside?

I drove slowly up to the house and turned the truck broadside to the door and windows. Easing out, I stood by the open driver's door, the rifle across the seat. I waited, watching the windows.

Leaning in, I beeped the horn. Waited. No one showed.

I beeped again, leaned on the horn longer.

This time I saw movement, a shadow passing the window on the right. I reached in and drew the rifle toward me.

The door rattled. It began to open. There was a boom inside, a shotgun. I pulled the rifle out, aimed it at the door. I heard Clair shouting from inside and I ran, kicked the door open and trained the gun on the gloom inside.

I heard Clair call, "Jack. It's okay. We're all set."

I stepped inside, smelled the gunshot smoke. My eyes adjusted and I saw Clair crouched by someone sitting on a broken down couch. I moved closer, saw it was a woman, dressed in a long denim jumper, beat-up running shoes. Her hands were over her face, her body heaving with sobs. The woman from the Belfast court. Cheree Wilton.

No one was shot. There was an old single-barrel shotgun on the floor behind Clair. I looked to the back of room, saw the blast hole in the dry wall.

"She missed," Clair said.

"I thought it was him," Cheree Wilton said, from behind her hands.

"Who?" I said.

"My husband," she said. "I thought Harland, he'd come back."

She lowered her hands, showing eyes ringed in purple and yellow bruises. One of her ear lobes was bloody, like an earring had been torn out. There was a cut at her hairline, a scab that ran through her hair. The backs of her hands were scratched and gouged.

She took a long, deep breath. "You police? What do you want?"

"I'm Jack McMorrow," I said. "Roxanne Masterson is my wife."

She blanched under the bruises, swallowed. "I'm sorry," she said.

"For what?" I said.

"For what he's doing. He's freakin' lost it."

"Who? Your husband?"

She nodded, started to cry again.

"It's okay," Clair said.

"It's not okay. It's a mess. It's the worst mess you could ever have. The kids. I'll never get them back. But it doesn't matter 'cause he's gonna kill me."

"Nobody is going to kill you," I said.

"He said it. He said it's my fault they took the kids. Why couldn't I cook? But I couldn't cook, there was no food. No food he'd allow in the house. He says if we don't get them back, he'll kill me. And he'll kill them, before he'd let them be raised by the followers of the Nazarean. That's what he said."

"Where is he?" I said.

"I don't know. In his truck someplace, maybe. He came home last night and said, why was I just sitting here? Well, where am I supposed to go? He said he was fighting to get the kids back and I was just laying around. Called me names and punched me and punched me. Look at me."

She looked like someone who staggers from the wreckage after a bomb goes off. "We can call an ambulance," Clair said.

"No," she said.

"Is he coming back soon?" I said.

"How would I know? He doesn't tell me. It's like I'm his servant, you know? Orders me around. If I don't do what he says fast enough, he slaps me in the head. That's how I got this."

She touched her scalp.

"Hit me so hard it tore the skin."

"Is he alone?"

"No, most of the time now he's with his friend. His only friend. The only one left."

"The guy who came to my house," I said. "Who got stuck with the knife."

She looked at me, seemed to almost cower. "I had to go, I had to do it. He told me if I didn't it would show that I was one of the fallen ones and he couldn't be responsible for my safety. My safety. Look at me."

"Why did you come to my house?" I said.

She hesitated. "Like I said, it wasn't my idea."

"But what was the idea?"

Another pause. She looked at Clair, then away from both of us. "He called it a raid. He . . . he thinks that if he has your little girl, he can trade her for Jeremy and Luc."

"Not a good plan," I said.

"You can't tell him."

"Who's his buddy?"

"His name is Carlton. Last name is Sirois or something like that. He joined the group near the end."

"The religion thing?" Clair said.

"It wasn't always like this. When we first met, Harland was so interesting. I mean, really. Like, he can tell you all about Egypt and Sumeria and the gods they worshipped and how the Catholic Church came about and all of this stuff. My first husband, he couldn't even tell you about New Hampshire. And then I meet Harland, and it's like he's from a different time, you know what I'm sayin'?"

"Satan and all that?" I said.

"Which, if you think about it, it makes so much sense, right? Or it did in the beginning. We had, like, twenty people who got together to talk and you learned so much. Did you know that the original gods were made into this awful evil thing so Christians could take over and make money and get all this power? Like all those Popes and cardinals and bishops, living like kings in the thirteen hundreds while everybody else starved? It's all there, if you really do the studying. Harland could prove it, that Satan was, you know, the creator. I mean, Satan wasn't really evil at all. And then they started making up all this stuff about him being the devil. He really isn't."

"But your husband says Satan is giving him his orders." I said.

"Does he order him to beat you up?" Clair said, still somber.

She sighed, shook her head. "He hears all these things now, stuff that's only real in his head, I think. He thinks the CIA is watching him, because the Pope ordered them to."

"The Pope?" I said.

"Oh, yeah. I mean, when a plane flies over, I mean any plane. A big jetliner going to England or someplace, he says it's surveillance. Either the CIA or the Vatican, or the Jews. The Jews are everywhere."

She wiped her eyes, touched the scab in her hair. "They hired this new girl down to the store over in Union, she's foreign or something, and he said he knew she was brought in by the Israelis to watch him. Stopped going there. And then he started saying they were gonna try to steal the kids, raise them Christian, stop the passing of the torch. And then they did, the lady from the state—your wife, I mean—she comes and takes Jeremy and Luc and it's like it's all coming true. Everything Harland said."

"But he beat your kids," I said.

"He said he had to discipline them to keep them from getting too weak. If you're weak, you're somebody the Christians can convert. It's what they did, like to the natives in Mexico. We studied it. Harland said we needed to know their methods."

"And he had to discipline you, too?" Clair said.

She didn't answer, just looked bone weary and defeated.

"You should call the police. Or I can call them for you," I said.

"Get police out here for this," she sighed, "and I'll never see the kids. Now it's way more than just me. He's just so angry. I think the voices in his head, they're driving him crazy. Yesterday he killed the dogs, threw them in the woods out back."

"The vultures," I said.

"He said the Jews had taken over their bodies, that the dogs were listening to us, telling the Jews what we were saying. He says it's Satan talking to him, but I don't think so because Satan wouldn't be talking to him *all* the time. I mean, he must have something better to do."

We stared at her, then glanced at each other. Clair reached for her shotgun, broke it open and pulled out the spent shell.

"He took all the rest of the guns," she said.

"Like what?" I said.

"Another shotgun, a double barrel. A .308 rifle. A handgun. It's an old revolver he got at a pawnshop in Augusta. Traded the lawnmower when we got the goat, but the goat died."

"What about the other guy?" Clair said. "He bring anything to the party?"

She shook her head. "Just money and a cell phone. Harland had to teach him how to shoot. Wanted to give him this shotgun but I told him it was busted."

"Why?" I said.

"So when he came back, I could shoot the son of a bitch. He's gonna kill somebody. But now I can't. He took all the shells. I only had the one in the gun."

"Come with us," I said. "We'll get you to a shelter."

"Hell, no. He's not driving me from my home."

Clair looked at me. I nodded. "Twelve gauge?" he said.

"Yeah," she said.

Clair jacked two shells from his gun, handed them to her. "Number six buckshot," he said. "He comes back, tries to hurt you again, aim for the belt buckle. Most people miss high."

28

There was a direct route home: up Route 105, hit 131 north to Searsmont, across Route 3, the main drag to the coast, and wind up Route 220 through Center Montville, Thorndike, and Prosperity.

But I wanted to drive the road Harland Wilton would drive, skulking around the countryside with his buddy, sleeping in his truck.

I said this to Clair and he said, "Up over Moody Mountain, down the other side and across Jam Black Brook. Tote roads in there, bogs and streams—you could hide out for years."

"Or at least until Satan gave you another assignment," I said.

"Until then," Clair said.

So we caught the Moody Mountain Road, six miles east of Camden and in another world. Deep woods, boulders strewn through them, the road running down into lowland covered with dense alder and swamp maple. I slowed so we could peer down the logging roads, looking for a truck, stuck back in the woods, maybe, waiting for night to fall. Nothing showed.

We drove north through Searsmont village—no truck there—and continued northward, over Thompson Ridge and up to Polands

Corner. It was like passing through some vast cemetery, the road signs like gravestones for people long dead.

And then we were climbing Knox Ridge, coasting down the other side, dappled swatches of forest and pasture spread out before us. It was the time when I ordinarily would feel my body relax, a delicious calm sweep over me. I was almost home and home was my refuge.

Not this time.

We slowed on our road, eased up to the places where a truck could pull into the woods. I drove down the path where we'd found Carlton and the Jeep but there was no truck.

"Doesn't look like anybody's been here since—"

Clair held up one finger. I let the truck coast to a stop. He got out and walked back to a place where the brush was low, grass and wildflowers mixed in. He walked in, started picking up branches, laying them back down. They were broken off. I walked back as he held a clump of Queen Anne's Lace to his nose, then held it up to me. I sniffed.

"Motor oil," I said.

"Truck's got a leak," he said. "Pulled in here and dripped."

"How long ago?"

Clair looked at the flowers, the broken stalks of wild asters. "This morning," he said. "Some stuff is dying."

"Waited until we left?" I said.

"Maybe watching the back of the house from the woods. Hears your truck pull out, thinks you've left the girls, gone to work."

"Goes in the house. We're gone."

"If he'd been smart," Clair said, "he wouldn't have left a trace. Wait for you to come back."

"He's just following orders," I said, turning back to the truck. "Sometimes Satan works in mysterious ways."

It was almost four o'clock and the house was standing, looked just as I'd left it. I eased the side door open. Listened. Clair and I stepped in. I was carrying the rifle, barrel pointed down but the safety off. Clair had his shotgun and he went through the kitchen, looked out the back. I started upstairs and he followed.

I checked our room. All was well. When I turned back, Clair had stepped into Sophie's room, where Twinnie remained impaled. I came in and stood beside him.

"One sick bastard," Clair said.

"At least one," I said.

"I'd bag the whole thing up. DNA, prints on the knife. Who knows what they'll find."

I left the room, gun still slung under one arm, and went downstairs to the kitchen. From under the sink, I took out a box of black plastic trash bags, yanked one bag from the roll. I was leaning down to put the others back when the phone rang.

Roxanne, I thought. Her first chance to call. Worn out by the swim, Sophie was taking a nap.

I grabbed the phone on the counter. "Hello."

No reply. "Hello," I said again.

"McMorrow," a man said.

I looked at the box. Same phone number, but not Wilton.

"You check on your girls lately?" he said.

"No, I haven't, Carlton," I said.

He didn't answer. There was a muffled hum, like he'd put his hand over the phone.

"We know where they are," he said.

"Is that right?" I said.

"You can run, McMorrow," he said. "But you can't hide."

"I'm not hiding," I said. "I'm right here. You're the coward hiding behind the phone."

"Kidnappers," he said. "Baby snatchers. Well, you'll see how it feels when your little girl, she's—"

"You're dead," I said. "Just so you know. Better start running now, Carlton. Give yourself half a chance."

"Do you know what Satan will—"

"Your buddy there, he's gonna owe you one, Carlton. No cops. No discussion. Not gonna listen to you whine and cry. Just a bullet in your head, bury you in a bog someplace."

"Who you think—"

"Open season just got underway on you, my friend. I'm gonna hunt you down."

He cleared his throat. I could hear whispering in the background, Wilton saying, "What's the matter?"

"Yeah, well," Carlton stammered. "Satan, he's gonna—"

"Two strikes, Carlton," I said. "That's all you get."

The phone went dead. I turned, the plastic bag still in my hand.

"Scare him?" Clair said, standing behind me, all the way down from upstairs and I hadn't heard him.

"Yeah."

"You were starting to scare me. But I think the other one might call your bluff."

"No bluff," I said.

"Figure of speech," Clair said.

I called Roxanne, left a message on her phone. Then I called the state police again, said I needed to talk to Trooper Ricci, and this time it was urgent.

"Is there something I can help you with, sir?" the dispatcher said.

"Maybe," I said. I explained about the threatening calls, my wife's job, that I had the number on my caller ID. I said I'd put the doll in a bag.

"What doll, sir?" he said.

"The one they stabbed with the hunting knife," I said.

"I'll see if I can get Trooper Ricci on the phone," he said.

Clair went home, said to call him if I needed him, if I heard anything outside. After he left, I walked around one more time, glancing at the phone, which didn't ring. Then I went to the refrigerator, took out a can of Ballantine Ale. I made a sandwich—Swiss cheese on pumpernickel—and I poured the beer in a glass. Leaving the kitchen light on, I moved to the study and dragged my chair around so it faced the kitchen and the sliding doors to the deck.

Then I went back to the kitchen, got the rifle, and sat in the chair and waited. The birds called; a phoebe over and over, a cardinal whooping from the top of a tree, a hermit thrush deep in the woods. There was a thump on the deck and I snapped the gun up—a stray cat crossed my sights.

I put the gun down. Took a bite of the sandwich, a sip of beer. Remembered the box of Mandi's papers, and picked up the rifle and walked out to the truck. I took the box out, closed the truck door. Walking down the driveway, I looked down the road, where the sun was dropping behind the trees and the woods were filling with shadows. I looked up the road toward Clair's, heard the cruiser coming before I saw it.

It came over the crest, slowed, signaled, and turned in. Ricci was at the wheel. She got out, reached back into the car for her hat. Putting it on, she came around the car, stuck her thumbs in her belt.

"Your day off," I said. "Thanks for coming."

"No problem, Mr. McMorrow," she said.

"Even put on your uniform," I said.

"Regulations," she said. "We're not supposed to go on police business out of uniform, unless it's authorized."

"Still, I appreciate it."

"I understand you had visitors," Ricci said.

"Yes," I said. "I'm sorry I missed them."

She looked at the rifle. "I can see that," she said. "Do some hunting?"

"Deer," I said.

"Season's four months off."

"Key to a successful hunt is preparation," I said.

She gave me a long look and I led the way inside.

I showed Ricci the bag. The chicken. The doll. The knife through its chest. It was the doll that did it.

Her expression darkened, anger almost coming through. She swallowed it down but then she'd look at the doll again, laid out on the kitchen table like it was ready for an autopsy, and her outrage would bubble back up.

"And your daughter, she's with Mrs. McMorrow?"

"Yes," I said. "He called all night. Roxanne couldn't take it anymore."

"And we have his number?"

I handed it to her, written on a page from a reporter's notebook. The number and times he'd called.

She walked to the phone, called in to what I figured was the Augusta dispatcher. She said she needed a cell phone trace, said it was important. Read the stuff off the paper and said, "I'll call back," she said, and she hung up.

"Where were you?" Ricci said.

"When?"

"When they were here, and your wife and daughter had left."

"I followed them to where they were going. Me and Clair, we did a staggered sort of tail make sure nobody followed them."

"Where'd they go?"

"A safe place," I said.

She gave me the look again. I wondered how she got so tough so young.

"So where were you?" Ricci asked again.

"Left them, came back."

"What time was this?"

"Got back around four-thirty."

"Where'd they go? Boston?"

"No," I said.

"So you just came right back," Ricci said.

I didn't answer.

"You're such a lousy liar you're not even gonna try?"

"We went to the Wiltons' compound, the place in the woods," I said.

A pause as that sunk in.

"What'd you find?"

"Cheree Wilson all by herself, two black eyes and bruises everyplace that showed."

"Who? Him?"

I nodded.

"But he wasn't there?"

"Left late last night."

"And now he's—"

"Out there somewhere," I said.

"What were you going to do if you'd found him?"

"Talk to him," I said.

"Were you armed?"

I nodded. "Dangerous out there," I said. "Gotta protect yourself."

"You shoot him, you go to jail," Ricci said. "You kill him, you go for a long time. You'd miss your little girl's entire life."

"I'll miss her if something happens to her."

"Well," Ricci said, "we're not gonna let that happen."

"That's right," I said. "We're not."

She glanced at me, walked to the phone and punched in a number. Waited. "Ricci," she said. "Watcha got?"

She listened, wrote something on the same piece of paper. She thanks whoever it was and hung up. "They do triangulation," she said. "Call made from between three towers, you can time the signal, tell where the phone was in relation to them."

"Where?" I said.

"Here," she said. "Or close by."

"Parked in the woods," I said.

"Except the last two. He was south of here, once south of Rockland, the second time near Brunswick."

"Headed for—"

"Portland?" Ricci said. "Who knows."

Ricci took the bag with Twinnie in it. Said the knife was bound to show something, maybe Twinnie would, too. Standing in the driveway, she said she'd prefer that I not have a loaded rifle on the premises. I said I'd prefer not to have to have a loaded rifle on the premises. She said if I thought they were around, I should lock the doors and call the police and sit tight.

"And then I'll call Clair," I said.

"What's your friend going to do?" Ricci said.

"Outflank them," I said.

She gave me the look. She said she was doing the best she could, that she'd talk to her patrol supervisor, put out a call for Wilton and this Carleton Sirois. Then she asked me for directions to the Wiltons' house, said she wanted to check in with Cheree Wilton.

"Be careful," I said. "She's got a shotgun and, last time I saw her, two rounds of buckshot."

"I'll call first," Ricci said. She drove off, cell phone at her ear. I went back inside, called Roxanne and left another message, this one more to the point. Call me, ASAP. It was 7:45. Where could they be?

I went to the chair. Looked down and saw the box on the floor. I opened it, took out a sheaf of papers. Flipped through, past the poems I'd read, the drawings I'd seen.

I came to a thin bundle of papers, held together by a paper clip. I unclipped them, flipped one open. It was a letter, written in a girl's showy hand, the paper faded and stained.

Syb- Yo, girl. Wassup? Can't believe your gone, all grown up and your own apartment, nobody telling you what to do 24-7. Babe I'm gonna come visit. Will watch TV, eat chips and get fat. I'm gonna be a fat pregnant lady someday. Lizard Lips says hi. She of the forked tongue. She is so forked up. Ha-ha. Yesterday after lunch she got on my case, said she was gonna right me up. I was gonna tell her to @#$#%*&* off but then I *remembered I want to come see you so I gotta behave myself. Hey, did I tell you I'm taking anger management? And doesn't it piss me off! Ha-ha.*

You take care, girl. Hugs!

Amanda

There were five letters from Amanda. The first four were small talk. She had decided to drop printing and switch to floral arranging. Some sort of vocational school? The last one was a terse note, the words slashed onto the paper:

I guess you don't care enough about me to write me back. Either that or your dead and can't. If your dead, sorry. If your not, I hope your happy, blowing me off, hanging out with your new friends. Me, I got the same old same old. It sux to be me.

Your former friend.

Amanda

Why would Sybill be dead? Where was Amanda? A boarding school? Reform school? Who was Lizard Lips and why would she be—

The phone rang and I jumped out of the chair to answer it.

"Hey," I said, my voice bright for Sophie.

"Jack?" was the reply.

"Mandi," I said. "You okay?" Looking over at the papers, I felt like I'd been caught rummaging in her underwear drawer.

"I'm okay, Jack," she said. "But I—"

She paused. "I was hoping maybe I could see you."

"When?" I said.

"What are you doing now?"

"I'm waiting for a call. I really can't leave tonight. Maybe tomorrow?"

"Oh. Okay."

"What's the matter? Other than the obvious?"

She hesitated. I heard the cat crying in the background and Mandi said, away from the phone, "Will you shut up?"

I waited.

"Sorry," Mandi said.

"It's okay."

"I just . . . I know you called. Before."

"Just checking."

"Thanks. I just had to kind of sort things out, you know? Everything's been so crazy, so way out of control. Roger, he was so upset."

"Maybe he'll get some help now," I said.

"But you know he's gonna tell on me, Jack. He's got to. That cop, that detective, he's gonna say, 'How do you know her?' and Roger's gonna have to tell him."

"You're probably right."

"So then I gotta move again and, I don't know, I kinda like it here. It's, like, the nicest place I've ever lived. And you and Roxanne and Clair—"

Silence, but for the cat. "It's not just that," she said. "It's—"

"It's what, Mandi?"

Or Sybill, I thought. Syb. Yo, girl, wassup? Why'd you leave your friends behind?

"There's another problem," she said.

"What's that?"

"You remember Marty?"

"Yeah."

"I don't know. He's kinda, I don't know how to say this, kinda like obsessed with me."

"Seems to be going around," I said.

"Yeah, well—"

"I thought you were afraid of him?"

"I am. 'Cause he's kinda nuts. But he's saying I should come live with him, stop working, he'll set me up good."

"What did you say to him?"

"I said no."

"And he said?"

"Kinda like Roger. Says he can't live without me. Says he's in love with me. Says he'll take me to Puerta Vallarta for two weeks. He has a time share."

"So he's not threatening you?"

A pause. "Not really. More like trying to guilt me."

"If you don't move in with him he'll—"

"Life won't be worth living."

"He didn't seem like that when I talked to him," I said. "Seemed more arrogant and nasty. A bully."

"Maybe that was for your benefit. He was following you. I think he was jealous."

"It's a control thing," I said.

"Now he's saying I'm all he has. His ex-wife is really on his case, I guess, over money. Wants half of everything. Has this lawyer out of Boston, threatening to turn him in to the IRS. He said he'd give her the money, if he could have me, he wouldn't need anything else."

I pictured the black Tahoe, the gold chains. My guess was that you'd have to pry the bling off his cold, dead neck. "What do you think of him?" I said.

"I think he's totally creepy."

"So tell him that. Tell him to get lost. Tell him to leave you alone."

A long pause this time. The cat crying.

"Or else what, Jack?" Mandi said.

Sure, it was tough for her to call the cops. But what was it Marty had said? A tiger by the tail. And not just in the sack. Seemed like a tiger would scratch his eyes out. A woman who would beat somebody with a crutch, stick a guy with a knife—why was she letting this guy push her around?

"Maybe you could talk to him again," Mandi said. "He listened to you."

I sighed, silently. "I don't know, Mandi. I have my own stuff going on."

"Is that guy still bothering Roxanne?"

"Yes," I said. "More than ever."

"The police still aren't doing anything about it?"

"They want to now but they can't find him."

"Jeez."

"Yeah. He assaulted his wife, killed his own dogs. He's really lost it."

"I'm sorry, Jack. If I could help you and Roxanne in any way. I mean, maybe if you needed somebody to watch Sophie for a little while. You could bring her over here."

I hesitated and she caught it.

"Maybe that's not a good idea, me being who I am."

"No," I said. "It's just that, well, I don't think Roxanne wants to be away from Sophie right now. Not for a minute."

"I understand," Mandi said, but her tone was chastened.

"It's not that," I said.

"Sure."

"Well, take care, Jack," Mandi said.

"Listen," I said. "So Marty isn't threatening you?"

"No, he's more threatening himself. But then he says he can't stand to see me with anyone else."

"If he can't have you, nobody can?"

"He doesn't say that but—"

"Where's he staying?" I said.

"Little place called Bayside," Mandi said. "He took me there once to see his house. It's this cottage, looks out on the ocean from across the road. This name is on the sign by the driveway says Smith. He's renting."

Bayside was an enclave just south of Belfast. I remembered cottages and a little yacht club.

"If I'm out that way, maybe," I said.

"Thanks, Jack."

"So just don't answer the phone."

"Okay."

"How you getting around?"

"A little better," she said, her voice oddly brighter. "One step at a time."

29

Roxanne called at quarter to nine. She said she was fine—a relative term—and that Sophie wanted to talk to me. There was a clatter and Sophie came on.

"Daddy," Sophie said.

"What, honey?" I said.

"We went swimming in a big, big pool."

"Really. Was it deep?"

"Yes. Deep like the ocean."

"Were there fish?"

She paused, thinking. "Yes, but you couldn't see them 'cause they were at the bottom. With the octopuses."

"Wow."

"And daddy."

"What?"

"Then we went to this place and had a dinner and it was fancy."

"Oooh," I said. "Did you get dressed up?"

"I wore my yellow dress. And my sandals."

"You must have looked beautiful."

"Yes. And I had macaroni. And there were lots of forks."

"Very nice," I said.

"And two spoons for the ice cream."

"What kind?"

"Chocolate with cookies in it."

"Yum."

"Yes. And now we're going to watch TV right in our bed. There's two beds but I'm going to sleep with mommy."

"I wish I could be there to watch TV with you."

"Maybe you could come," Sophie said.

"I'd love to but I can't tonight," I said. "But you have fun with your mom."

"You want to talk to her?"

The phone clattered, Sophie saying, "Daddy wants to talk to you." Then there was a smooching sound as she kissed the phone goodbye. Then Roxanne.

"Hi," she said.

"I've been trying to call you," I said.

"I know. Just got your message. Cell doesn't work in the room."

"Where are you?"

"Using the room phone."

"Sophie sounds happy."

"For now," Roxanne said. "Until the excitement wears off. How are things there all by yourself? Quiet?"

"Well—"

"What, Jack?"

"Sophie right there?"

"She's playing with the mini-bar."

"And you call yourself a good mother," I said.

"What is it?" Roxanne said.

"Don't worry, because everything is okay."

"Tell me," she said.

I did. The chicken. The doll. The knife. The phone calls.

"Portland?" she said.

"They have no idea. Just that he's driving south. Could be headed for Key West for all they know."

There was no reply and I could picture Roxanne closing her eyes, trying not to show Sophie anything.

I told Roxanne about Trooper Ricci, how when she saw the doll she seemed to get fired up for the first time. And after a deep breath, I told her about going to the Wiltons' house.

"Oh, Jack."

"At that point, Ricci hadn't even called back. I had to do something."

"But Jack, what if—"

"Clair was there. And anyway, now we know who the second guy is, the guy with the Jeep in the woods. They'll pick them up soon, I'm sure."

"But if he'd been there—"

"And he'd pointed a gun at me? I would have killed him."

I heard her swallow.

"I can't just sit here and let him come after you and Sophie. I can't."

"I know, but it puts me in such a difficult place."

"This is a difficult place, honey," I said. "No matter how you look at it."

"So we shouldn't come back?"

"Let's talk tomorrow morning."

"I've got to call the office. God, this is insane. And it's so hard with her right with me."

"I know," I said.

"So nothing else I need to know?" she said.

"Just Mandi, she called and—"

I heard water running and Roxanne called, "I'll do that, honey." To me she said, "I've got to go. I'm going to give her a bath, get her in bed. I don't want her all turned around, up all night."

"Okay."

"Was there something else? Mandi, you said?"

"It can wait," I said. "You take care of yourself."

"You, too. And remember I love you."

"I love you, too. You know what they say. This, too"

"—shall pass," Roxanne said. "But how, Jack? And when? I don't like not knowing, Jack. I don't like it at all."

Ten o'clock. Full dark, inside the house and out. I sat in the big chair with a cup of tea and the loaded rifle. My eyes had adjusted to the darkness so instead of blackness, I saw shadows. The house, the yard, the woods.

The shadows were alive with sounds: crickets, night birds, rustling at the edge of the trees as voles dug in the moldering leaves.

I got up and went to the screened door and listened, heard a faint thud, then scratching. A flying squirrel had landed on a birch by the bird feeders. The squirrel launched again, a pale flicker like a bird flashing through headlights. I heard it hit the feeder, the seeds showering down. I eased the screen door open, moved slowly out onto the deck.

When my shoe touched the wood, the squirrel leapt, climbed the birch trunk, and was gone.

I waited. Listened. Catalogued the sounds, filing them under categories of things you should hear in the woods at night. And then there was the sound of a step, the faint scritch of a shoe on gravel. The driveway.

I eased down the steps, moved across the grass to the trees at the rear of the yard. I flicked the safety off, moved to my right, then toward the driveway, staying at the edge of the woods. Peering into the shadows, I took two steps. Waited. Another two steps. Waited again.

Another sound, something hitting the hard-packed gravel in front of the garage. A kicked stone?

I let my breath move in and out slowly, calming myself. Put my feet down carefully, feeling for branches or twigs. Beside the garage, I paused. Listened. Heard a barred owl in the woods.

Then a soft rustle. Fabric rubbing. Behind me.

"It's me," Clair said.

I exhaled slowly. He stepped up beside me, a different shotgun cradled in his arms, this one all flat black, from barrel to butt. He was wearing a dark camouflage sweatshirt, black fatigue pants.

"Was that you out front?"

"Just checking."

"Good thing I didn't shoot you," I said.

"You learned to shoot?" Clair said.

"Sometimes you get lucky."

"Speaking of which, you see the flying squirrel?"

"Yeah. Raiding the birdfeeder."

"Always figure seeing something like that is a gift," he said.

"See anything else?"

"Fox in the ditch out front. Other than that it's clear," Clair said.

"Phone trace shows them nearly out of the state, anyway," I said.

"No. The phone trace shows the phone nearly out of state. Doesn't tell you who's holding it."

"True," I said. "Guess we'll know when they get picked up, some Georgia highway patrolman."

"Or he's out in your woods with night-vision goggles right now."

"This isn't gonna help me sleep," I said. "Been a long day."

"Take a couple of hours," Clair said. "I'll stand watch."

"They've got that armload of guns. I could stay with you."

"Rather know that anything I hear out here isn't you," Clair said.

"You think they'll play night sniper?" I said.

Clair thought for a couple of moments, then shook his head. "I picture more like a gallon of gas, pour it on the house, use a cigarette for a fuse."

"I'll sleep well," I said.

"Like a baby," Clair said.

I turned, walked to the house, eased the screen door open, and squeezed back in. I sat back down in the big chair, leaned the rifle against the arm. Watched the darkness for a minute, two.

Sleep? In a while.

I went to the kitchen and put the kettle on. When the water boiled, I made tea and a peanut butter sandwich. I sat at the kitchen table and reached for my notebooks.

My hurried scribbling from the first conversation with Mandi, sitting on the bench. Seemed like a lifetime ago but it had only been a week. A beating ago. A bunch of threats. A guy waving a pistol. Another guy saying he had to have her.

I flipped through the pages. A quick story. "Ha," I said, and then I came to the page with the VIN from Mandi's car.

I considered it, got up, and went to the counter for my wallet. I took out a credit card, came back and sat back down. Reached for my laptop and powered it up. Waited for the browser, then found the CarFax page.

I signed up for 30 days for 35 bucks. I carefully typed the number into the search box. I waited while the wheel went around. Looked out at the woods, a black shadowed wall. Looked back as a list appeared.

The car had been last registered in Maine seven months ago, back in January. Sybill Lasell, 14 Ellsworth St., Portland. Eleven months before that, February, Sybill Lasell, this time living at 138 Beach St., Old Orchard Beach, south of Portland. A year prior to Old Orchard, a Sybill LaSalle had registered the car in Seabrook, New Hampshire: 544 Beach Road, No. 2, a cheap off-season rental? Two months before New Hampshire, the car had been registered to Jane Aire, 879 Ocean Rd., #4A, Revere, Massachusetts. The list ran out in Worcester, Massachusetts.: Marie Delgado, 1123 Boston Highway.

Jane Aire? A memento of high school English? Even if she wasn't Jane, and that was a previous owner, Mandi was working her way up the coast.

I printed the page. Stared at it some more in the blue glow of the computer. It told me what I already knew: that she was a transient. Told me what I suspected: that her name was Sybill but it wasn't necessarily Lasell or LaSalle. A plan formed: call the city tax offices, get the names of the owners of those properties. Call and inquire about Sybill: "I'm a landlord in Portland, Maine. Sybill Lasell gave me your name as a reference. . ."

A half-hour of my Clair patrol time had passed. I shut the computer down and looked out at the darkness. Shapes formed, nothing moving. I felt drowsy, and, as Sybill circled, I reached for the gun, leaning against the chair. I made sure the safety was on and then leaned back, closed my eyes, and slept.

A police radio. A woman's voice calling numbers. Three-twelve to three twenty-three. A man answering, more numbers. Then, "Augusta, I'll be off." It played, background music to my dream, and then I needed to answer them but I had no radio. I was running from room to room looking for—

I sat up. It was light. The radio noise was still there. A motor idling. It came to me in a rush: there was a cop out front. I bolted from the chair, thinking of Roxanne and Sophie, that something had happened. I ran to the side door, unlocked it and yanked it open.

Just as Raven lifted his hand to knock.

"Morning, Mr. McMorrow," he said.

"Hi," I said.

"Sorry to bother you."

"It's no bother," I said.

"The A.D.A. wants to see you."

I looked at my watch. It was 7:10, sunny but still cool. Raven wore a blue cotton jacket over his blue polo shirt. A blue unmarked cruiser waited behind him like a faithful horse.

"Your prosecutor works early," I said.

"She," Raven said. "Ms. Tibbetts. And yes, she does. Young and ambitious."

"Good thing for a prosecutor."

"Sometimes."

"You could have just called."

"That's okay. Pretty morning for a ride in the country. Nice little hideaway you got here."

"Thanks," I said. "You want to come in? I can make coffee."

"Rain check on that one, Mr. McMorrow. Ms. Tibbetts, she has court at nine and she wants to talk to you before that."

"You gonna drive me in?" I said.

"Sure," Raven said. "We can talk."

"You'll have to drive me back."

"That's okay," he said, smiling. "We can talk some more."

He waited outside as I brushed my teeth, put on a clean T-shirt, a denim shirt over it. I grabbed a notebook and pen from the desk, my phone from the counter. As I turned away, I saw a note stuck to the outside of the sliding glass door to the deck. I opened it, pulled it off.

0420 hours. Sun coming up. Gone home. Quiet night.

Clair.

Outside, Raven was standing by the cruiser looking up at the trees.

"Know what just flew over?" he said.

"No," I said.

"My namesake. I always consider that a good omen."

"I hope you're right," I said.

He gave the sky a last glance.

"Maybe they'll pick up those two numbskulls," he said, opening the driver's door, climbing in. I got in on the passenger side, Raven grabbing a notebook out from under me.

"You heard about them?"

"Talk around P.D. this morning. Anything with kids, you know? And this one, the state worker, too, the wife assaulted. I heard there was a knife stuck in a doll."

"That's right," I said.

Raven backed out and pulled away fast. "People are twisted," he said.

"Yes," I said, and after a moment or two I asked, "What do you think of the way the state police are handling it?"

"By the book," Raven said, one hand on the steering wheel, the other rubbing his jaw. "The way they teach 'em now, at the academy." We took the left onto the Dump Road and Raven hit the gas, accelerating. The radio squawked, the roadside trees were a blur. "Of course, doing things by the book—that's not always a good thing."

"No," I said.

"'Cause people don't really fit into a textbook."

I didn't answer. We swung onto the paved road and turned east. There was a car up ahead, a Chevy chugging along, an old country couple sagging into the seat. Raven hit the lights and the car pulled off so we could pass.

"Like this guy, Roger," he said, half to himself.

"He's obsessed with her," I said. "My expert assessment."

"And Miss Lasell. Beats the guy's head in, but he did come to her apartment with a gun. Did it to save you, but then, if she hadn't gotten this guy into such a lather, none of it would have happened."

I shrugged.

"Real femme fatale," Raven said.

"You know who really scares her?" I said. "Marty, the ex-cop."

Raven touched the brakes, a curve ahead.

"Where was he a cop?" I said.

"You could ask him," Raven said.

"I don't think he likes me."

"See? Love triangle number two. Kinda like geometry. Miss Lasell is the common point in two intersecting triangles."

"I'm not her lover, more her babysitter."

"Some people combine the two," Raven said.

"Not me."

"If you say so," he said.

"I know so," I said. "And I think Marty's crooked as hell. Retire or get drummed out?"

We were climbing a hill, passing a tractor trailer filled with wood chips. They flew out of the back of the truck like confetti. A parade of one.

"You know we caught a guy, he had a compartment built in a trailer like that, under the chips," Raven said, one hand on the wheel, arm flung over the seat back. "Hauling a hundred and fifty pounds of pot in from New Brunswick every week."

"Retire or drummed out?" I said again.

"Guy was making five grand a week just for bringing the stuff across. Only got caught 'cause the truck breaks down, trooper stops to help, happens to have a drug dog in the car. Dog goes flippin' crazy. Murphy's Law."

I waited.

"Retire or—"

"Martin B. Callahan," Raven said. "Mass. corrections."

"Really," I said.

"Google's a wonderful thing," Raven said.

30

The assistant district attorney had an office in the courthouse, the same place where Cheree Wilton had shown up for her hearing, her husband waiting in the truck outside. We stood for a few minutes in a hallway with a water cooler but no cups, and a vending machine that sold bright orange cheese and crackers. Raven eyed it for a minute, then walked over and dropped in two quarters. The crackers fell down and he picked them out, tore the cellophane open and offered me one.

I declined. He ate one in two bites, was halfway through the second when the door opened. A very young woman in a dark blazer, slacks, and pumps stepped out and said, "Come in," and turned away. We followed.

By the time we got inside, she was behind her desk, which took up most of the cramped office. She had dark-rimmed glasses and reddish permed hair that fell in long ringlets. Her hands were on the desk. They were small, like a little kid's.

"Sandra Tibbetts," she said. "I'm assistant district attorney."

I glanced at the wall to her left: a framed diploma said University of Maine Law School.

"Jack McMorrow," I said.

"The reporter," she said.

"That's right."

"Except you don't write for any papers around here," she said.

"Not usually."

"They're crappy papers, anyway," she said.

"I'm sure they're doing the best they can," I said.

There were two chairs in front of the desk. Ms. Tibbets remained standing so we did, too. She looked at me like I was a math problem she had to figure out. Nobody smiled.

"You have a lawyer?"

I shook my head. "I didn't think witnesses needed one."

"Most times not," Tibbets said. "We can get you one if you want."

I shook my head again.

"Okay, then let's get right to it. I've got to be in court."

I nodded.

"Tell me what happened."

I did, the abridged version. She listened, didn't blink. Her eyes were green. She had more mascara on the left than the right. Maybe she hadn't been wearing makeup that long.

Raven looked at me, then at her, then back at me, enjoying the show. Then it was her turn. "When you walked in, what did you think Mr. Wilde was going to do?"

"I didn't know that was his name," I said.

"Roger David Wilde," Tibbets said. "The third."

"Huh," I said.

"So he had the gun on his own temple?"

"Right. Like he was going to shoot himself. I think he was distraught."

"But he turned and shot at you?"

"Right. I startled him. He just whirled around and fired. Pretty wildly."

"He wasn't trying to harm himself at that point?"

"No. He just sort of blasted away. I don't think he'd had much experience with guns and an old forty-five like that, has a bit of a kick. He missed by a lot."

"So when you tackled him—"

"Pretty tough for a reporter," Raven said.

Tibbets looked at him, obviously annoyed at the interruption, then back at me.

"I tried to get the gun away. We struggled for it."

"Was he trying to harm himself at that point?"

I considered it. "He was trying to get loose. I don't know what he would have done if he had."

"Did he point the gun at Miss Lasell?"

"No."

"Did he point the gun at you?"

"Eventually. I had his wrist and we were sort of arm wrestling."

"Did he say anything? I'm gonna kill you?"

"Never said a word. You know how it is in situations like that. Just a lot of grunting."

"And you're saying you were still struggling when Miss Lasell intervened?"

"Yes."

"And then what happened?"

"I told you. She hit him in the head with her crutch. More than once. It became clear that he was disabled."

"Somebody gave him a damned good whack," Raven said.

"Somebody?" I said.

"He says he can't remember anything," Tibbets said. "Remembers walking in there to talk to her. Next thing he knows he's in the hospital."

"With his head wrapped up like a mummy," Raven said. "You know they let him out this morning? Christ, you have open heart surgery now, you're home before lunchtime."

She gave him another look.

"What are you getting at here?" I said.

"Trying to get at the truth," Tibbets said.

She had her hands folded on the desk in front of her, like she was playing the teacher in a high school play. *Now class . . .*

"I told you the truth," I said. "What did Miss Lasell say?"

They both looked at me, hesitated.

"She says she clubbed him when he was on the floor," Tibbets said.

"Well, there you go," I said. "He came in with the gun. It was self-defense no matter what. Fact is she may have saved my life."

"Which brings me to another question," Tibbets said.

I waited.

"What is your relationship with the victim?"

"Acquaintance," I said.

"Is she your lover?" Tibbets said, the word rolling off her tongue like we were in a soap opera.

"You've got to be kidding."

"Was she Roger's lover, then?" she said. "I mean, guys don't usually try to kill each other over a girl who's just a friend."

I didn't answer, Tibbets leaned forward, her child's hands on the wooden desktop. "Let's get real here, Mr. McMorrow," she said. "Somebody was screwing her."

"What would your parents say if they heard that dirty talk?" I said.

"People assaulted," Tibbets went on. "Shots fired on Main Street in Belfast, Maine. Men coming and going."

I looked at her. I said nothing.

"She's a prostitute, isn't she, Mr. McMorrow?" Tibbets said. "A call girl."

I didn't answer.

"My first guess was a drug dealer," Raven said.

"Or both," Tibbets said. "You're protecting her or she's protecting you. Or you're protecting each other. You use drugs?"

"Ballantine Ale," I said. "But I have it under control."

"You do have a heck of a reputation, McMorrow," Raven said. "Play it close the edge. Have for years. Well, you don't play it that way around here."

"Ain't room in this town for the both of us?" I said.

"Reckless conduct with a firearm," Tibbets said.

"That's all you can get him for?" I said.

"No, that's both of you," she said. "He says you got the gun away from him, fired one shot, over his head and into the ceiling."

"I thought you said he couldn't remember."

"It's coming back to him," she said. "In pieces."

"He's lying. I tried to get it away from him but I couldn't. He still had it when she clocked him."

"He says he got it back off of you," Tibbets said.

"Your prints are on the gun," Raven said.

"I picked it up," I said.

"You tell us what's really going on in that apartment and we let you walk," Tibbets said.

"Let me walk?" I said.

"I think you don't want to tell us 'cause your wife will go ballistic, she finds out you were having sexual relations with that young girl," Raven said.

"She knows better," I said.

"So you're not going to cooperate?" Tibbets said.

"I told you what happened."

"You told me what happened in that exact instance, or at least one version of it. You didn't tell me what was really going on."

I looked at her.

"Grand jury sits Wednesday," she said.

"You know the old saying," Raven said. "You can indict a ham sandwich."

"I've got bigger problems than this," I said.

"And I've got to be in court," Tibbets said.

She was gathering up folders and legal pads from her desk. "Indictments go in the newspaper," she said. "Heck of an embarrassment for your family, especially for a spouse with a job that's in the public eye. Not exactly a career move for you, either."

"My career moves were a long time ago," I said.

"Think the *New York Times* will like their reporter on the front page? Mixed up in this? 'Cause you know they'll hear all about it. Amazing thing, the Internet." She started for the door. "Of course, maybe you don't need to work. Maybe you have money."

"A lot of that around here these days," Raven said.

I thought of Roxanne. *"I don't want to do this anymore."*

Tibbets was out the door, her heels clicking down the corridor. Her perfume wafted to me and hung in the air. Raven popped another orange cheese cracker into his mouth, like he'd been waiting for her to leave to eat.

"She's young, but she's tough," he said.

"Watches way too much *Law & Order*," I said.

Raven smiled as we turned to the door. "Know what I like about that show?" he said. "The way the people get squeezed and squeezed."

I looked at him.

"You know what else?" Raven said.

"No, what?"

"It's starting to look like a boat," he said. "For a while it was just a lot of pieces of wood."

31

I told Raven I'd find my own way home. He said, "Shoot yourself," and ambled over to his cruiser and drove off. I started walking up the street toward the downtown, my stomach growling.

There was a corner café just past the newspaper and I needed a cup of tea. As I walked by the newspaper office I saw the front page taped to the window: "Man Injured in Main Street Fracas," the headline said. The story was above the fold, just under a story about the lobster catch. It was down. One photo showed Mandi being led by the arm out of the front door of her building by a cop, her sweatshirt hood down over her face.

"You go girl," I said to myself. "Take you on a perp walk, the bastards."

I stepped into the newspaper office and grabbed a paper off the pile on the counter. Dropping a dollar bill, I walked out into the cool summer morning.

So the word was out. That was why Tibbets was so hot to charge Mandi with something that lived up to her reputation. This probably meant Mandi would be moving on, no way to live on Main Street with the scarlet W on her chest. Her next move would have to be way up the coast.

If they let her go.

At the corner, I stepped into the café. There was canned classical music playing. Pachelbel. I ordered a tea to go, and the woman behind the counter—green apron, white blouse— looked at me closely before turning away. She poured the water into a paper cup, slid the tea bag and lid across the counter.

"You were in the paper," she said.

"Is that right?" I said.

I held the paper out. She took it from me, flipped it over. There, on the back page, was the jump to the shooting story. They'd lifted a headshot of me off the Web. The caption said, "Jack McMorrow, of Prosperity, uninjured in Main Street shooting.""People are saying it's one of those crack houses," she said.

"That's not true," I said.

"I didn't say it was true," she said, swirling a towel over the wooden counter. "I just said it was what people were saying."

"I'm sure they are," I said. "Do you know the young woman who lives there?"

"I've seen her around," she said. "The sad girl, right?"

I looked at her.

"Yeah. The sad girl," I said. "She's not a crackhead. You can spread that around town. Say you heard it from a reliable source."

She looked at me warily, said, "Right."

I took my tea, chose one of the empty tables and sat. As I started the story, the door swung open, bell ding-a-linging. A woman strode in: fifty-ish and silver-blonde, tight khaki skirt, clingy sweater, heeled sandals. Her jaw was clenched, face pink, and she waved the rolled-up paper like a club. She went directly to the counter, thumped the paper down.

"Coffee, Charlotte," she said. "I have to vent. I want to know why don't these people just go back under whatever rock they crawled out from under."

Charlotte put down a mug, poured. Glanced over at me.

"I don't know, Jackie," she said.

"This is our town," Jackie said. "We work out butts off to make it a good place to do business, for people to come and retire, and then these lowlifes come in. You know this story just cost me a big sale?" she said. "Dentist from Pennsylvania. Just divorced. Very good looking, too. Like an older George Clooney. Looking for vacation property, this close to making an offer on a beautiful contemporary, bay view, wrap-around porches, granite counter tops. Fully modernized. He saw that story in the paper, said maybe he'd go with a house in Camden."

Charlotte shook her head.

"We don't need druggies and whores on Main Street," Jackie said. Charlotte looked toward me. Jackie turned. Her face was flushed with anger, her cleavage, too. It appeared to me she'd had some work done.

"Hey, aren't you the one—?"

She started unrolling the paper. I flipped money onto the table, got up, and started for the door. Then stopped. Looked at them as they stared.

"Let she who is without sin cast the first stone," I said, and pushed through the screen door, let it slam shut behind me. The bell jingled.

I took a right toward the harbor. There were other people on the sidewalk and I walked slowly, feeling or imagining their scrutiny. So the small-town paper had tabloid instincts. My headshot; Mandi's covered face.

I glanced up and across the street as I passed the apartment.

Sure enough, Lulu was in the window. She was surveying the people, the slowly moving traffic. Nothing bothers a cat. But I wondered about Mandi, the last phone call, the odd, upbeat quality in her voice. What was she thinking?

I'm on the front page of the local paper as the focal point of a brawl where shots were fired. Word is getting out that I'm a prostitute and drug addict. But then again, I broke a crutch over a guy's head, saved somebody's life. Mandi, the heroine.

I continued on.

And there was the black Tahoe, parked fifty yards down, Mandi's side of the street. There was nobody in it, no Marty in sight. I turned back and the cat was still there. I kept walking, touched the hood as I passed. It was cold.

The town was pitched toward the harbor, everything flowing down to the bay. I walked down the street, skirting summer people standing in front of the shop windows in clumps. At the end of the street, I crossed the little park, took out my phone. I sat on a bench, right next to the one where I'd first interviewed Mandi. Sipping the tea, I opened the paper. Went right to it.

Police called to a building on Main Street after neighbors reported hearing shots fired. Three people were found in the second floor apartment, including one with a head injury. A firearm was recovered. The three people were: Sybill Lasell, 25, of Belfast, the occupant of the apartment; Roger Wilde III, 32, of Annapolis, Maryland; Jack McMorrow, 40, of Prosperity. Police said Wilde was injured but it did not appear he had been shot. He was taken to the Waldo County Memorial Hospital for treatment. The reporter called the hospital later that day and Wilde had been released. The investigation is ongoing, said Detective Brian Raven.

I put the paper down.

No mention of an escort service. No hint that Roger had gone up there and threatened to blow his head off. Nothing about who had fired the gun, about Mandi beating Roger with the crutch.

What kind of newspaper was this?

I looked out at the harbor. The breeze was brisk out of the northeast, the remnant of the rain that had passed, and the boats were turned stern-first toward the docks. They swung on their moorings and a big two-masted sailboat eased out of the harbor under power. I watched it absently, then caught sight of a guy moving around in the cockpit of a powerboat as the sailboat passed by.

Something white on his head. Not a hat—a bandage.

Roger.

The boat was moored in the middle of the harbor, to the south toward the bay. It was big, forty feet or more, a classic type, all varnished above the white hull, the kind of boat that required a lot of work. There was a white dinghy tied at the stern.

I got up from the bench and walked to the railing above the floats. Leaning there, I watched him. He sat in the upper cockpit, where there were controls atop the boat. He was facing the harbor front, wearing sunglasses. I felt like he was looking right at me. And then he moved slowly down a ladder, into the cabin and out of sight.

Dropping the tea and the paper in a trash can, I walked to the gate that led down the ramp to the floats. A sign said, "Only Boat Owners And Their Guests Beyond This Point." I went through, anyway, walked down the sandpaper ramp to the floats. There were dinghies upside down on the deck, a few tied up alongside. Some had small outboard motors. One was beat-up, with an empty Budweiser can floating in the rainwater. That one had oars.

I undid the rope, stepped over the bow, felt the water in my shoes as it sloshed toward me. I sat on the seat, put the oars in the locks, and pushed away from the float. The water sloshed back to the stern as I spun the boat around and started to row.

Crossing the harbor toward Roger's boat, I turned to navigate between the moorings. Halfway there, I looked over my shoulder. I could see the name on the stern now: *Jolly Roger*, Chesapeake Bay. I changed course, headed just north of his boat. I passed it, seventy-five yards off to my left. There was no sign of him, just the dinghy swinging gently in the wind. When I was upwind and fifty yards off, I stopped rowing. The boat slowed and then began to blow and I touched an oar to the water to steer it.

In a couple of minutes I was drifting past his bow. I could see the helm through the big windows, the others covered by blue curtains that matched the canvas awning over the sitting area at the stern. And then I was alongside, feathering the oars to keep from banging his hull. As I closed on the stern, I pulled the oars in and laid them in the bottom of the dinghy, reached up and grabbed the gunwale with one hand. I held the big boat off, stood and swung up and over and in. I reached back and grabbed the dinghy's line as it started to drift away, tied the rope to a davit.

Stood and waited.

There was a weather radio playing somewhere inside the boat, a robot voice talking about low pressure, waves three to five feet. I walked under the awning and looked in. There were canvas director's chairs, in matching blue. Beyond that a little doorway that led below. I took two steps closer, waited for my eyes to adjust. Bent over and stepped down and in.

"Freeze," a voice said.

He was sitting on the edge of a bunk to my right, an orange flare gun in his right hand, pointed at my chest. His face was pale; up close, the bandage was held on with flesh-colored tape.

"You," he said.

"Roger," I said. "Good to see you again. How you feeling?"

"What do you want?" he said.

"I'm feeling pretty good, too, considering some dipshit took a shot at me."

"I didn't mean to. I mean, I didn't know I was going to do that. It just sort of happened."

"I'm glad you just sort of missed," I said.

I looked around. "Okay. Now put that thing down before you burn this tub to the waterline. And after that, I just want to talk."

"About what?"

"Mandi."

"I don't want to hear it," he said, the flare gun still pointed at me.

"The gun," I said. "I'm not here to fight."

He looked at it, put his hand, with the gun, down on the bunk cushion.

"What don't you want to hear?" I said.

Roger looked at me, then looked away. It was dark in the cabin but I could see he was wearing the same clothes from the apartment, blood stains on his shirt. This khaki shorts were rumpled his feet were bare.

"Any of it," Roger said.

"Any of what?"

"What she does. Why you come see her."

"I'm a reporter," I said. "I came to her to write a story. That's it."

"She went to live with you," he said.

"She stayed with a friend down the road because she couldn't do stairs. His sixty-year-old wife was there, too. I'm happily married. I have a child."

"She likes you," he said, his tone flat and discouraged. "Why didn't you tell her to stop doing this?"

"I told her she could do something else."

"She doesn't have to do anything," Roger said. "I have money. Lots of money. She'd never have to work again."

"Huh," I said. "Nice boat."

"My great-grandfather had it built in 1938. In East Boothbay. Brought it down to the Chesapeake."

"He was Roger, too?"

"Yeah, but he wasn't jolly. My father wasn't, either."

"You're not exactly a barrel of laughs yourself. You work at all?"

"No, not really. I mean, I work on the boat. My sister and I have the house in Delaware. That needs attention sometimes. And there's another house in Georgia, on the coast. We inherited it from my father, who inherited it from my grandfather."

"Was that your grandfather's gun? The forty-five?"

He hesitated, looked down. "The gun came with the boat. The police took it. I'm actually sorry about that."

"That you lost the gun?"

"No, that I shot at you. I thank God I didn't hit you."

He said it like he'd swerved his car and missed a deer.

"Me, too," I said. "Do you know the prosecutor is saying you said I took a shot at you?"

He looked frightened. "No, no, no," Roger said, shaking his head. "I told them I couldn't remember much. Still can't. This pain stuff, I'm still in sort of a fog. They said, 'Could McMorrow have taken the gun and shot at you?' I said, 'I suppose. But I can't remember.'"

"Gotcha," I said. "They're fishing."

"I'd ask Mandi, but I'm not supposed to talk to her. Doesn't matter 'cause she won't talk to me anyway," he said.

"Since when?"

"Since I told her I loved her."

"Maybe you should have eased into it."

"But it's true," Roger said. "I've never met anyone like her. She seems to know things."

"Like what?"

"Lots of things. Like she knows me. She can tell what I'm thinking, what I'm feeling. I know we're meant to be together. When we were dating, I mean, it was so easy."

I considered him. A nice-enough looking guy, but something soft about him, naïve. Kind of hapless. A bit of a doofus.

"You took her to the amusement park?"

"She'd never been to one. Can you believe that? I mean, you get talking to her, there's all these things she hasn't done. Never swam in the ocean. Never been on a boat. Never been to New York City. I told her we'd spend a week, a month. Stay at the Carlisle. It's where I always stayed with mom and dad. I said we could see a show every night. She could go shopping. She likes clothes. I told her we could go to Paris or London. Here's another one, for you. She's never flown on a plane. Not ever."

He looked at me, incredulous.

"There are a lot of people who haven't flown," I said. "Maybe she grew up poor."

"I don't know how she grew up. 'Cause she never talks about herself. If I ask she changes the subject. When we were out, she mostly just talked about me. Like she was interested."

A hundred bucks an hour interested, I thought.

"I mean, other women, it's just so much work."

"Roger," I said. "Did you beat her up? Last week?"

"God, no. I wouldn't touch her. I wouldn't even yell at her. I mean, Jack—if you don't mind me calling you that—Jack, I love her totally."

"No hard feelings about her hitting you on the head?"

"Of course not. She saved me from myself. She saved my life."

That makes two of us, I thought.

A motor started up somewhere near us. There was the sound of an outboard, approaching, then receding. The boat rocked gently. Roger looked down at the flare gun like he'd forgotten it was there. He pushed it away.

"So who beat her up, Roger?"

He looked down at his pudgy bare feet. Wiggled his toes. Took a deep breath. "The guy from Massachusetts," he said.

"Marty?"

"I don't know. That's all she said. She said he was a Masshole. She said he hit her because she wouldn't do something."

I left that alone. I started to turn to go but Roger said, "Wait," like he wanted company.

"I wonder, I mean, when she's sleeping. Have you heard what she says?"

"No," I said. "I haven't seen her asleep."

"She comes out here, I don't know what it is. The motion of the boat or something, but she's out cold. And then she talks. She says the same thing. She says, 'I'm sorry, Hildie.' Or Hiltie. Hard to tell. But she says it over and over. And then gives out this crying sound."

"Did you ask her?"

"I did. It was right here, right before I told her I loved her. She just said she had to go. So I got the 'I love you' part out and she never said a word back. And I rowed her in and she didn't talk the whole time and then she walked up the ramp and that was it."

"Just like that?"

"Yeah. So—"

He hesitated. "So you think you could give her a message?"

"I guess."

"Tell her I really do love her, I still do, and I'd like to talk to her."

"Okay. And you do something for me, okay Roger?"

"What?" he said.

"We never had this conversation, if the cops ever ask you."

"Okay."

"They might get the wrong idea."

"Right."

"Deal then?" I said.

I held out my hand and he took it and we shook on it.

"Deal," he said, smiling like I'd picked him for the team.

"I'm glad I didn't kill you, too," I said.

"Thanks," Roger said.

I started to leave again and again he said, "Wait."

I did, standing at the hatchway, looking back into the darkness.

"You know the saddest thing?" he said.

"What?" I said.

"When she got beat up?"

"Yeah?"

"She said she deserved it."

That was sad and it made two things on which we agreed.

"But she doesn't," Roger said.

That made three.

32

I called a taxi and asked to be picked up on Main Street, outside Momma's Pizza. They said it would be twenty minutes. I called Roxanne and got voice mail, left a message asking her to call. I waited a minute and she didn't, so I circled the block.

The Tahoe was still in the same spot, but Lulu the cat was gone, her window closed and the curtains drawn. I walked around back and saw the Camry still parked in the lot. Circling back to Main Street, I came around the corner—and saw Mandi and Marty walking down the block.

He had her by the arm and she was limping. He was carrying a small bag. I broke into a trot.

They stopped at the Tahoe. He opened the door for her and she got in. He hurried around to the driver's side, got in and started to back out. Traffic was steady and he waited for cars to pass. I came up to the passenger side, saw Mandi staring straight ahead.

I knocked and she started, turned to me. Her eyes were swollen and red, even under the fading purple bruise. I tried the door but it was locked. Mandi fiddled with the window and Marty popped out of the door on the other side, stood and pointed at me.

"Get away from her," he barked. "She don't need you."

"Where are you taking her?" I said.

"I'm not *taking* her anywhere. I'm getting her outta here so the goddam yokels won't be bothering her. You saw that fucking rag?" "I saw the story."

"She's lucky you didn't get her killed, you and that other fucking wingnut. Oughta lock the both of you up and I told 'em that. Now get the hell outta here. Leave her alone."

"I need to hear it from her."

"She doesn't need—"

The window opened. Mandi looked up at me, her face drawn and pale without the veil of dark window glass.

"Jack," she said. "It's fine."

"Where are you going?"

"Just getting away from this goldfish bowl."

"You could come back to Clair's."

"That's okay, but thanks."

"You sure you're alright with this?"

Mandi hesitated, looking up at me sadly, then nodded.

"You have your phone?"

She tapped the bag on her lap.

"Call me if you need anything. Anything at all."

"Sure," she said. "I will."

"Really. And you know you could come with me right now."

"I know. Thanks." She managed a strained smile. "Thanks, Jack. Thanks for everything. Tell Clair and Mary. And Roxanne and Sophie, too. Give her a hug for me."

"What about the cat?" I said.

The window hummed up.

"Satisfied?" Marty said.

"No," I said.

"Tough shit," he said.

"You hurt her, I'll come after you."

"Make my day, chump," he said, and swung into the seat, jammed the truck into gear and backed out, the tires squealing as he pulled away.

I stood on the sidewalk for a minute, then walked past the apartment and looked up. The cat was back on the windowsill, which told me they weren't going far or that she expected to be back soon. But then why had her goodbye seemed so final?

Crossing the street, I stood on the sidewalk in front of the pizza shop. The phone buzzed in my pocket like a bee.

I took it out, flipped it open.

"Yeah."

There was a rustling, a whispering. I pictured Mandi sneaking a call, saying come get me.

"Daddy."

Sophie's breathless voice, the drama princess.

"Honey," I said. "How are you?"

"Good," she said. "We went to the kid's museum and I got to go in the fire engine and there was this boy, he was bigger than me, and he peed his pants in the space ship."

"Oh-oh."

"Yes. His mamma was really crabby."

"Too bad," I said.

"And we went on this big pirate ship and we played store except it wasn't real money and we're coming home."

"Really. When?"

A clatter, more whispering, then Roxanne.

"Hey," she said.

"You're coming home?"

"On our way."

"Great. What—"

"David called. They picked up Carleton Sirois in Wilmington, North Carolina."

"What about Wilton?"

"He said he put him on a bus for Florida. Their truck broke down and Wilton didn't want to wait."

"What's in Florida? The annual Satan convention?"

"I guess there's a much bigger group than in Maine. He said he got the bus to Tampa."

"They check to see if he got on the bus?" I said.

"Yes. They said it appears he did."

It sunk in. "So he's gone," I said. "For a while."

"We can get back to normal," Roxanne said.

"Great."

"So things must be quiet there."

"Well—"

A pause and Roxanne said, "Where are you now?"

"Belfast," I said.

"Why?"

"It's a long story."

"Everything okay?"

"Yeah. Okay's a good word for it."

"Should we still come back?"

"Yeah," I said. "This has nothing to do with you."

"Let me guess who it does have to do with," Roxanne said.

"I'll see you at home in a couple of hours," I said.

"Will you be alone?"

"Yes," I said.

"That's good," Roxanne said. "I'm tired and I'm not in the mood for company."

"Okay."

"But those two things aren't necessarily related."

"I understand."

"I hope so, Jack," she said. "I sure hope so."

The Belfast taxi, a decommissioned State Police Crown Vic, dropped me at the end of the driveway. I went inside, cleaned up Sophie's room and changed the sheets. If she asked for Twinnie, I'd say I spilled something on her and had to send her to the doll laundry. She'd be back in a few days.

I hoped to hell they didn't cut Twinnie up when they did the doll autopsy.

Back downstairs, I wiped off the counter, hung the towel on the rack. Checked the refrigerator for milk and found a half gallon and three cans of Ballantine. I took one out, went through the study on my way to the deck.

Stopped. Went back and picked up Mandi's bin of papers and walked back to the sliding door. Opened it and stepped out into the sunshine.

"Getting ready to write your memoirs?" Clair said. He was sitting in an Adirondack chair in the corner by the clematis, legs stretched out in front of him, running shoes off. A humming bird flitted above his head.

"More like a biography," I said, moving to the chair next to his, dropping the bin on the deck. "Mandi's."

"She hired you as a ghost writer?"

"Not exactly," I said. I opened the beer, handed it to him.

"A little early?"

"One of those days," I said.

I went back inside for another, came back. Clair had a sheaf of Mandi's papers on his lap and was beginning to read. I opened the beer and watched him. Took a guilty swallow.

"Why'd she give this stuff to you?"

"She didn't," I said. I told him where the papers had come from.

"So she doesn't know," Clair said, putting one poem down, picking up another.

"No," I said.

"No wonder you're drinking in the afternoon."

"That's not the half of it," I said.

I told him about the day: the assistant D.A. and Detective Raven, Roger on the boat; Mandi taking off with Marty; the odd finality of her goodbye.

Clair put another paper down, picked up a drawing of a woman holding a spear above her head, looking down at her own bare belly.

"This girl really hates herself," he said.

"But I'm not sure why," I said. "She's attractive, pretty smart, kind of thoughtful and philosophical, even."

"Read it all?" Clair said.

"No," I said.

"Invasion of privacy?"

"It's what I've done for twenty years. And I'm trying to help her. This may help me figure out how." I took out a stack of papers and notebooks. Clair sipped his beer and started reading. I sat beside him and did the same. When we'd finished our stacks, we switched. In an hour, we looked up.

"The friend who wrote to her," Clair said.

"Amanda," I said. "If you're dead, sorry."

"She couldn't come see her, apparently."

"Stuck with the same old people, while Mandi, or Sybill, was enjoying a new crew."

"What kid writes letters anymore?" Clair said. "They call. Text or E-mail. Leave messages on Facebook or whatever it is."

"I still get letters," I said.

"And I'll bet I can guess from where."

I thought for a moment. "A guy I know in prison, for one," I said.

"Right. Here's what I think. Amanda and Sybill did time together. Sybill got out first."

"She's a loner. Maybe came out and her family was gone."

"Or estranged from her," Clair said. "Moved on."

"What would she have done?" I said.

"Young girl like that? Drugs, maybe. Prostitution to feed a drug habit? Slipped right back into it?"

"I've never seen her have anything at all. Doesn't even smoke. Wine in the apartment but it looks like a tool of her trade."

"Could have kicked drugs inside," Clair said.

"And if she's done time, that would be why she stuck old Carleton without blinking an eye."

"Survival skills."

"And now she goes off with Marty."

"The ex-cop," Clair said.

"No," I said. "Not exactly. Ex-corrections."

There was a pause, all of it sinking in. "Huh," Clair said. "So they'd have that much in common."

"At least," I said.

I put the papers down, got up from my chair and went inside. I looked up the Massachusetts Department of Corrections online, went through the directories. I found the number for human resources, went to the phone and started punching numbers.

I got electronic directories, dialed one and two, now. A recorded voice asked if I knew the party's extension. I stayed on the line. A woman answered, sounded harried.

"This is John Malone," I said. "I'm calling from Maine. I run a security company, JM and Associates, and I'm checking on the job history—"

A click. Ringing. A guy answered, said, "Please hold." I did, listened to country western.

"Yeah," the guy said.

I gave him the pitch. "Hell of a nice guy so I'm sure there's no problem, but we can't make exceptions in the security business. And to whom am I speaking?"

"This is Jacob," he said. "And those requests should be made in writing."

"Oh, Jake," I said. "Do you think you could just check? I need to use him tomorrow," I said. "It's a special detail. The art museum in Rockland, Maine. I really could use someone with his experience."

A deep sigh, like a doctor had told him to take a breath.

"The name?"

"Martin Callahan. Middle initial is B, as in baby."

"D.O.B.?"

"Um, hard to read his writing. The year looks like sixty-six. Or maybe that's a nine."

"Retired recently?"

"A couple of years ago," I said.

Another sigh. The sound of tapping keys.

"It's sixty-six," he said. "First hired in eighty-six. What else you need to know?"

"Oh, just where he worked, which facility. We do some private jail contracting and it sounded like Martin might be pretty versatile."

He cleared his throat. "Three years in Walpole, that's maximum security. Two years in Deer Island. That's minimum, a lot of intake. Then left. Says he went to Plymouth County."

"Which is—"

"Big county jail. Adults and juveniles," he said. "I guess he liked that 'cause he stuck with it right to the end."

"Huh," I said. "Is this facility all male?"

"No, it's both, but it's all women working on the blocks."

"And he said his rank was—shoot, where is it? Hang on a sec. I'll find—"

"Sergeant," he said.

"Which is supervisory?"

"Yeah. He'd be supervising a shift, corrections officers one and two. Those are levels."

"But he'd be among the inmates, not just in an office someplace."

"Oh, no, a sergeant's out there working. Gotta be to keep your finger on the pulse of the facility, know the current climate, be alert to any problems might be bubbling up."

"Would he know the female inmates?" I said.

"Sure. Not as well as the female officers, maybe, but yeah. What're you securing, anyway? A girls' school?"

"Yeah," I said. "Kind of like to have the right guy for the job."

"A girls' school in Maine. Sounds pretty cushy."

"Still gotta be vigilant."

"That's right," he said.

"Listen," I said. "You probably can't tell me this, Jacob, but I'm assuming Martin was honorably discharged."

"We don't do that," he said, but there was a change in his tone, a new guardedness.

"So how do I know if a person was fired for gross negligence or if he got the medal of valor?" I said.

"Google," he said. "But I didn't tell you this."

"No."

"You'll pick up the heroes. You'll pick up the real bums. The rest of the great unwashed, they don't show up anywhere."

"Oh, yes, they do," I said. "They show up here."

And I heard a car door closing. The rattle of the side-door latch.

I put the phone down, went to the door, notepad still in my hand.

"Mr. McMorrow," Trooper Ricci said. "I'm sorry to bother you."

"What is it?" I said.

"I'm afraid I've got some bad news," she said.

33

She stared at me from under the brim of her hat.

"Oh, no," I said.

Ricci held up her hands. "No, no," she said. "It's not your wife. It's Cheree Wilton."

"What about her?" I said.

"Is Mr. Varney here?" she said.

"Yes. Out back."

"I'd like to see him, too," Ricci said, then stepped in and closed the door. I led the way to the back deck, where Clair was still sitting.

"Everything alright?" he said, Mandi's papers on his lap.

"Cheree Wilton," Ricci said.

"Tell me again about how you left her."

I hesitated, glanced at Clair. "She was afraid of her husband," I said. "She shot at us with this old shotgun, thinking we were him. He'd beaten her and then left, and she was afraid he was back."

"So she fired her gun. In the house?"

"Yeah," I said.

A humming bird, iridescent green, buzzed by us. Ricci didn't seem to notice. "Did Mrs. Wilton seem despondent?"

It started to become clear, like someone moving toward you through fog.

"She's dead," I said.

"Yes," Ricci said.

"And you want to know if she was threatening to kill herself?" I said.

"Among other things," Ricci said. "Detectives will want to talk to you, too."

"She was upset," Clair said. "All beat up. Bruises on her face."

Ricci waited.

"But more angry than despondent," I said.

"She said she wanted to kill him but now she couldn't because she only had one shell for that old shotgun and she'd used it shooting at me," Clair said.

"So she was fine when you left her," Ricci said.

"Relatively," I said.

"I gave her two shells from my gun," Clair said, half to himself. "So she could protect herself."

"What kind?" the trooper said.

"Double Aught Buck. Low recoil load."

He stared off. "So it didn't protect her," he said.

"No," Ricci said.

"When?" I said.

"Two, three hours ago. I just left there. Crime scene people are there, homicide."

"We should have made her come with us," Clair said.

"Yeah," I said. "He'd cut her ear, face was all bruised, her eyes swollen."

I looked to Ricci. "Well, you saw what she looked like."

"No," she said. "She didn't show herself when I stopped there last night. I went back this morning."

The meaning hung in the air, surreal against the blue sky, the flowers.

"Point blank," I said. "In the face?"

Ricci nodded.

"Was there a shell left in the chamber of her gun?" I said.

Ricci hesitated, then shook her head slowly.

"She missed," Clair said.

I looked at him.

"He's back."

"Daddy!" Sophie shouted, sandals flapping, arms outstretched. She crossed the kitchen, hit me at a full run. I swung her around once, hugged her tightly, kissed her on the cheek.

"That was a juicy smacker," she said, wiping her face, sitting in the crook of my arm.

"I'm glad to see you," I said.

"Mommy's coming. She's—"

Sophie stopped, looked at Ricci. "You have a big hat," she said.

"Yes," Ricci said. "It keeps the rain off."

"You're a policeman except you're a girl. You're a police girl."

"That's right," Ricci said. She smiled, a gentle expression I hadn't seen on her before. "Girls can be police, too."

"Do you put bad guys in jail?" Sophie said.

"Sometimes," Ricci said. "When they're really bad, I put them in jail."

"Like a time out?"

"Right. A long time out."

Sophie looked at Ricci.

"Are bad guys here in my house?"

Ricci hesitated.

"No," I said. "There are no bad guys—"

I heard the suitcase drop to the floor. Roxanne appeared in the doorway, saw Ricci and said, "Hello." She turned to me and said, "What's going on?"

"Hey, Punkin Pie," Clair said to Sophie. "I'm thirsty. You can get me a drink."

"There's juice," Sophie said.

She took him by the hand and led him into the kitchen.

"So," Roxanne said. "Tell me."

Ricci did, the story of the death of Cheree Wilton, cops undecided whether it was suicide or homicide.

"She wouldn't kill herself," Roxanne said. "She was cowed by him, but she loved her kids."

She took a deep breath. "Somebody's got to tell them," she said.

"You?" I said.

"I'll call and find out," she said.

Then it was my turn: Clair and I at the compound, Cheree Wilton beat up, Clair leaving her with the two shells for her gun.

"So you think he killed her?" Roxanne said, her work face on.

"I do," I said. "Nobody's seen him in a couple days."

"Said he got on the bus to go south," Ricci said.

"Could have been anybody," I said.

"Or he got off at the next stop, took the next bus north," Roxanne said.

"Or he never left at all. His buddy dropped him in Portland and kept going, hang-up calls along the way to throw us off."

"I don't want to take Sophie back to Portland," Roxanne said.

"We'll pick him up if he's around here," Ricci said. "We want him. We'll be going all out."

"We'll stay with Clair and Mary," Roxanne said.

"Retreat to the stockade," I said. "But for how long?"

"Until he's in jail," Roxanne said. "Until he's—"

"No longer a threat," I said.

Ricci looked at both of us. "Be careful," she said. "I hate to see guns around children."

We told Sophie that she had just finished her city vacation and was now going to start her Clair and Mary vacation. She ran upstairs to get new toys and books. We heard her shriek.

"Twinnie," I said.

We went upstairs, found Sophie standing in the middle of her room. There were stuffed animals and books strewn on the floor around her feet like an offering.

I picked her up. "Twinnie," she sobbed. "Where is she?"

I took a deep breath and told my daughter my carefully rehearsed lie, not the first, not the last, but painful still.

"She'll come back when she's all cleaned up?" Sophie said.

"Yes," I said. "When she's all cleaned up."

We packed her bag, then one for ourselves. Sophie stayed with us every second, asked me to carry her downstairs. I put a sweatshirt on her against the cool evening coming on, and carried her out to Roxanne's car. She rode in the front. I went back to the house, got the rifle and put on a canvas field jacket. I poured bullets into the jacket pocket, and felt their weight swinging as I walked out to the truck.

Clair made popcorn, then slipped away. I sat with Roxanne, Sophie, and Mary on the couch and watched *Muppet Treasure Island.*

The Muppets were still at sea when Sophie sagged into my shoulder, sound asleep.

I carried her up to our room, one of three bedrooms at the front of the house. There was a double bed and a cot and Roxanne started to lay Sophie down on the cot.

"I'll take it," I said. "I may be up and down."

She looked at me, and understood. When Sophie was tucked into the big bed we both kissed her goodnight, my lips lingering on her forehead. I closed the windows and locked them, looked out on the road. It was dark and deserted, the moon peeping through the big maples on the front lawn. I closed the shades. Then we walked into the hallway, alone for the first time since Roxanne had gotten home.

We embraced. "Oh, I missed you," she said, her face against my neck.

"I missed you," I said. "Both of you."

"I feel like we're on different planets."

"I know," I said. "It's been kinda crazy and—"

I paused. Roxanne leaned back, knew me so well. "What?" she said.

I hesitated, then told her the rest of the story: the D.A. squeezing me, Roger on the boat, saying he never touched her. Mandi leaving with Marty. The box of papers.

"I asked you to stay away from her, Jack," Roxanne said, a cold flatness in her voice.

"I feel responsible."

"You are," she said. "For us."

"It's not that easy," I said.

"It never is with you. Once, just once, I wish—" She didn't finish the sentence.

"Someone will get him," I said.

A long pause, Roxanne swallowing her anger down.

"Soon, I hope," he said. "That poor woman."

"And I think Mandi will be moving on. It's her pattern."

"Soon, I hope," Roxanne said again.

34

Clair had the walkie-talkies, the kind families bring along when they're skiing. There was one radio on the kitchen table. I picked it up and called.

"Where are you?" I said.

"Barn," he said. "Upstairs."

Mary was in the den, the shades drawn. Roxanne was on the phone, talking to her supervisor about the Wilton kids. I got her attention, mouthed to her that I'd be right back, and went out the kitchen door, across the dooryard to my truck. I took the rifle out of the scabbard behind the seat. Turned to the barn, which was dark.

The stairs were at the back of the workshop. I felt my way along in the darkness, across the room and up, carrying the rifle. On the second floor was a loft that smelled of hay and oil. On the end facing the house there were double doors. They were open to the night. Clair was sitting by them, silhouetted against the sky, which was gray-blue in the moonlight.

I walked over and stood beside him. His deer rifle, a Mauser with a scope, was across his lap. The shotgun was leaning against the wall to his right.

"Hey," I said.

"Can see most of the back lawn, the field all the way to the treeline," Clair said. "Don't think he'd walk up to the front door."

"You wouldn't think so."

"Then again, he is taking orders from a higher power," he said.

"What are you going to do if you see him?"

"Shoot him," Clair said. "Put him down. For good."

"I can take a shift," I said.

"I'm fine for now."

"You just don't think I can shoot straight."

He smiled. "Did this for a long time, Jack."

"She's my daughter," I said.

"She's mine, too," he said. "You all are."

We stared out at the night. A bat slipped by us and flitted away, a late sleeper.

"I made a big mistake, Jack."

"She didn't want to go."

"Could have picked her up and taken her with us."

"Maybe," I said.

"Old junk gun. Inside of the barrels all rusted, probably. That'll affect the spray pattern. Maybe she got off one shot, missed. You know, people think a shotgun, all they have to do is point it in the general direction."

"Way it works on TV."

"Close range like that, all the way across the room, the shot would have spread maybe four or five inches. You still have to aim."

"You tried to tell her," I said. "And I left her there, too."

"Talk, Jack," Clair said. "It's cheap."

We were quiet. I got a crate and moved it over and sat. A half-hour passed and neither of us spoke. My butt was getting stiff and

I shifted. Clair was motionless, still and silent as a Sphinx. I took a deep breath, listened more than looked.

A barred owl. A bat that flitted in, made a couple of circuits of the loft and slipped back outside. Mosquitoes hummed faintly. Clair reached in his pocket and handed me a small bottle of bug dope. I put it on my face and neck.

Another fifteen minutes. And then there was a rustle in the trees. Then another.

"What's that?" I whispered.

"Deer," Clair said, and a small doe materialized in the field.

"If there's deer moving out there, he's not."

"Probably right. Why don't you go in, get some rest. You have the radio?

"Yeah."

"I'll call when I need you."

"Don't wait that long," I said, and I turned and started across the loft toward the stairs.

Mary was watching the news on TV, the sound turned down. I left the rifle in the hall, poked my head in. Mary said, "She went up to check on the baby."

I said goodnight. Picked up the rifle and went upstairs, my footsteps nearly silent on the carpeted front stairs. There were back stairs going up from the kitchen, a door at the end of the hallway, to the right. I walked down the hall, checked the door. It latched with a hook and I dropped it in place. It wouldn't stop him, but he'd have to rattle it to get it open.

I walked back to our room, where the door was ajar. I pushed it open and it creaked. I stepped in, heard the whisper of their breathing in the dark.

My eyes adjusted. Roxanne was asleep on top of the covers, still in her shorts and top. Her arm was laid across Sophie, who was on her back, her mouth open. I watched them for a minute, then turned and leaned the rifle against the wall. I put the radio on top of the bureau and fingered the switch, making sure it was on. I took off my jacket, draped by the radio. Then I stretched out on the cot, stared at the ceiling.

I listened to them, Sophie's breaths coming quickly, Roxanne's longer and deeper. There was a distant yapping outside, coyotes way back in the woods. More time passed. I heard Mary come upstairs, her footsteps receding down the hallway. Her door closing. I wondered if Clair had told her where he was going, or if, after all their years together, she just knew. Did she know what he was feeling? Why didn't I feel it as strongly. Was it wrong that I still partly blamed Cheree Wilton? Maybe she was there when Twinnie was stabbed. Maybe she was driving the car. Why didn't she leave him? Why did she let him control her? Maybe . . .

I opened my eyes. It was lighter, not yet dawn.

"Jack," Roxanne whispered. "There was a noise."

I rolled off the cot, grabbed the rifle.

Listened.

A banging.

The front door.

I picked up the radio. Pushed the button. "Front door," I said.

I slipped from the room, down the hall, and the stairs. Another rattle at the front door, someone trying the latch. I moved through the house quickly, went out the side door. Behind me, I heard the barn door open, turned and saw Clair emerge, rifle ready. He motioned to the back of the house, then made a circle with his hand. He'd go around the far side, I'd approach from the driveway.

I counted to five, let him get in position, then moved across the grass. Paused at the corner of the house and eased out, the rifle pointed.

Another rattle at the door—the latch again. There were rhododendrons across the front of the house, blocking the view of the front door. I raised the rifle to my shoulder, stepped out.

A figure stood with its back to me in jeans and a dark hooded sweatshirt, the hood up. I took another step, said, "Freeze right there. Hands on top of your head. Move slow."

The person froze. The hands moved up, clasped on top of the hood.

"Turn around," I said. "Go slow or I'll shoot you." I moved closer as the person turned. Clair came around the far corner of the house.

"Jack," Mandi said. "It's me."

"I didn't know where else to go," Mandi said. "I've been driving around and around, for hours."

We were in the driveway, me and Clair. Mandi was leaning against the black Tahoe, her bad foot drawn up. She was pale and disheveled and looked small and young, the tomboy little sister of the sexy call girl.

"I didn't want to bother you, really I didn't. But he was crazy. I couldn't stay there. I had to drive with my left foot."

"What did he do?"

"He had a pistol, drinking whiskey, Jack Daniels out of a big bottle. He started out saying he was gonna kill his ex, she wasn't gonna get his money. Then he started in on me, said maybe I was just after his money, too, maybe he'd have to kill me. And he laughed, like it was funny."

"You shouldn't have gone there," I said.

"He said, at first, maybe he'd give me the house up here, would I come and see it. Then we got there, it was more, I could stay for free when he wasn't here. Of course, when he was here, I could stay, too."

"It was okay until he got drunk. He's got a real bad temper and this time he just got meaner and meaner, and crazier, too, saying all this stuff. First he was saying he had money and he had clout down in Mass., he could get me a real job, he had a friend in real estate."

"And then?" I said.

"I said I didn't want to live in Mass. and he got mad and said I was blowing it, he was my big chance. And maybe I just liked being—"

She paused. "He said some pretty nasty things."

"Hasn't he beaten you up before?" I asked.

Mandi didn't answer.

"Why do you go back for more?"

She sighed, looked away.

"Did he touch you this time?" I said. "Let's call the police. Lock him up."

"No," Mandi said. "It's okay. I just had to get out of there."

"Where was he when you left?"

"The bathroom. I took the keys and kind of limped out, real quiet."

"Where was the gun?" Clair said.

"In his hand," Mandi said. "He only put it down when he poured more whiskey. At one point he took some of the bullets out and put it up against his head and pulled the trigger."

"Russian roulette," I said.

"Then he told me I should try. Every time I did it and didn't die, he'd give me ten thousand bucks. I said no way and he put it on his forehead and just kept pulling the trigger. I said to stop, but he kept going."

"It was empty," Clair said.

"Yeah, he said I'd just blown eighty grand. Then he put the bullets back in. That's when he started talking about really killing himself, maybe taking me with him. Then he started in on his ex, said she was screwing around on him and that's why she wasn't gonna get any money in the divorce. Then he started saying maybe he'd shoot her and then shoot himself, wasn't gonna do time for her, not as a policeman."

"He wasn't a cop," I said. "He was in corrections."

She looked at me. "How do you know that?"

"I checked. Corrections his whole career."

"Like a prison guard?" Mandi said.

"Yeah."

"He told me he was a detective. Undercover. Drugs and stuff. I figured he made his money knocking over drug dealers."

"I don't think so," I said.

"So he lied," Mandi said. "Everybody lies. Like Roger and his rich family and his boat."

It struck me that she'd very quickly changed the subject.

"That's true, about Roger," I said. "You saw the boat."

"How do you know that?"

"I talked to him. On the boat, in the harbor. He said to tell you he still loves you."

"See? Lies," Mandi said.

"What makes you say that?" I said.

She looked away, pulling her hood tighter. I tried again.

"Marty. He was at Walpole. Deer Island. But mostly he worked at a county facility," I said.

"Prison guard," she said. "That would suck."

"You think?" I said.

"I don't know, but it seems like it'd be really boring," Mandi said. "So Roger really said that?"

I nodded. "I believe him. I also believed him when he said he never touched you."

Mandi looked away, put her hands in her pockets. "Yeah, well—"

"Why'd you pin it on him?"

"I didn't pin anything on anybody."

"You said it was Roger, when it was really Marty, according to Roger."

"I was scared," Mandi said.

"Of Marty?"

She nodded.

"That he'd hurt you again?"

A hesitation, then another nod.

"But you went with him yesterday."

"He could be nice, sometimes."

"How'd you first meet him, Mandi?" I said.

She shrugged. "He called, like everybody else."

"Huh," I said. "You didn't know him from anywhere else?"

She frowned. "Heck no. Wish I didn't know him now. Hope I never see him again."

"Gotta get his car out of here," Clair said.

"We'll just leave it in Belfast somewhere," I said.

"You want me to leave, I will," Mandi said. "I was afraid, if I just went back to the apartment and he woke up—"

"Probably be out for a while," Clair said. "Let's go in."

We started for the door, then turned back. Mandi was hobbling after us and I offered her my arm, a little grudgingly now. She took it and hopped and half-skipped her way to the side door, where we paused. Clair got on the other side and we helped her up, Mandi in the middle, the guns on the outside.

I looked up, saw Roxanne in the window, and then she was gone.

"If you don't mind my asking, what's with all the rifles?" Mandi said.

"The guy who's been bothering us," I said. "He's around."

"Give me one, then."

"You've handled a gun?" Clair said.

She looked at him, seemed to think about it, just for a moment.

"No," she said. "But I can learn."

35

Roxanne was upstairs, sitting in the chair in the bedroom. Sophie was asleep, head thrown back, her throat exposed. I had an awful thought, Wilton coming in, seeing her and—

I shook it off. Roxanne got up and we left the room, went down the hall. We stopped, face to face.

"What is she doing here?" Roxanne said.

I explained, the best I could.

"She should go to a shelter. Her foot is fine now."

"I know. But I guess she thinks of this as a sort of sanctuary."

"It is—for us. If she wants to live like that, associate with people like that, she can find someone else to rescue her."

"I know."

"What if he comes here looking for her?"

"We'll take care of it," I said.

"We've got one homicidal maniac to worry about, Jack. We don't need two."

Roxanne's eyes were dark and angry. Her lips were pursed and pale.

"I understand," I said. "So we've got to get rid of his car."

"We don't. She does."

"She can barely drive. She had to use her left foot."

"She got it here. She can take it away."

"She needs to sleep for a while," I said. "She's been up all night."

"Join the fucking club," Roxanne said. Then she turned and walked back down the hall, into the bedroom, and closed the door.

I sighed. Went downstairs, glimpsed Mandi curled up on the couch in the den, a blanket over her legs, her sweatshirt hood still up, and her back to the door. I continued on to the kitchen, found Clair making coffee. It burbled in the machine, trickled down into the pot. He got out a mug and poured some for himself. I went to the counter, took a teabag from the porcelain jar.

I filled the kettle, put it on the stove and waited.

"His car," I said.

"We both can't leave," Clair said. "Roxanne?"

"Won't do it. She's not too happy that Mandi is back."

"Mary could follow you in, drive you back."

"Or we could drive it out in the woods and torch it," I said.

"Now you're talking," Clair said.

"I can do the barn duty for a while," I said.

"Full light, should be able to take a break. Maybe a couple of more hours."

"Let me get my tea," I said.

The water boiled. I poured it into a travel mug that said Quantico on the side. I was letting the tea steep when I heard it.

A car door closing. I went to the doorway and looked out.

Raven was standing by the rear end of the Tahoe, looking at the license plate. He had his radio out. He was talking.

"I think we just found a way to get rid of his car," I said.

We went out to the driveway, left the rifles inside. Raven saw me, kept talking on the radio. When we got close, he said, "Ten-four," and put the radio in his jacket pocket.

"She here?"

"Sleeping," I said.

"Been here long?"

"About an hour. Did he report it stolen? Because I think there are extenuating circumstances."

"No, he didn't report it," Raven said. "But what might those circumstances be?"

"She said he took her over to his house in Bayside, got drunk, started waving a handgun around, threatening to shoot anybody and everybody. Tried to get her to play Russian roulette. When he went to the bathroom, she took off. Came here because she was afraid he'd come to her apartment."

"I need to talk to her," Raven said.

"Come on in," I said.

"No, I think we need to go back into town." He was somber. No chitchat about boats.

"I'll go get her then," I said.

I went inside, through to the den. Tapped Mandi on the shoulder. She jumped, jerked her arm up to protect herself.

"It's Jack," I said.

She rolled over, looked up at me, bleary-eyed.

"Police are here. They want to talk to you."

It took her a moment to process it, and then she said, "Did you tell them I was going to give the car back? It's not like I was stealing it."

She was sitting on the couch, scuffing on her sandals. "I have a car. I don't want his car."

She started to get up, winced. I stood beside her and she put her hand on my shoulder hobbled down the hall, through the kitchen, and outside, where the sun was bright and the breeze was out of the west. I held her up as she eased down the stairs. Raven came to her.

"Miss Lasell," he said. "We need to talk."

"I wasn't going to keep the car," Mandi said. "It was just that I had to get out of there. He had a gun and he was drunk and yelling and I didn't know what he was gonna do. So when he was in the bathroom, I just took the keys and—"

Raven held up his hand. "It's okay. We can talk back at the station."

"The police station?" Mandi said, eyes widening. "I didn't do anything. I just borrowed it. You can take it back right now. I used some gas driving around—God, I drove for hours—but I'll pay for it.

She turned to me. "Jack, can you get my bag. I have cash. It's in—"

The hand again.

"Hey," Raven said. "I have to ask you to come with me. Right now."

"Okay, but I don't see why—"

"Mr. Callahan is dead," he said. "We found him a little while ago."

Mandi reeled on her feet, grabbed for my shoulder. She started to take short, shallow breaths, like she was hyperventilating.

"Easy," I said.

"Oh, my God," she said. "Oh, my God. He said he was gonna kill himself or his wife or me or all of us, but I thought he was just drunk. I just didn't want the gun going off or—"

"Please, let's get in the car, Mandi," Raven said.

She looked at me.

"It's okay," I said. "Just tell them what happened."

"He was crazy," she said, as Raven led her down the driveway. "Whiskey. It does things to people, they turn into maniacs. He was just out of control, you know?"

He eased her into the back of the cruiser and closed the door. Walked back to me.

"We'll need a statement from you, too."

"I can tell you right now," I said. "At least from when she got here. And I saw them leaving the apartment together in the afternoon."

The hand. "State police are helping with this one. They'll want to hear it."

"So I take it he didn't choke on a bite of steak."

"When I left they were picking pieces of his brain off the wall," Raven said.

"Huh," I said.

"How 'bout you come down and tell us what you know."

"Okay," I said.

"The whole story," Raven said.

Our eyes met. I nodded. "Right."

"I'd let you ride with her but I don't think that's a good idea, until we get your statements. Oh, and a wrecker is on its way for his truck. Got the keys?"

"Never saw them. I think they're probably still in it."

He walked over and looked in the window. Turned back and nodded.

He looked up at the sky, vivid blue beyond the swaying trees, the breeze cool and dry and pure.

"Beautiful day," he said.

"Yes," I said.

"Great day to be on the water. Won't be long, I'll have that boat ready to launch."

"Good for you," I said.

"Couple more little things to be done," Raven said.

"Great."

"Makes it all worth it," Raven said, "when everything starts to fall into place."

It was Raven and a balding CID detective, his last name Lawrence. I'd seen it in news stories over the years and now I had a face to put with the name. He had a weak chin, and he'd missed a spot on his left cheek when he'd shaved that morning. He was matter of fact and efficient, legal pad at right angles to the table, pen laid neatly on top of it.

There was a digital recorder on the pad and he picked it up when I sat down. He turned it on, put it on the table, and slid it toward me. Gulls cried outside and I wondered if the recorder caught that.

"Okay, Mr. McMorrow," Detective Lawrence said. "From the top. When did you first meet Miss Lasell?"

I took a deep breath and started at the beginning. The idea for the story. The ads in the paper. My calls. Mandi in the pizza shop.

Raven smiled. He'd won at last.

But not quite. I told them about finding her beside the bed. I told them about her staying at Clair's. I said I didn't know much more about her, that she seemed to want to listen more than she wanted to talk about herself.

I answered their questions, but they never asked if I'd gone to her former apartment in Portland. They never asked if I'd CarFaxed her Toyota. They did ask about Roger and I told them about our conversation on the boat. I told them what Marty had said to me. I told them everything Mandi had said about him that morning.

"Kind of a dangerous business she got herself into," Raven said.

"Yes," I said. "All by herself, too."

"You believe her story, that he was drunk and crazy but alive when she left?" he said.

I shrugged. "What's the forensics say?"

"A little early," Lawrence said. "We're supporting the investigation with informational interviews. Medical examiner will make the determination of cause of death."

He reached for the recorder, turned it off.

"Was he shot from ten feet away?" I said.

"No," Raven said. "Muzzle was pressed against his right temple."

"Right-handed?"

Raven smiled. "Yes," he said.

"Time of death?"

"Not long. Neighbor called it in. Said he heard something, then he fell back asleep. Woke up and decided he hadn't dreamt it. Dead maybe an hour when we got there at four-ten."

"Was he sitting up when he got it?"

"In a recliner," Raven said.

"Any other prints on the gun?"

"They're working on that," he said.

"That sort of information really can't be disclosed. It's part of the investigation," Lawrence said.

He stood, picked up his legal pad.

"At least we'll get her prints run quick now," Raven said, ignoring him. "Sent them in a week ago, but the state needs a little incentive,

you know what I'm saying? A guy with his brains all over the wall—
now that tends to get their attention."

36

Sophie wanted to play "Chutes and Ladders" so that's what we did, with the board set up on the kitchen table after the dishes had been cleared and washed. The idea of the game was to make your way from one end of the board to the other without having bad things happen to you, like catching a cold or being scratched by a cat. There was no skill. Like a lot of life, it was all in the roll of the dice.

Mary, Sophie, and Roxanne played, Sophie on her knees on her chair, hunched over the board and counting intently. Clair and I shared the red piece, rotating in and out so we could take a walk. Sophie guffawed when we broke dishes or fell through the ice. She couldn't understand why we'd want to leave and miss all the fun.

At eight o'clock, Sophie had won and was rubbing her eyes. The three of us went upstairs to the bedroom and tucked her in with stuffed animals lined up beside her, bears, a cat, a giraffe poking their heads out from under the blanket. It looked like bedtime on the ark.

"I want to go home when I wake up," Sophie said.

"Me, too," Roxanne said.

"We'll see," I said.

"Maybe Twinnie is there," Sophie said.

"Soon," I said.

We kissed her softly, left a desk lamp on, the shades drawn. In the hallway, I reached over and took Roxanne's hand. She stopped. Stood. Turned and fell into me, her arms wrapped around me. I wrapped mine around her.

"I'm sorry," I said. "I'm sorry for all of it."

"I just want things to go back to normal," she said.

"Normal. What's that?"

"When I can do my job and not have it follow me home. When you can write your stories and be done with it."

"Not have them sleeping on the couch," I said.

"Yes," Roxanne said.

"I wonder what happened with her today."

"She tells her story and she leaves, right? I mean, they have ways of determining this stuff."

"The gun, the wound, the angle of the entrance. His state of mind. Whether she seems like she's telling the truth."

We were standing in each other's arms, Roxanne's forehead against my shoulder. "You believe her, don't you?" she said.

"About this? Yes. But her whole story? I don't know. There are gigantic holes."

"They would have brought her home?"

"I'm sure."

"You know my theory."

"Yes," I said. "She was abused. Blocks out a big part of her life."

"And you don't agree."

"I don't know. How do you leave your whole life behind?"

Roxanne was quiet. "Maybe I'd be more sympathetic another time. But now—"

"I know."

"Will you be up all night?"

"We'll spell each other," I said. "At least I'll try. Clair is in full combat mode. He told me he's stayed up seventy hours before."

"Because there was no choice," Roxanne said.

"Because he was responsible for his men," I said.

"And now he feels responsible for us."

"And Cheree Wilton," I said.

"So he'll stop Harland and it will be even?" Roxanne said.

"Not even," I said. "But closer to it."

"Why can't we see the police?" Roxanne said.

"They're around. Saw a car pass on the road on the way home. But it's better if you can't see them. If we can't, Wilton can't."

"Be careful of yourself, Jack," she said.

I pressed her to me, said, "Don't worry."

"If anyone hurts our baby . . . "

"Don't even think it," I said, and gave her a last hug. Then we parted.

Clair moved around most of the night. An hour in the barn loft and then he'd melt away into the woods. Scanning the fields, the trees from the barn, I knew he was out there, but, like a bittern in the reeds, he was invisible.

He came and went. I went inside to say goodnight, found Roxanne and Mary had gone to bed. I went back to the barn, sat in the chair in the loft door and listened. I looked at my watch at 2 a.m. At 3:45, I woke up and Clair was in the chair beside me, his rifle across his lap.

"Your gun's behind you against the wall," he said. "I was afraid you'd drop it, make a racket."

We sat and were quiet. And then in a little while it was dawn, the birds starting up, chickens clucking in the coop, trees emerging from the blackness. The sky turned from indigo to gray to rose-colored in the east, beyond the trees. Clair listened, heard a car approach, then fade into the distance.

"Trooper," he said. "Shift change at six."

We sat. I stood. Clair was frozen, listening again.

"What's that car?" he said.

It was a small motor, moving slowly from the east end of the road. It stopped, idled, then started up again. Then it slowed and stopped again. I headed for the stairs.

When I came out of the barn, the rifle at my side, I saw headlights approaching, then the car itself. It was a small sedan, a Toyota. It slowed again and then turned into the driveway. The lights were glaring and I couldn't see the driver.

Until Mandi turned the lights off, then the motor, and opened the door.

She swung her legs out. Swiveled her foot. I came over and stood. She looked up at me. Drawn, gray, exhausted.

"I can't sleep there, Jack," she said. "Even with Lulu, it's like I can't stand to be alone. I'm sorry. I think I've got that post-traumatic thing."

"Take the couch again," I said.

"I feel like I'm losing it. They brought me home, helped me up the stairs. I said, 'I'm fine. I'm fine.' And then when they left and the door shut I just started to shake. I was just shaking all over. For half an hour. I mean, what's the matter with me? Am I cracking up?"

"Get some sleep, you'll feel better."

"He didn't come, did he, Jack?"

"No."

"I could help. I could look after Sophie, give Roxanne a break. I mean, I don't want to be in the way."

"You won't be."

"You're a good friend, Jack McMorrow," Mandi said.

"Am I your only friend, Mandi?" I said.

She stopped talking, looked at me. "I don't know. What do you—"

"You must have somebody you can go stay with. Not tonight but sometime. I mean, away from here."

"Not really," she said.

"Why not?" I said.

"I don't know," Mandi said, the vagueness creeping in. "I guess I'm sort of a loner."

She reached back for her bag, and I helped her up the stairs and inside. Despite it all, she seemed stronger than the previous day and she hobbled into the bathroom on her own. I put the kettle on, and when it had boiled, I made tea. Wearing the same sweatshirt and jeans she'd had on when Raven took her away, Mandi sat at the table and sipped. I brought out blueberry muffins and she ate one, then half of another.

"When did you eat last?" I said.

"Lunch yesterday, I think," she said.

Her eyes began to droop and she said, "I think I do need to sleep."

"Let's go then," I said. I helped her up from the chair but she dropped my arm and made her way down the hallway to the den. She closed the door and I heard the couch creak.

I sipped. Wondered where Clair was.

Reached for her bag.

A wallet. ID with the Portland address. Cell phone, turned on. I looked at the list of incoming calls: eight different numbers all days old. Two outgoing calls, both to me.

I listened for noise from the den. Opened the photo folder on the phone, then began to select. I didn't want to see pictures of her at work, but there weren't any. There were twenty-one photos in the folder. All of them were Mandi, self-portraits, slight variations on a theme: Mandi, holding the phone out at arm's length and snapping her picture. Scowling. Screaming. Crying. In none of them was she smiling.

I quickly pushed the buttons, punched in my cell number. Sent one of the photos to myself. There was a rustling in the den and I put the phone back, dug around quickly.

Felt something hard and pulled it out.

A small hunting knife, like guys I knew carried in sheaths on their belts. Six-inch blade, leather-wrapped handle.

So what, I told myself. With what had happened to her, I shouldn't have been surprised to find a Glock, much less a knife.

Seven o'clock, asleep in a chair by the kitchen window. A touch on my shoulder, and I started, saw Clair standing beside me, heard the shuffle step of Sophie coming down the front stairs.

Clair put his shotgun behind the door. I got up and put my rifle there, too. There was the sound of slippers on the pine floors, Sophie accelerating, sliding into the kitchen and throwing herself at me.

I swung her up into my arms. She hugged me and slid down. "I'm hungry," she said, and she climbed into a chair at the table. "Please."

There was more stirring upstairs, footsteps coming closer. It was Mary, in her bathrobe, saying, "I don't know what got into me. Look at the time."

"Day's half gone," Clair said. "Jack and I already milked the chickens."

Sophie grinned. "You can't milk chickens," she said.

"Sure you can," Clair said. "Where do you think they get chicken broth?"

Sophie looked at him, cocked her head. Just then Roxanne came into the room, wearing shorts and one of my T-shirts.

"Mommy, do you get chicken soup when you milk the chickens?" she said. "Clair says—"

There was a rattle from the direction of the hall. The den. Roxanne turned and looked. Turned back to me.

"She was freaked out, alone in the apartment," I said. "She got here at four-fifteen."

"And walked right in?" Roxanne said. "That's reassuring."

"We heard her car coming down the road," I said.

She looked at me, was silent for a minute. Clair poured Fruit Loops into a bowl, added milk, and put them in front of Sophie.

"Yum," she said, and started shoveling them into her mouth like coal into a furnace.

"What do you say?" Roxanne said.

"Thank you," Sophie mumbled, still crunching.

"I'm going down to the house," Roxanne said.

"I'll go with you," I said.

"She'll be fine here," Clair said. "If I were you, I'd walk down the road."

"Why?" Roxanne said.

"High visibility," he said.

"Is visibility a good thing?" she said.

I glanced at Sophie but she was intent on her cereal.

"Let's go, then," I said. "We'll be back."

I picked up the rifle outside the door. We walked down the drive and started down the road. Sparrows flushed in the grass and flitted ahead of us.

"You know, I was reading about someplace," Roxanne said. "I can't even remember where it was. The Philippines. Someplace like that. People in this village carry their guns everywhere because they're fighting the rebels. Or maybe they are rebels. I don't remember. But they said they'd leave their clothes behind before they'd leave home without their machine guns."

"And you think that's what we're turning into?"

Even as I said it, I found myself turning to scan the woods, sweeping the rifle across. A car started and we spun around. An unmarked police cruiser eased out of the mouth of a tote road and turned toward us.

Trooper Ricci was at the wheel.

She pulled up, stopped beside us.

"A little news for you, folks," she said.

"Somebody who fits Harland Wilton's description got on a bus in Augusta yesterday morning, heading south. Bought a ticket for Fort Lauderdale."

"But was it Wilton? What'd his ID say?

"Guy said his name was Pazuzu," Ricci said.

"So," I said.

"I went online," she said, the cruiser idling, her arm out the window. "Pazuzu is a Sumerian demon, supposed to protect children. It was in *The Exorcist,* the movie."

"And common knowledge, if you worship Satan, I suppose," I said.

"Where's the bus?" Roxanne said.

"Pennsylvania. He got off in New York. Ticket the rest of the way is good for two days."

"What are the chances?" Roxanne said.

"Of it being another whacked-out devil worshipper?" I said.

"Not very good," Ricci said. "As soon as we pick him up, I'll call you or come find you."

Ricci put the car in gear and drove off, toward Belfast.

"I've been praying," Roxanne said.

"Don't stop now," I said.

37

Ricci's news had lifted a weight from Roxanne. She played with Sophie that day, more "Chutes and Ladders," called the office while Sophie took a nap. I heard Roxanne say, "I may be in tomorrow. I'll call you. How are the kids? No, I think I need to be there."

Mandi got up for breakfast, then went back to sleep on the couch. Roxanne was civil to her, if not friendly. Sophie had Mandi play a round of "Chutes" and patted her on the hand when she lost.

Clair and I switched off patrolling that day. He was out back when the mailman came in the afternoon, pulling up in a Jeep with the flashing yellow lights on the roof. I took the Varneys' mail and ours and walked back up the driveway.

There was a *New Yorker*, some bills, a catalogue from Agway and a couple of credit card offers. They didn't know I hadn't worked in a week, I thought, as I continued to flip through the mail—and saw the letter with the handwritten address:

Christian/Jew Power Center

c/o *Roxanne Masterson, state agent*

I looked at the postmark: New York, N.Y. 10008. The date: July 20. Yesterday. Good mail service.

I went inside and looked for Roxanne. Found her reading to Sophie on the bed upstairs.

"What?" she said.

"You need to read to your friends for a minute," I told Sophie, "and Mommy will be right back."

As we went into the hall, we heard Sophie "reading" the animals a story she knew by heart. I showed Roxanne the envelope.

"I don't think you should open it," I said. "It could be a letter bomb or something."

Roxanne took the envelope from me.

"New York," she said.

"Yesterday," I said.

She ran her fingers over the envelope. Held it up to the light. Brought it back down and tore it open. Unfolded what appeared to be several sheets of paper.

Roxanne scanned one, handed it to me.

It began:

Dear Jew Bitch Masterson, Christian Gustapo Agent from Rockland, Maine,

This message is to inform you of our rejection of your government and you, as its official agent and there fore abducter of the children of Harland and Cheree Wilton. There is bodies of the spiritual world that are out of your control and forces that are beyond the "religions" Nazarean and Moses and Mohammad: and Christianity, the hoax that is being played on the people of this earth for the last 2,000 years by the powers of FEAR, needing to FEAR themselves because the DAY OF RECKENING is coming and it is coming hard and fast. It will come for all Jew/Christians but it will come to you, BITCH MASTERSON!!!!, and you alone swifter than you think it possible.

This is your only warning. We are sorry that you have chosen the path that has taken us here but man has the god given right (true god, not the Nazarean) to protect his children against the GUSTAPO ABDUCTERS. The serpent gives us the knowlege and the demons they protect us as true believers in Satan's goodness.

"Why is it these people can't spell?" I said.

I flipped the pages. There were drawings of snakes and flowers and something that looked like it was supposed to be a pyramid. More about Jews and Jehovah and the evil Catholic Church, and the state of Maine and the Nazis who work in Augusta.

"You're Jewish and a Nazi."

"Who's it from?" Roxanne said.

I turned to the back of the last page.

"Harland Wilton, Follower Of Satan, Respecter of his Demons."

"Wrote it on the way down," Roxanne said.

"Mailed it in Manhattan."

"Maybe he got lost looking for a mailbox, missed the bus."

"Let's hope he gets on his soapbox in Times Square and gets locked up," I said.

"How would we know?" Roxanne said.

"He'd come up a hit when they picked him up, if he's carrying ID. Be sought in connection with a possible homicide in Maine. No ID, it'd take longer."

"I wish he'd made the bus and kept going."

"I wish it had run him over," I said.

"But all in all, this is good," Roxanne said. "We always say at the office, it's the ones who don't call up and yell and scream that you have to worry about."

"A barking dog can't bite," I said.

"Is that some old saying?"

"I just made it up."

"I don't think that's true," Roxanne said. "A dog barks and then he bites."

"Okay."

"It should be, a dog can't bite you if you're in Maine and he's in New York City."

"Not quite as catchy," I said.

"But at least it's true," Roxanne said, but I was thinking of something else.

"His guns," I said. "I wonder where he left them."

The house was still, the air stale. Our footsteps echoed as we crossed the kitchen. I put down the rifle, threw open the door to the deck. Roxanne opened the refrigerator, started sorting through food. She turned over yogurts, checking expiration dates, pulled out a bag of romaine and tossed it into the trash.

"I'm ready to be home," she said.

"I know," I said.

"We can't hide forever."

"Yeah—"

"It's been three days. It's not good for Sophie. She has no routine at all and she's starting to get cranky. And—"

Roxanne paused. "We need to be in our own house, just us."

"Mandi," I said.

She didn't answer, held up half of a cucumber in a plastic bag. Tossed it.

"One more night," I said. "Maybe they'll pick him up."

"She's like a pleasant stranger. She talks, but she doesn't really say anything, not about herself, anyway. I mean, who is she? Who is she really?"

"I know."

Roxanne opened the milk, sniffed it. "One more night at Clair's, then," she said. "And then we come home. And she finds another place to stay."

Roxanne went to the laundry room behind the stairs and took clothes from the dryer. I heard the washer lid shut and the water turn on. I went to the study, saw the answering machine light flashing. I pushed the button: Myra at the *Times*. "Jack. Where you been? Got a couple of stories for you. It's a little after ten, Saturday night. Yes, pulled the weekend. I'll be here another hour. Back to the grindstone tomorrow. Isn't Sunday supposed to be a day of rest? Call me."

Ah, yes. Work. I'd almost forgotten. What had the plan been? Crank it up, make more money so Roxanne could stay home?

I went to my desk. Looked at the list, nothing checked off. Down at the floor: the tub of Mandi's papers.

I heard Roxanne going upstairs, probably with clean laundry. Her footsteps were over me now. Sophie's room. I heard the basket hit the floor, a drawer open.

I sat, pulled the tub to me. Roxanne was right; Mandi revealed next to nothing. I picked up the stack of papers, separated the half I'd already skimmed. Started working through the other.

More drawings: women with flowing hair and flowing dresses. A whole set of a bride and groom, the bride's gown trailing behind her, the groom in a tux, his head cocked as he looked at the woman. No wedding on the horizon for Mandi. Why the pictures?

Another poem, some sort of haiku:

This room
holds me
so tight
I can
 not breathe.

And another, written on the same page.

My imagination
is the window
they cannot close
or lock
or pull the shade
or put a screen over
or shut in with steel bars.

I see the sky
when it's not there
sometimes blue
sometimes clouds
some blow fast
and some just float
take me away like the dandelion fuzz
that the wind carries
but when I land
and open my eyes
I'm still here
Until I dream
Again

Bars. A sky she can't see. A suffocating room.

A jail cell.

Upstairs drawers were opening and closing. The closet door slammed shut.

I put the poems aside. Leafed through a bunch of wrinkled clippings from *People* magazine, 2002. Britney Spears and the Backstreet Boys. Jennifer Aniston and Keanu Reeves. A story about Cameron Diaz, one sentence underlined. "Cameron was so skinny when she was young, the kids called her 'Skeletor.'"

Someone had written: "And now you're famous! F--- them!"

Roxanne passed overhead, headed for our room. She called down, "Jack, you call this making a bed?"

I kept flipping through the papers. More poems. What looked like the start of a story, written in pencil on yellow legal paper: *Marisa liked to take walks in her neighborhood and pretend it was Paris. She talked to herself as she walked, speaking what she thought sounded like French. But Marisa didn't speak French. She had never been outside of Massachusetts. The only foreign language she heard was Porchagese (???), from the old guy who lived two doors down from her house. She didn't know what he was saying to her but when she was 13 and started to get boobs she decided he was sketchy.*

The story ended there. I kept going.

A yellowed newspaper photo: Ben Affleck at Fenway Park, the word "hottie" written under his face. I turned the clip over. July 9, 2002. *The Quincy Patriot Ledge*, a newspaper from outside of Boston.

Then a page from what must have been a journal. No date.

Who decides who we are and what we are? Do we have a choice? Or are we made, like cookies. You put the dough on the sheet. It has no choice of whether it's gonna be chocolate chip. It just is. What made me what I am? If it was my mother, I still love her, I guess.

Roxanne tossed sheets down the stairs. I was almost through the stack. More *People*: a picture of Jennifer Lopez, a story about Reese Witherspoon. Scrawled on the clipping: *I want your life.*

Stuck to the back of Reese Witherspoon, a folded piece of paper. I unfolded it and another newspaper clipping emerged. I unfolded that, too, like a set of nesting dolls. It wasn't a story: just a picture. A woman in handcuffs, standing by a deputy. It was a perp walk photo, a cruiser behind them, another cop closing the back door from which the woman had just gotten out, presumably on her way into court.

The woman wore jeans and boots and a baggy sweatshirt. Her face had been cut out of the clipping, leaving a small, round hole. I looked at the cop's uniform. Reached for the desk and took a magnifying glass from the drawer. The cop had a name tag but I couldn't make it out. The cruiser looked brown but the picture was black and white. The door was open and the insignia wasn't in view.

"Damn," I said.

I turned it over. It was going to be partly cloudy and 60-65 degrees. The *Patriot-Ledger* Weather, Tuesday, August 12, 1999.

More sheets came down the stairs. I reached for the phone. Got directory assistance and got the number for the newsroom. I called. A young guy answered, said, "Newsroom."

"Photo desk," I said.

He transferred the call. The phone rang. A woman answered, a smoker's rasp. "Photo."

I told her my name.

"Yup," she said.

I said I was working on a story for the *New York Times.*

That got her attention.

"There's a picture on a clip," I said. "Looks like it's page one. Cop leading a suspect into court. A woman."

"Yeah."

"I just need to know who the woman is. It's cut off on the clip I have."

"Our archives are online," she said. "You can—"

"I don't have a name to search for. All I have is the date."

"Well, listen, I'm kinda busy right now."

"It's August 12, 1999. You must have a photo log."

A long pause. A sigh. "Gimme your number," she said. "I'll see if I can find somebody to look it up. It'll be a while. What I'm saying is, don't sit by the phone."

I gave her my number, then said, "One more thing."

"Yeah?"

"The weather in your paper. What page is that on?"

"The weather? You mean, like the forecast, with the graphics?"

"Right."

"Back page, A-section," she said.

"Okay."

"But are you talking about now or back then?"

"Back then. The same paper, '99," I said.

"Used to be on page two, top left. They just changed it, along with everything else."

"Then the photo I have, it ran page one. This women was big news."

"She was that day," she said. "It's all relative, as you know."

I did know it, and I thanked her and hung up as Roxanne came into the study, a new swish in her step. She came over and kissed my forehead, and smiled for the first time in a days.

"We're going to celebrate when they lock him up," she said.

"Right," I said, mustering a smile back.

"Drinks and dinner and maybe Mary and Clair will keep Sophie for a couple of hours after we get home."

Roxanne leaned down and kissed me again. Saw the papers on the desk, the bin on the floor.

"What's that stuff?" she said.

"You know that question you had? It's part of the answer."

38

Roxanne peered at the faceless photo. "It could be her, but she would have been a kid. Fourteen or fifteen."

"Built like her," I said.

"Could be her mother," Roxanne said. "Maybe her mother had her young. This person could be thirty, a little older. Slim."

"Maybe her mother killed her father. Doing twenty-five to life. Leaves Mandi with nobody. That would explain why she's so closed about everything."

"So she drifts. Gets into a bad crowd. Ends up doing what she does."

"Gets used to being alone," I said.

"But what about the rest of it?" Roxanne said.

"Room could be in rehab or something."

"No letters from her mother."

I looked at the papers. "No. But Mom kills Dad? Maybe you don't have much of a relationship after that. Maybe it was Dad she was close to. Now that would be a good story. When one parent kills the other, what happens to the children?"

We both looked at the papers. "You think it's strange that I have this? I mean, she is sort of our friend."

"Your friend," Roxanne said, playful no more. She put the clip down. "I think you need to put this stuff away. We need to get back."

I wrote the number in a reporter's notebook, stuck it in my back pocket. We locked up, took the path through the field, not wanting to be predictable. I carried the rifle and Roxanne carried a knapsack with a change of clothes for Sophie and a few books, enough for the afternoon— and her briefcase. We walked single file, Roxanne hurrying in front of me.

"She's fine," I said. "Clair's there. Nobody could even get close."

"I'm not worried about that," Roxanne said, and picked up the pace.

We crossed the field, sparrows flushing from the grass, and Clair stepped out from behind the barn behind us, shotgun draped across his chest.

"Hey, there," he said. "Come to spell them?"

"From what?" I said.

"When I came out, she'd won fourteen straight games. They got playing for crackers and she's got a pile in front of her."

"We got some news," Roxanne said.

We showed Clair the letter, the envelope.

"So maybe he's gone," Roxanne said.

"Maybe," Clair said.

"Traveling alone," I said. "In New York City yesterday. Why would he leave just to come all the way back?"

"Good question," Clair said.

Roxanne said, "I'm going in," and headed for the house. Clair waited until she was out of earshot, then said, "Could be because the voices tell him to."

"Seems unlikely," I said.

"Don't see much likely about this fella. An eccentric turned into a nutjob turned into a psychopath."

"What's next?"

"That," Clair said, "is the question."

Roxanne was in the door. Clair started to turn back toward the barn.

"Another question," I said, and I told him about what I'd found in the bin, the photo with no face.

"Will be interesting," he said.

"People make mistakes."

"Some mistakes you can't undo," Clair said. "If they're big enough, they define you."

I looked toward the house, where Sophie was with Mandi.

"When are they going to call?" Clair said.

"Didn't say. It's a newsroom. May not be a priority."

"Call them back. Make it one."

"That her mother went to jail?"

"Or something," Clair said, and he looked at the house, too, then turned, scanned the woods once, and started back to the barn.

I left the rifle outside the door on the porch and stepped in quietly. They were at the table in the kitchen, Chutes and Ladders underway. It was Mandi's turn and she rolled the dice.

"Five," Sophie said, and she clapped her hands.

Mandi counted out the five spaces and her face fell into an exaggerated frown.

"Rats," she said.

"Oh-oh," Sophie said, grinning. "You go back all the way."

Mary picked up the dice.

"You want me to roll for you, Mary?" Sophie said. "I'm good at rolling."

She did, and Mary zipped ahead.

"You are a good roller," she said.

"Yes, you are," I said, and Sophie turned to me and said, "You want to play?"

"In a minute," I said. "I need to talk to Mom."

Mary pointed to the dining room. I walked in, found Roxanne seated at the table, her briefcase open, DHHS papers spread out.

"Trying to figure out my life," she said.

"Good luck," I said.

There was a burst of laughter from the players and Roxanne looked up, not smiling. "I wonder when they'll call," she said.

"I'll give them an hour and call back," I said.

Roxanne turned away.

I moved to the back porch, sat in the chair by the back window, scanned the woods. Every few minutes, I moved to the front window and looked out at the road. A log truck passed. A red Chevy pickup, the retired guy from the house by the corner, on the way to the dump.

I turned on the radio: opera from the Met. "Don Giovanni." I didn't know what they were saying, but it was inscrutably beautiful. The time passed. The hour was up.

Mary opened the door, said she'd made lunch. I came in and Sophie was at the table, Chutes and Ladders back in the box. Mandi and Sophie were at the table. Sophie was eating a peanut butter and jelly sandwich and there was a pile of Goldfish crackers next to her plate.

"Daddy, I won a lot of crackers," she said.

"Good for you, honey," I said. "Are you going to eat them all?"

"No, I'm going to show them to Twinnie when she gets back. When is Twinnie coming home?"

"Soon."

"Are we sleeping at our house tonight?"

"Yes, Soph. It's time to get back in your own bed."

"I liked sleeping with Mommy in the big bed at the hotel," she said.

"I'm sure."

Mandi smiled at her.

"When you were little did you sleep in a big bed with your mommy?" Sophie said.

"I don't think we ever stayed in big-bed hotels," Mandi said.

"Where did you stay?" Sophie said.

"When I was your age? An apartment."

"You didn't have a house?"

"No. We lived in a city, honey."

"Where?"

Mary came with tuna sandwiches, laid the plate on the table. She handed small plates to me and Mandi. Mandi took half a sandwich and put it on her plate, poured a glass of ice water.

"Where?" Sophie said.

"Massachusetts," Mandi said.

"Is that near Portland? We went to Portland. They had drinks in your bedroom."

"Isn't that nice," Mary said, putting down a bowl of fruit salad.

"Did you grow up right in Boston?" I said.

Mandi looked at me, seemed surprised. But she seemed to catch something in my tone, my expression. She blushed and smiled, seemed resigned to something. "Near Boston," she said. "Not right in the city."

"But you said it was a city," Sophie said. "If it wasn't in the city, how could it be—"

"Enough questions, young lady," Mary said. "You know, my grandchildren, they ask questions like you. After a while, they tire me out."

Sophie took a bite of sandwich, a sip of milk. "I'm not tired," she said.

"Well, I am," Mandi said. "I couldn't get to sleep. I think I'm going to take a nap."

"Grown-ups don't take naps," Sophie said. "Naps are for kids."

Roxanne came into the kitchen and said, "Sure, grown-ups take naps, you silly. Grown-ups get tired, too."

"Not you and Daddy."

"Well, maybe we should start," Roxanne said.

Mandi had gotten to her feet, pulling herself up with her good hand.

"Excuse me, Roxanne," she said, eased by, and started for the den. Roxanne sat and we ate, the four of us. I told Sophie she couldn't eat all the grapes in the salad but Mary said it was okay, that there were more. I finished my sandwich, got up and caught Roxanne's eye. I went outside and stood in the driveway. Clouds were moving in from the southeast and the air was heavier, that stillness that comes before a heavy rain.

I put in the number. Waited.

It rang and the newspaper's receptionist answered. I asked for the photo desk again, and the phone clicked and connected. It rang five times, six and seven. In the old days, the photographers would be in the darkroom, but now—

"Yeah." My raspy-voiced friend.

"Hi," I said. "Me again."

"*New York Times*. I left you a message."

"I'm out. You must have left it at the house."

"You want me to give it to you again, I suppose," she said.

"If you don't mind."

"And what if I do? Just kidding. Things were a little hectic down here. You must know the feeling."

"Sure," I said. "Worked in a newsroom for years."

"Well, it's okay now. So the picture—I should have known when you told me what it looked like. I think I'm losing it, thirty-two years in this business. I mean, I really should have known just by the date. I guess I wasn't really listening."

"August 12, 1999?"

"I shot it. She was going to court for her arraignment. Just a kid, really. That's what I remember. This girl, I mean. What was she, fourteen?"

"I don't know," I said, my stomach tightening. "You tell me."

"It was really sad. I mean, this was a kid never caught a break."

"What was her name?" I said, but she was still talking.

"Luck of the draw, you know? Some kids get born into good families, loving home, go to school, college, the whole nine yards. Others, just have shit for luck right outta the chute."

"Is that right?" I mustered.

"Listen, you really should talk to a reporter, except the guy who covered it, he left the paper to write a book or something. I have no idea where he is."

"Then tell me what you remember?"

"Hard to forget. I mean, some are, some aren't. This one, this kid Louise, I remember thinking she really got the short straw. Mother was a drunk, pretty woman but hardcore alcoholic. Father was a junkie. You sure you don't know this story?"

"I don't think so."

"One of these kids, one foster home after another, kicked around their whole lives, nobody wants 'em. I've seen it so many times. See it in their faces, you do crime stuff."

"Yes," I said. "I know the look."

"Long story short—you can Google it, *Globe* came in did a big story of their own—anyway, nobody really knows what happened. She says she doesn't even remember. Of course, the poor foster mom, nice lady by all accounts, she wasn't going to shed any light on it."

"Why not?"

"Why not? 'Cause she was dead, that's why not. Louise took a hammer to her. Good-sized girl for her age. You know how some girls grow early. Well, she wasn't small."

"Louise killed this person?" I said, my voice small and low.

"Killed? You look it up. Medical examiner said this woman was hit so many times with this big framing hammer—husband was a contractor—that she was flat. Every single bone in her body broken. M.E. said he hadn't seen those kinds of injuries except when somebody got hit by a truck, then run over, too."

"And Louise did this?"

"Didn't deny it. Couldn't explain, either. Said she liked this new foster mother okay, only been there a couple of weeks. My theory, I think she'd been knocked around so much by her real mom, used to beat the living crap out of her, that's what they said in court. Belittled her something awful. I think she just didn't know how to react when somebody was nice to her. Something went haywire inside her head."

I stood there in the driveway under a darkening sky, the story rolling over me like waves.

"You sure you didn't hear about this?"

"Sounds vaguely familiar."

"What do you do when a murderer is fourteen? And this isn't some gangbanger shooting guns in the air, bullet comes down on somebody's head. This is a girl turned a human being into steak tartar."

"So—"

"You sure you want to hear all this? I mean, I kinda get going on this one."

"It's okay," I said. "I'm interested."

"Alright. So the judge stews over it for months. I mean, people saying, 'How can you let this kid loose? What if she does it again?' She says she doesn't even know why it happened. I mean, this is literally a walking time bomb."

"What was the sentence?" I said.

"I was there," she said. "Judge reads this long statement. Smart woman. I mean, you could tell it tore her up. Victim's family there, the foster mom was like Mother Theresa, you know what I mean? Her kids all grown up, she decides to help the underprivileged."

I waited.

"Judge decides to sentence her as a juvenile. Keep you until your twenty-one, then off you go, free and clear. Courtroom went crazy, everybody crying."

"So she's out," I said.

"Somewhere," she said. "I've always wondered about that. I mean, is she bagging groceries? Is she taking care of old people in a nursing home? Is she somebody's babysitter? Gotta do something, right? I'm sure she can't go around saying, 'And, oh, by the way. I'm a murderer.'"

"No," I said.

"One of those interesting situations," she said.

"Yes. Very."

"So there you have it. In a nutshell."

"One more thing," I said. "What was her last name. Louise what?"

"Lilly," she said. "Louise Lilly. Isn't that a pretty name?"

39

It could have been someone Mandi met in jail. Her sister. A friend from school.

I started down the road, then broke into a trot. Jamming the key into the lock, I got the door open, went straight to the computer in the study. I turned it on, stood over the desk as I waited, clicked through.

Typed the name: *Louise Lilly,* then *Quincy, Massachusetts.* Hesitated, then touched the key.

I waited. The list popped up.

Boston Globe, August 20, 1999. *Teen Showed No Sign of . . .* I took a breath. Touched the keyboard.

The story. Foster mother brutally murdered. Quiet fourteen-year-old girl arrested. Investigators said she told them she didn't know why she did it. She liked Mrs. Martini. There had been no argument that young Louise Lilly could remember. Police said she told them her new foster mother was bringing in groceries and the hammer was in a tool belt in the entryway. The girl said she took it out of the holder and just started swinging. Once she started, she couldn't stop.

Then into the bio part. Born in Medford, no father in the picture . . .

I scrolled down. Mother couldn't hold a job because of drinking, moved every couple of months, dragged her daughter with her. Nine different schools, all around Boston, before she was eight. Removed from home when she showed up at school showing welts that turned out to be from the cord of a hairdryer.

I scrolled again. The Martinis' children were grown. This was their first foster child. They wanted to give back to the community. The dad fixed up a room, new paint and paper and furniture, so the girl wouldn't feel like she was living in hand-me-downs . . .

I didn't care about that. I just wanted to see—

The girl walked two miles to a fire station, told firefighters she had just done "a very bad thing."

—the picture.

Neighbors and friends devastated. The girl's mother too distraught to comment, but a former classmate at Tompkins Middle School in Revere said . . .

And there it was.

The caption said, "Louise Lilley."

Younger, slimmer. Her hair longer.

Mandi.

I pulled away from the screen. Swallowed hard. Leaned back down and bookmarked the page. Closed out and shut the computer down. I was out the door when it clicked off.

Hurrying back down the road, I tried to put it in order.

A horrific crime, fourteen years old. A child who killed an innocent and well-meaning woman for no apparent reason. A girl who continued pounding Mrs. Martini long after she was dead.

Every bone in her body.

Chutes and Ladders. Mandi, at home in our house. Sophie, eyes wide and bright: "Mandi's here!"

The loner who purveyed this false sort of relationship. The young woman who didn't want anyone to love her. Roger, on the boat, "She said she deserved it."

The sentence had been six years in a juvenile jail. But was Mandi still punishing herself? Eight years since it had happened and nothing since. Or was that true? Marty, with a bullet in his head

Back to Clair's, I started up the driveway. Roxanne was at her car, taking something from the back seat. Sophie and Mandi were at the side door, holding hands. Sophie's hair was in short braids.

The rifle, loaded just inside the door.

"Daddy," Sophie said. "I got braided."

A car approaching, the mailman's Jeep again, yellow roof lights flashing. A package, I thought. I stopped.

A rifle shot.

Behind the barn.

Another shot. This one a shotgun.

Closer.

They froze, then Roxanne ran to the house, scooped Sophie up, and yanked the door open. They were all inside when I reached them.

"Get inside, call the police, stay down," I said.

I grabbed the rifle and leapt the stairs, saw the Jeep at the end of the driveway. I waved him off, ran across the yard, around the end of the barn. Clair was behind a farm trailer, shotgun aimed at the woods.

"Get in here," he said.

I ran in a crouch, threw myself behind the cart.

"Edge of the woods," he said. "First shot just missed, over my head. Returned fire, but no accuracy with this thing."

Boom, another shot, a simultaneous crack in the wall of the barn above us.

"His rifle's sighted high," Clair said. "Why you always sight a gun. Police?"

"Roxanne's calling."

"If he'd been smart, he would've tried to get closer. Crawled through the grass. You see him through that scope?"

I slid the barrel through the slats of the trailer, peered through the scope. I found the edge of the trees, ran the scope left, then right.

Nothing, then movement. A block of leaves along the trunk of an oak.

"Got him," I said. "He's in camo. Left side of the third tree to the right of the big maple."

Boom again, the slats splintering three feet to our left. I put my eye back to the scope.

"Still see him?"

"Yes. Same place."

"Must've not seen the rifle, thinks I can't reach him with this."

"Here comes another one," I said.

We hunched lower. A shot, this time close, above our heads.

"Take him," Clair said.

A door slammed at the house.

"They must be getting out," I said.

Another shot from the woods, a snap as the round hit the barn between us.

"Got him?"

There was a shriek. From the house.

"Sophie," I said.

"I'll take it," Clair said.

I moved out from under the rifle and slid it over to Claire. He fixed his eye to the scope as I reached around him, took the shotgun.

"There you are, you son of a bitch," Clair said.

He took a breath, exhaled slowly and held it. I was crouched, ready to go.

He squeezed the trigger. There was a boom and Clair still looked through the scope. He nodded.

"Go," he said.

I did, running with the shotgun down the back side of the barn. I heard Clair going the other way, and I circled, came out first, ran across the dooryard, down the driveway.

The Jeep was backing out.

Roxanne was behind the wheel, Mandi in the front seat beside her. As the car swung into the road, I saw Sophie, the top of her head, and Wilton holding her, his hand over her mouth.

40

Clair was getting into his truck. I ran for the passenger side, yanked the door open as he started off, took a couple of steps to keep up, and threw the shotgun in, then heaved myself up.

The Jeep had gone left, past my house, headed east. We caught a glimpse of it ahead, then it went over a rise. Clair slammed the big Ford through the gears, hit fourth and kept the pedal to the floor. We launched over the crest of the rise, the truck coming off the ground, hitting hard.

I steadied the guns, my feet against the dash.

"We can't shoot."

"We'll stay with him," Clair said. "Just hope the cops come in this way."

"I'll call," I said.

I got my phone out, flipped it open. The truck bounced and skidded.

No service.

There was a plume of dust ahead, a dry stretch of road, the Jeep somewhere beyond it. I braced myself with my feet, one hand on the gun barrels, the other holding the phone.

I punched in 911.

Call failed.

"Shit," I said.

"Hang on," Clair said.

We slammed over potholes and the truck veered left. Clair pulled it back. I looked through the dust, saw brake lights flash on and off.

"He's got Roxanne booking it," Clair said.

"He's got Sophie," I said.

We were gaining, the Jeep showing closer as the dust subsided. It bounced, slid, straightened, then slid again going into a downhill turn.

"Maybe we should back off," I said. "They're gonna go into the woods."

It was big trees on this stretch, stone walls in the brush along the road. All of it rushing by, the motor roaring. We made the downhill turn, started up the other side, Clair downshifting, flooring it.

We crested the hill. The intersection was ahead, the Jeep running the stop sign, tires screeching, a small silver car sliding past, the kid at the wheel fighting to stay on the road. We braked, slid to a stop, watched as he hit the ditch and the car bounced.

They'd gained on us, and Clair turned, ran through the gears, kept the pedal down. It was four miles to the main road and we needed to have them in sight when they turned. The motor screamed. I tried the phone again. Still nothing. We caught glimpses of the Jeep before it disappeared into curves.

We saw it go right, up on two wheels, nearly rolling over.

"Jesus," I said.

Traffic now, trucks and cars, two lanes and no place to pass. The Jeep braked behind a log truck then went right, passing in the breakdown lane, spraying gravel. The trucker hit the airhorn, the brakes. Hit the horn again as we went by.

A rust-pocked pickup pulled out in front of us, a white-haired driver going slow. We slowed, and Clair started to go right but the man pulled over. Clair went left and the man veered back.

"Come on," I said.

Clair hit the horn and the man held up his hand, flipped us off. Clair stayed behind him, cars coming at us, a chip truck barreling past. When the old man finally turned off, the Jeep was gone.

"You take left," I said.

We drove on, looking down side roads, behind houses, into the woods.

"There," I said. They'd gone right down a narrow dirt road. Clair braked and backed up and we followed. Dust showed the way, and when the air cleared, we knew they'd turned again.

Again, Clair braked. Again, he backed up.

I looked right. This time he saw them, a flicker of brake light. It was a single lane through the woods, probably leading to somebody's back field. We turned in, pounded down the rutted path.

And there they were.

There were boulders blocking the road and the Jeep was stopped, doors wide open.

I was out before we stopped, rifle in my arms. I ran to the Jeep, saw Sophie's sandal on the back seat. There was a path on the far side of the little cul de sac and we ran down it, Clair first, shotgun in two hands in front of him. The path went uphill through dense scrub trees, then opened into an overgrown pasture.

We stopped.

Looked out. There were clumps of poplar in the field, big and thick enough to hide behind. But the grass didn't show that anyone had run through. I turned, looked to the left and back.

"Lay 'em down," Wilton said.

He was coming out of the woods alongside the path. He was driving Roxanne and Mandi in front of him, Mandi limping. Sophie was in his arms, one little foot bare, his hand over her mouth. He was dressed in black jeans and a black long-sleeved shirt. The revolver was black, too, the barrel pressed to her head.

Her eyes were closed, like she was already dead. Roxanne was ghastly white. Mandi was silent,

"It's okay now, honey," I said, in case Sophie could hear me. "Daddy's here."

"Sure it is," Wilton said. "Soon as you put those guns down on the ground."

We didn't move.

"Or I kill the little one right now."

"Oh, my God," Roxanne said. "Oh, my God."

We lowered ourselves to a crouch, placed the guns on the path.

"Your god ain't gonna do nothing, 'cause he don't exist," Wilton said. "They been selling you a fairy tale."

"Don't hurt her," I said. "Just take the car and go."

"The car," he said. "You think I did this for a goddamn car? A fucking car? This is about my children. This is about the children the Gestapo bitch here abducted from me. Where are my kids, bitch? Where are my fucking kids?"

"We can bring you to them," Roxanne sobbed. "They're fine. They are. Just let her go."

"No, no, no," Wilton said, grinning. "Don't pull the crying thing with me. Crying Christians and tricky Jews. Well, what we're gonna do is you're gonna tell me where they are. And we're gonna go there and you're gonna go in and take them out of fucking state incarceration and bring them to me."

"Okay," Roxanne said.

"We're gonna bring them back here and you're gonna be tied up and taped up, just like the mailman. By the time you get loose, I'll be gone."

"Fine," Roxanne said.

"Is she asleep?" I said.

"Some sort of shock," Clair said.

"She'll be sleeping permanent, you don't do what I say," Wilton said.

Sophie was sliding down in his arms and he boosted her back up. I saw her eyes start to open.

"Goddamn," Wilton said.

He dropped her to the ground and I saw the wet stain spreading down his jeans.

"Brat," he said, and he raised the gun.

Mandi jumped in front of Wilton, raised her hands over her head as Sophie ran for Roxanne.

"Shoot me," Mandi said. "Go ahead."

Sophie's arms were outstretched and Roxanne lifted her and spun away, started to run. Wilton moved for a clear shot but Mandi moved with him, blocked his shot.

"Shoot *me*," she said, five feet from the gun. "I mean it."

I dropped to the ground and reached for the rifle, Wilton snapped off a shot, a deafening boom, dirt spraying. I dodged back and he turned, saw Roxanne and Sophie a hundred feet down the trail. He raised the gun, both hands now, but Mandi jumped in front of him again, bouncing up and down and waving her arms like a kid desperate for the teacher to call on her.

"Shoot me," she said. "Go ahead. I dare you, you goddamn freak. You piece of crap."

He looked puzzled, lunged at her, flung her back, started running after Roxanne and Sophie. I grabbed the rifle as he stopped and aimed again, then Mandi hit his legs, screaming, pulling him. Wilton staggered, slashed at her with the gun, aimed it at her head.

There was another boom. The pistol kicked up. Wilton straightening, feet coming off the ground as Clair's shot lifted him, spun him, and he fell, landing face down.

Clair was on his knees, the shotgun at his hip. Mandi sagged to all fours, her head lowered. There was a moment of utter stillness. Then Roxanne's scuffing footsteps in the leaves.

And then a deep breath from Mandi, a long sigh. I put my hand on her shoulder.

"You okay?" I said, as I looked at Wilton, the black puddle spreading from underneath him.

"Yeah," she said, face to the ground. She looked up at me and there was blood running from her scalp down her forehead.

"You know, don't you?" Mandi said.

"Yes. But maybe you're even now."

She shook her head, looked away. "No. It's like I told you, Jack. I'm damaged goods. Damaged goods."

I squeezed her shoulder once and started after my wife and child.

41

It was big news, in all the Maine papers, television, the *Globe* and the *Times,* CNN.com. "Abduction of Social Worker, Child, Ends in Fatal Shooting." Roxanne took a leave of absence. We stayed home. For a couple of days Ricci and another state trooper were posted at each end of our road to keep the press away.

We took the phone off the hook. And we held Sophie tight. Roxanne and I. Mary and Clair.

For two days, Sophie held us, too. She didn't speak. She didn't cry. She slept in our bed and when she woke up, one of us had to be there. Roxanne's boss called a couple of times, told her there was counseling available.

"I'm okay," she said, "but I'm not so sure about my daughter."

Clair said he knew how Sophie felt. We were on the deck, watching the swallows and bluebirds. It was a dark red sunset behind the trees. Roxanne was giving Sophie a bath, and Mary was finishing the dinner dishes.

"Strange thing, good and evil," he said. "An odd human invention."

"Do you think Wilton was pure evil?" I said.

"I did, but I changed my mind," Clair said. "Now I think he was just sick."

He watched the birds, sipped his drink.

"How you doing?" I said.

Clair smiled. "Gets harder every time," he said. "I mean, the first one. Vietnam. That was tough. To take a life, see it end right there in front of you. And then, well, stuff's flying and you're just protecting your guys, trying to make it out of the chaos alive. Then you get good at it, it becomes a job."

"One shot in the field," I said.

"That guy. Wonder if he knew what he was getting into."

"Best not to think about it,"

"Easier said."

We both were quiet for a moment.

"I have no regrets," I said. "You saved her."

"Mandi saved her," Clair said. "I just pulled the trigger."

Sophie was up late, her clock still out of sync. We read books, played games. Candyland. Chutes and Ladders. She was intent and silent, moving her pieces across the board.

Finally, after midnight, she fell asleep in my arms. We put her in the middle of the bed, climbed in ourselves. Our hands clasped.

"How are you doing?" I said.

"Better than this afternoon," Roxanne said. "Which was better than this morning." She looked at Sophie, her hands raised over her head.

"She's so precious," Roxanne said. "She's a gift."

"And so are you. Every moment."

"Will we ever be normal again, Jack?"

"Sure. We just won't be what we were before."

"Maybe we'll be better," she said.

"Yes," I said. "Maybe we will."

She was quiet, her fingers rubbing mine, both of us listening to Sophie's miraculous breaths.

"You can go see her, you know," Roxanne said.

"I know," I said.

"Why don't you? Go in the morning."

"I know you didn't want her—"

"My gut," she said.

"I understand."

"But I turned out to be wrong."

"Nothing is black and white," I said. "Is it?"

I left at seven. It was raining softly and Roxanne and Sophie were asleep. The police were gone from the end of the road and I drove slowly, sipping tea from a travel mug. Over the ridge, down the roads that had once been trails through the woods. I saw two deer, a fox, an old woman picking up bottles from a ditch. And then the horizon to the east, glimpses of the bay shrouded in pale gray mist.

And then I was running down the road to Belfast. I sat at the light, punched in Mandi's number again, the same number that had been in the paper. "Mandi. Personal Escort. Companionship."

I heard her voice. "Hi. This is Mandi. I can't answer the phone right now . . . "

The bright-slickered summer people were up, walking from their cars to the cafe on the corner for coffee and the paper, their lifeline to the world. I drove past them and down the block to Mandi's apartment. I pulled in and parked, looked up.

Lulu was in the window. She looked down, as if she'd never seen me. I got out and tried the door. It opened and I walked up.

There was a broom and mop and cleaning stuff in the hallway. A pail with some odds and ends of food. Tomatoes. Cheese in a plastic envelope. An open bottle of white wine. Half full.

I knocked at the door. Nobody answered and I pushed it open. I stepped in. It looked like when I'd left it, with Roger and the gun, Mandi on the floor. Except it had been neatened up. There was a light on in the bathroom, the sound of water running. I walked across the room, knocked on the door jamb.

A guy appeared. Thirties, muscular, baseball hat. He was holding a sponge and the sponge was dripping.

"Yeah," he said.

"Just looking for Mandi," I said.

"Flew the coop," he said.

"Huh. Looks like she didn't take much with her."

"Hell, all this stuff goes with the place. I rent it furnished."

I looked behind me, the couch and pictures, magazines. Lulu jumped down from behind the window shade.

"What about her cat?" I said.

"Lulu?" he said. "Original owner was two tenants ago. She comes with the place, too."

"Huh," I said.

"You know where she mighta gone?" the landlord said.

He squeezed the sponge into the sink. Gave it a scrub.

"Why?" I said. "She owe you money?"

"No, she's all paid up. I was just gonna see if she wanted the rest of her stuff. She left some behind."

He pointed back into the living room. I turned and saw a plastic bin. It was filled with papers and notebooks. On the top was a drawing of a woman with long flowing hair.

When I came out, Raven was leaning on the hood of my truck, arms crossed.

"Hey, there," he said.

"Hey," I said, walking toward him. He straightened, held out his hand. I took it and we shook. He leaned back and looked up at the apartment windows.

"Poof," Raven said. "Gone."

"I just heard."

"Know where she's headed?" He looked at me, watching my face. I shook my head. "District attorney wants to talk to her. Came by because she didn't return my calls."

"Me neither."

"Not sure whether they'll be able to go to grand jury, if they can't talk to her again."

"Too bad," I said.

"Saved by the bell, huh?"

I didn't answer.

"Heard she sort of helped save your little girl."

"Not sort of. Did."

"Jumped Wilton or something?"

"More like made herself a shield between him and Roxanne and Sophie."

"Dared him to shoot her? Is that right?"

"More than once."

"Impressive," Raven said. "You don't see that."

"I think he was so surprised he wasn't sure what to do. And then she ended up trying to tackle him."

"And your buddy took him out."

I hesitated, thinking of Clair. I nodded.

"Good friend to have in that situation," Raven said.

"In most situations," I said.

He didn't answer, just looked up at window where Lulu had climbed back on the sill.

"Aren't people strange?" Raven said. "Turns out to be some sort of heroine or whatever. After everything else."

He turned to me, met my gaze, and held it. Then smiled. "We both know, don't we?" he said.

"Yes."

"How'd you figure it out?"

"Little things," I said. "One thing led to another. You?"

"Prints came back," Raven said. "I guess you can't really call that detective work."

I shrugged.

"M.E.'s report said the deceased was pounded flat as a frog in the road."

"M.E. said that?"

"Not the frog part," Raven said. "But can you imagine? That little girl?"

I shook my head. We stood, the tourists bustling past us.

"Got a copy of the sentencing report. Know what they said she had?"

"No," I said.

"Conduct disorder. No kidding. For that they get a hundred bucks an hour."

Raven smiled. I didn't.

"I have another theory I'm working on," he said.

"What's that?" I said.

"You know Marty Callahan worked in the same facility where she was incarcerated?"

"I figured."

"But she didn't like him. You said he scared the crap out of her."

"Beat the crap out of her, too," I said.

"Yeah, good riddance to bad rubbish. No tears here. But I've been picturing it. She's in town. He happens to be here, has his summer house, paid for with money from some goddamn graft and corruption. And there she is, living under an assumed name. Doing what she does."

I waited.

"So he says, 'If you don't want the whole town knowing you were a child murderer, a teenage psychopath, then you do what I say.' I figure she was like his slave."

"I don't know," I said.

"No, that much I'm pretty sure of. It's the ending I'm working on. It's like the boat's nine-tenths done."

I didn't answer. He looked up at Lulu.

"Guys like him, they don't kill themselves. They're too self-centered. Too domineering. Things get tough, they go beat somebody up so they can feel better. They like to win. And putting a forty-four to your head and pulling the trigger isn't winning. That's giving up."

"What about the Russian roulette?"

"I can only see it if he's playing with her head. No, I think Mandi, Sybill, Louise, she figured he was gonna rat her out anyway. Or maybe she just got sick of being pushed around."

I shrugged.

"I think he got sloppy drunk, passed out with the gun in his hand, and she took it and put it to his head and kaboom. No more problem."

"What'd the M.E. say?" I asked.

"Suicide."

"Blood on her?"

"Coulda cleaned it up."

"Her prints on the gun?"

"Nope."

"That's that then," I said.

"Could be her second victim," Raven said. "Maybe there've been others. Maybe she's a goddamn serial killer."

"All I know is she saved my little girl."

"You're gonna let a possible homicidal maniac walk 'cause of that?"

I looked at him, then turned and walked to my truck. He watched as I backed out. When I drove past him, I waved. He didn't.

42

The car was backed into the woods at the side of the road. I glimpsed it as I passed, looked into the rearview mirror and saw it pull out and follow. I pulled over and stopped and it pulled up behind me. Mandi got out, walked up to my truck and got in.

She was blonde, hair cut in a bob that made her look even more like a 40s film star. She was wearing jeans and a black top and sandals. She'd had her toenails done. Blood red.

"Hey," I said.

"Hi," Mandi said.

"I'm glad to see you."

"Me, too."

"I went to the apartment."

"I moved."

"Where to?"

Mandi shrugged.

"I like the hair," I said.

"Do you?" she said. She flipped the visor down but there was no mirror. She flipped it back up. "I needed a change,"

"Becomes you," I said.

"Do you really think so?"

"Yes."

"Would you say so if it didn't?"

"Probably not," I said.

We sat. Yellow and black butterflies wafted around the milkweed at the roadside. Mandi folded her hands in her lap.

"So how is everybody?" she said.

"Okay. Takes time."

"Sophie?"

"Very quiet. But I want to thank you. You saved her—"

She held up a hand to stop me.

"No, what you did was—"

The hand went over my mouth.

"It was nothing, Jack. Nothing at all."

I pulled her hand off my mouth. Turned it and held it in mine.

"You saved my family."

Mandi looked away. "I couldn't let him—"

"I owe you. I'll always owe you."

She shook her head. The blonde hair gave a little shake and then was still. "Nobody owes me, Jack. Never will because I'll never get back to even. Dug myself way too deep a hole."

We were quiet for a moment. I still held her hand.

"With Marty? Were you digging yourself out or in deeper?"

She looked at me, then away.

"He had a list, Jack. Girls from back there. He was looking them up one by one."

"Blackmailing them into—"

"He told me who was next. If I didn't work out. He knew she was a friend of mine. She used to write me letters."

Amanda, I thought.

"So you stopped him? Stopped him from preying on people?"

Mandi looked down at our hands, clasped between us.

"I don't do things. They just happen."

She took a deep breath.

"Do you ever wonder why we are who we are? Of all the people I could be, why am I this person? I mean, why not somebody else? Anybody else?"

"No," I said. "I guess I don't."

"Can I tell you something?"

I nodded.

"I'm just going to say this once. Never again."

She paused.

"A big part of me wishes I was Roxanne. Living in a pretty house in the country. Having your babies."

Mandi smiled.

"I even thought about it once, how I could take Roxanne's place."

"I don't think it can be done," I said.

"I know. I think crazy stuff sometimes. Like I said, it was really just once. Just to have a life like that."

"You can."

She smiled, shook her head.

"Yeah, well, maybe someday."

"You're going?"

"Yeah."

"Coming back?"

"Maybe someday."

"You want to come to the house, say goodbye?"

"Thanks, Jack, but no. I'm terrible at goodbyes."

She gave my hand a squeeze, opened the door and got out. I looked at her but she didn't look back, just walked to her car, got in, started it, and did a U-turn in the road. I watched in the mirror until she disappeared from view.

43

It was two days later and Sophie still hadn't spoken. She and I were in the woods, walking from the big pine to the pond. I had her on my shoulders and she ducked beneath the branches, her arms wrapped tightly around my neck. As we brushed underneath a maple, a beetle peeled off and landed on Sophie's leg. It was black with red spots and it was moving toward her knee. I flicked it off.

"That bug crawled on me," Sophie said, her voice small and hesitant, like talking might hurt.

I smiled at the words, pulled her tight. "Yes, he did," I said. "But he didn't hurt you."

I waited.

"He was a nice bug, wasn't he, Daddy?" she said.

"Yes, honey, he was."

We kept walking, Sophie hanging on as I bent under branches. She leaned down and said, "Can we go see Mommy? I need to tell her."

"What do you want to tell her?" I said.

"It was black. It had red spots. It crawled on me but it didn't bite."

I turned, started back up the trail toward the field and the house. Sophie clung to my neck like a jockey.

"When's Twinnie coming home?" she said.

"Soon," I said. "I'll call again today."

We walked. She was quiet.

"He was a bad guy," she whispered, like she knew.

"Yes. He was very bad. But now he's gone."

"Is Mandi gone?" Sophie said.

"I don't know, honey," I said.

"Mandi wasn't bad," she said. "Mandi was nice."

I pulled her closer. In the dark woods, there were shadows, myriad shades of gray.

ABOUT THE AUTHOR

Gerry Boyle is the author of a dozen mystery novels, including the acclaimed Jack McMorrow series, and the Brandon Blake series. A former newspaper reporter and columnist, Boyle lives with his wife, Mary, in a historic home in a small village on a lake. He also is working with his daughter, Emily Westbrooks, on a crime series set in her hometown, Dublin, Ireland. Whether it is Maine or Ireland, Boyle remains true to his pledge to send his characters only to places where he has gone before.